Star Pack

By Dawn Napier

Ink Smith Publishing

www.ink-smith.com

Printed in the U.S.A

The final approval for this literary material is granted by the author.

All characters appearing in this work are fictitious. Any resemblance to real persons, living or dead, is purely coincidental.

ISBN: 978-1-939156-89-1

Ink Smith Publishing
710 S. Myrtle Ave Suite 209
Monrovia, CA, 91016

First and foremost, for my husband Bill, my first reader and number one fan. I probably wouldn't have finished it without your encouragement. Pineapple.

Also a shout-out to the Antioch Writer's Group, who kindly listened to snippets and told me that there's nothing silly about trying to sell a book about space-faring alien werewolves.

Part One:
The People of Garou

Year 175: Ledra and Nedrra

Syrrsa was exhausted from the long hours she'd spent birthing, and her whole body ached as though she'd been beaten. Her mate Gyrr was out of the room, observing the medical hunters as they tested the cubs for health and liveliness. They'd both let out a good strong squall after emerging, and they'd each taken a nipple with painful enthusiasm. Now Syrrsa only wanted to rest and prepare herself mentally for life with two small children.

The nest she lay curled in was pleasantly heated, and the fluffy bedding smelled of milk and living blood. Syrrsa closed her eyes and listened to the distant beeps and chimes of the medical center's function. It sounded like a chorus of singing cubs.

Her wrist emitted a gentle tone reminiscent of a wolf's howl. Syrrsa lifted her arm and peered at her wrist eye, a portable screen used to communicate with other hunters or call for help in an emergency. The wrist eye enclosed her forearm in a light, strong alloy that could survive fights, falls, and even the vacuum of space. The screen flashed with the image of Gyrr's face. She bared her teeth at it. Why had he called her when he had been just down the hall? Not that coming into her nest and disturbing her would be any less irritating, she supposed.

"Were you sleeping?" his voice came from a tiny speaker below the screen.

"Not yet." Syrrsa's tone was rough.

"I show my throat. But the medical hunters would like to test the cubs' genetics. Shall I approve it?"

"Approve whatever you like." Of course the Medical Research Council would want to know if the cubs were born of one egg or two. Such information would be useful to them for all sorts of reasons. But Syrrsa didn't care about anything but sleep.

She pressed down on a black button next to the speaker, and the screen flashed red as Gyrr's contact was terminated. Then she tapped it twice more, telling the device to block all further communication.

This might be the last proper sleep she got for a while. She needed to make the most of it.

*****

According to the tests, Ledrra and Nedrra were not identical twins. But their mother could not be convinced of that. The two little girls grew at the same pace, fed the same way, and were so alike physically that she had to resort to her sense of smell to tell them apart.

Syrrsa was worn out by their birth and their nursing habits, and when they were a year old she made the appointment to be evaluated for sterilization. Gyrr pretended to be hurt.

"Is there something wrong with my seed?" he asked, wrinkling his nose in a joking expression.

Syrrsa snorted. "Not at all. Your genetic material is so superior that my ovaries decided it would be wasted on only one child. And now I am worn out by their delusions of grandeur."

Gyrr nuzzled her hair. It felt good to joke with her again, after a year of physical and mental exhaustion. The babies had been born small, like most twins, and Syrrsa had insisted on caring for them entirely on her own with no help from Gyrr or any of their friends. Sometimes new mothers were overprotective, to their own detriment.

The Southeastern Territory was flat, grassy land perfect for farming. Gyrr, like his parents before him, was a farmer of ungula. He was well-known for his skills at evaluating the beasts for health and temperament, and business owners traveled from all four Territories to buy his pack animals. Ungula that did not meet his standards were culled and sold to the paradises for meat.

It had been a grueling year for him. Since the twins' birth, Syrrsa had been physically incapacitated and unable to catch or kill her own food. He'd dipped into his own stock to provide for her and the babies, and now he had to work harder to make up the loss of profit. As proud as he was to have fathered twins, he wasn't sure he wanted to do it again.

Gyrr and Syrrsa snuggled up in the family nest in the living room. The girls slept peacefully, and their parents savored the rare quiet. This was the first evening they'd managed to spend together in weeks.

"Full moon tomorrow," Gyrr commented.

"Yes." Syrrsa stretched, dozing a little.

"Busy day for me. I have to lock up the ungula."

"Will you go out? Are you going hunting?"

"Will you go with me?" For the past year Syrrsa had taken tranquilizers and stayed in when the wolf came out.

Syrrsa considered. "I don't know if I should leave my babies."

"They'll sleep all night. They always do. You should go out. Celebrate your impending freedom from reproduction."

"What if there's a rogue wolf?"

"There hasn't been a rogue wolf in this territory in years, but we'll lock the house securely before we go."

"Then we will lock ourselves out, too."

"Only until morning. You should go out."

Syrrsa finally agreed. She had been cooped up for the last ten changes, locked in the house with baby twins while the wolf whined and scratched. It would feel good to run on all fours again.

On the wall eye they watched a video story about a family of ungula genetically engineered to hunt like wolves. Syrrsa laughed at the antics of the sharp-toothed beasts, and Gyrr had to shush her before she woke the babies. It was an enjoyable evening.

*****

As Gyrr had said, the next day was a busy one for him. In addition to his usual tasks—feeding and cleaning up after the ungula, inspecting the calves, and training the beasts suitable for pack work—near the end of the day he had to bring all the ungula into the main barn and lock them up. He fed them drugged treats to keep them calm and tolerant of the crowded conditions, and he bolted all the doors and covered the windowpanes. Younger wolves with poor control were likely to attack anything that looked or smelled like food.

He got home from the barn just after sundown. Syrrsa had already fed the babies and put them to bed; they both slept deeply in the family nest. "They'll be fine," Gyrr whispered in her ear. "Come on. My teeth are itching."

Syrrsa felt it too. The moon was rising; they could both feel it in the backs of their eyes and in their teeth. It was time to go.

She locked and shuttered all the windows, and she locked the door as she stepped outside. The air was cool and breezy, and she felt her sense of smell sharpening. The wolf was awake, and she was anxious to run.

She followed Gyrr away from the house and the farm. By the time they reached the edge of the trees the full moon was well into the sky. The itch in Syrrsa's eyes and teeth was agony now, and it was with deep relief that she gave up control of her two-legged body and let the wolf take over.

The old familiar pain crackled through her skull, her face, and her joints. It rippled through her, shattered and liberated her. When it was over, Syrrsa threw back her head and howled her delight to the star-studded sky.

She and Gyrr ran together through the cool, breezy night. The children were safe, sleeping soundly behind locked doors. Tonight belonged to the wolf, and tonight the wolf was her.

There was a lake nearby, and Syrrsa went there. Gyrr followed her into the damp undergrowth at the water's edge. They hunted together for waterfurs, the slick-coated water-dwellers that made their nests in tunnels along the banks. They were juicy and delicious, and their bodies were well-padded with fat to insulate them against the cold water. Gyrr found a colony of them and dug it up, and the two wolves had a fine time pouncing and snapping at the scrambling, fleeing creatures. They each caught half a dozen before the survivors tunneled too deep to dig out again.

Bellies full, Syrrsa and Gyrr padded through the dark, silent trees. The usual ground and tree-dwellers were silent tonight; they knew that the wolf was awake and running. Syrrsa savored the cool silence and felt grateful to her mate for convincing her to do this. She hadn't felt this good in months. The wolf really needed to run, to stretch her legs and feel live game between her jaws. Sleeping in the family nest with the babies had never felt this relaxing.

Gyrr growled. Syrrsa's ears pricked up. Something was coming. It was stealthy, as silent and slinking as a wolf. But it wasn't a wolf. Syrrsa could smell it, a wild, gamey scent. Her hackles rose.

Gyrr growled again, louder. It was getting closer. It smelled pungent and aggressive; it was the scent of a hunter. But Syrrsa was puzzled. Wolves were the dominant predators on Garou. But this creature was larger—and it smelled fiercer.

Syrrsa saw it just before it lunged out of the brush at them. It leaped like a flying thing, a fluid, night-colored creature of muscles and teeth and claws. It tackled Gyrr to the ground and sank its teeth into his neck. Gyrr screamed.

Syrrsa threw back her head and howled for help, a wailing cry that all wolves in the area would recognize. But they would come too late, and this she knew. She steeled herself and rushed in to defend her mate, knowing all the while that she was too weak to fend the monster off.

Her last thoughts were of her children.

*****

The Council for Alien Affairs had an emergency meeting. Outsiders were told that it was to discuss a possible budget cut for the new space-exploration program. The reality was too strange and frightening to release to the general population.

Usually the meeting hall was filled with chatter and gossip before the meeting, but this time the long cave was silent as death. Council members stared at their hands or tapped at their wrist eyes and waited for the business to start.

Council Alpha Stefrra opened the meeting with a question. "Has anyone seen it yet?"

"Not yet," said Hrraz, her mate and second in command.

"Good. Physical evidence?"

"The medical investigator found three hairs and a fair amount of saliva."

"Take possession of the samples immediately. Exert authority if you must. Those samples must be kept in the Council's possession."

"Yes, of course." He would feel strange pulling rank on a respected investigator, but Stefrra was right. This was not the first alien sighting in the history of Garou, and records indicated that such sightings sometimes brought plague and panic. The safety of the world-pack was their first concern.

Jerr was the officer in charge of the samples. He was a gentle little fellow easily impressed by authority, and he handed the hair and saliva samples over to Hrraz without a word of argument. "I'm so glad someone important is doing this," he said as he handed over the small plastic cylinders. "I seem to have forgotten everything I know about genetic analysis. My teeth are not sharp enough for these samples."

Hrraz left him with instructions to report to the Council immediately should he feel ill or feverish in any way. "Were the samples infected?" Jerr asked. His mild grey eyes widened.

Hrraz didn't want to panic the little hunter, but he didn't want to lie, either. "We just don't know. Did you use a mask and full protective gear when you took the samples?"

"Of course!"

"And what happened to the bodies of the two unfortunates?"

"I was given instructions to incinerate them, and I did so immediately after the exam. Was that correct?"

"Perfectly. You should have nothing to fear."

Stefrra read Jerr's notes on the samples and studied them for several days. Though their son no longer needed constant attention, Hrraz stayed home with him while Stefrra lived and worked in the Council's private laboratory. He told the neighbors that it was to keep him company in his mother's absence. He did not tell them that Stefrra's research could possibly mean a deep change to life as they knew it on Garou.

When she was satisfied with her findings, she called another meeting.

"This isn't the same creature as the one discussed in the library records, but the DNA markers are similar. It is from the same type of animal, the same type of ecosystem, as the one in our records."

"Do you have a hypothesis?" asked Yrrix, an elderly councilman. He looked old enough to ride the ancestor train, but his body was still healthy and his mind as quick as a cub.

"Some sort of genetic modification experiment is a possibility. But it is unlikely that such a large project could be kept secret for so long. I suspect, instead, an actual alien visitation."

"But we've seen no intelligence. How could they have come here from another world without a keeper?"

"Each time a visitation has occurred, the animal has always vanished without a trace afterwards. Something intelligent is protecting these animals."

"What should we do?"

Stefrra considered, and her fellows waited. "Nothing for now," she said. "Destroy the samples and preserve the notes for the library. Watch and wait."

"And what about the children?" Brrina asked. She was the youngest council member, a female barely out of Council Academy.

"They have already been sent to live with cousins on the Northeastern Territory."

"Did they have any contact at all with their parents' bodies?"

"No. Jerr destroyed the bodies the night they were killed."

"Poor cubs," Hrraz said. He thought of his own son, who had just started primary academy. "Too young to howl for their parents."

"True," Stefrra said. "But the good news is that they are young enough to adapt to their new situation. They'll never know what they lost."

Years 175-180: Ledrra and Nedrra

Syrrsa's twins were sent to the Northeastern Territory, where Syrrsa's cousin Keerra lived. She was an older female who had never raised her own cubs. Her father had been a rogue, and his abuse had left her sterile. She had not had a mate in many years, and the Council for Pack Health was concerned about her. Giving her a family of her own was considered the perfect solution.

As soon as they entered her home, Keerra told them, "You should be grateful. After a lifetime of sterility, I'm one of the few people willing to take in someone else's damaged offspring. You should always be grateful to me and thankful for your pack." Ledrra was very tired from the trip, and she yawned during Keerra's words. Keerra bit her on the shoulder as punishment. Nedrra whined at the sight of the blood flowing down her sister's arm, and their new mother bit her too.

The bites and blows were frequent, but they rarely left marks. Nobody outside the family cottage realized how badly the twins were being treated. Even after the girls started primary academy, their instructors thought that they were just naturally shy and attached to each other. Twins were usually like that.

The cubs' only reprieve came once a month, when Keerra went out for the change. She left them alone, locked in her cottage while she ran under the moon in wolf skin. The girls always trembled at the thought of their rogue aunt running wild, possibly attacking and injuring other hunters, but it was a relief to sleep untroubled for once.

As soon as the door clicked shut, Ledrra scrambled out of her nest and climbed in with her sister. Keerra never let them sleep together or with her; each of them had her own sleeping nest lengths away from the other two. Many of the beatings the cubs had received had been Keerra's attempt to keep them apart. "You must never rely on someone else for comfort!" she'd shouted between whacks. "It will only lead to loneliness and suffering!"

But on this night, at least, she had no control over their nighttime sleeping arrangements. Nedrra clung to her sister with all four limbs, and slowly they relaxed in the peaceful darkness.

"She's going to kill us someday," Ledrra said.

"Maybe not. Maybe someone will come get us." Nedrra was always hopeful of this. Someone had gotten them once, when their parents had gone out hunting and never come back. It might happen again.

"We should run away. Go back to our own territory and find someone else to feed us."

"She would find us and take us back. Then she'd bite our faces."

"Then we should run away into space." Ledrra rolled over onto her back and looked at the locked window. Beyond the glass, the stars were like sharp, brilliant eyes. "We'll get on one of the deep space ships that leaps across the whole galaxy. There's no scent in space. She'll never track us."

"I'd rather run away to the Medical Center." Nedrra snuggled against her sister's side, enjoying the fantasy. "I'll hide in an empty nest and pretend to be sick. And when nobody's around to see I'll use the research lab to create a cure for the rogue wolf. Then we can fix her, and we'll all be happy."

"There's already a cure for the rogue," Ledrra said ominously. And they both shuddered. Keerra was sick and frightening, but she was the only pack they knew.

They curled up tightly together in the nest and fell asleep, clinging to each other like leaves in a rain storm.

*****

When they were four, Ledrra knocked over a platter of ungula-cheese that Keerra had been saving for dinner. "Such ingratitude," Keerra said. Usually she bit them on the back or legs, but today she lost her temper. She punched Ledrra across the face with both fists, bloodying her nose and swelling her eyes shut. Then she bit Nedrra on the neck as punishment for not controlling her sister. "Now both of you can sleep outside without dinner tonight. Perhaps tomorrow you'll have a better understanding of how good you have it here."

A passing neighbor heard the children whimpering and took them out of the cold, wet garden. Once they were safe and warm in his cottage, he called rogue control and reported Keerra. The twins were taken to the medical center where they were treated for dehydration and emotional neglect. An ancestor who worked at the center, Grrifa, came to their room and slept in their nest while they were being treated. She talked to them and played with them during the day, distracting them from their condition and offering what comfort she could. Nedrra was cautious, but Ledrra attached herself to the ancestor immediately and clung to her like a newborn to the breast.

The psychological examiners studied Keerra's file and history, and they discovered that both her father and brother had been rogue wolves. With such a poor upbringing and faulty genetic material, they decided that she could not be rehabilitated and sentenced her to euthanasia. The investigators agreed that it was good that she was sterile. Had she produced cubs, rogue control would have had to make a hard decision about the fate of those cubs.

The ancestor Grrifa was assigned to be her comfort guide. Keerra was tightly strapped to a soft bed, and Grrifa sat in the chair nearby. Outside, they heard the usual beeps and chatter of the medical center in full swing, busy with the job of life. But in this room, all was silent.

Muscle relaxers, painkillers, and a stealthy poison dripped into Keerra's vein in a concoction of death. It didn't hurt, but Keerra's limbs felt numb and heavy, and she was terrified. She lifted her head, as well as she could for the straps, and bared her teeth at the ancestor. Grrifa ignored it. Keerra growled curses and mocking questions about her ancestry, and Grrifa accepted it all with stoic silence. Finally, in a last attempt to elicit a reaction, Keerra lunged and snapped at Grrifa. She never got close, but Grrifa finally reacted. She stood up, caught Keerra's jaw in one hand, and shoved her down onto her back. She pressed her forearm firmly against Keerra's throat and spoke quietly.

"I am sorry for you, in spite of what you've done. You came from a pack of rogues, and you suffered under their hands and teeth. But I will leave you to die alone, if that is what you wish."

Tears welled in Keerra's eyes, and she shook her head. Grrifa released her and sat down on the edge of the bed.

Keerra used what little freedom of movement she had to press up against Grrifa's hip and leg. There, curled up like a cub, she fell asleep and never woke up.

*****

The girls next went to Karrev and Hesrra, a couple who had mated for life. Their own child, Cavrra, had just gone away to secondary academy. They would have no more children after losing a son to the wasting disease, and they were thrilled to welcome Ledrra and Nedrra into their empty nest.

Grrifa was gratified that they had gone to hunters she knew. She was able to watch them grow up from her position as family friend and occasional babysitter, and no matter how long they were parted they always remembered her. Whenever they saw her, even in between the five-month sessions at secondary academy, they greeted her with hugs and nuzzles.

While they were in secondary academy, Grrifa was instructed by the Council for Pack Health to tell the cubs what had become of their parents. Grrifa argued. They were happy and healthy girls now, and they seemed content with the knowledge that their parents had become "lost" when they were babies. Grrifa's concern was overridden. The Council leader, Durra, told her that it was better for them to find out now that their parents had been killed than to find out through gossip later.

The official story was that a wolf had gone rogue under the moon and taken both parents by surprise. Grrifa told them this with dread in her heart for how they would react. But she was surprised.

"We already knew," Nedrra said.

"We knew they were dead," Ledrra added.

"You never talked about them."

"You talk about everyone, except for people who died."

Grrifa embraced them both, which they accepted readily but didn't seem to need. After thinking it over, she realized that she had no reason to believe that they would be upset or confused by this revelation. Their earliest memories were of being beaten and starved. They already knew that the world was a scary, unsafe place.

Though they looked identical, Ledrra and Nedrra grew in different directions as secondary academy drew to a close. Nedrra showed an early aptitude for biology and medicine, and Ledrra looked to the stars— literally. Math and astronomy became her passions, though she shared her sister's interest in biology as a hobby. When they graduated from secondary academy near the top of their class, Ledrra made plans to stay in the North-west and attend the Flight Academy. Her dream was to join a star ship as a medical officer or xenobiologist.

Nedrra protested. Her own plan was to move back to the South-east to attend the medical academy. She'd hoped that her sister would join her. Nedrra liked routine and continuity, and she was terrified at the thought of separation from her twin.

Ledrra refused. They argued about it for days, and tempers grew heated. Grrifa spoke to them both, but even she could not make peace between them. Matters finally reached their climax with Grrifa's departure on the ancestor train.

Grrifa's cottage was small and spare. It was taken up entirely by the family nest, which had held no family in the girls' lifetime. Youngsters from around the community came to Grrifa for advice and comfort, so the nest still saw frequent use. Grriffa lay there now, embraced on both sides by two grown females who still thought of themselves as her cubs.

"It's not fair," Nedrra said.

"Dear, it's my time," Grrifa said. "I knew last month, when the change hurt me so badly my heart almost gave out."

She squeezed Nedrra's shoulder. Then she turned to Ledrra. "Do you still intend to join the flight academy?"

Ledrra nodded. She could hardly bear to think of staying here on Garou, where it seemed bad things kept happening for no reason at all. Her parents had been taken from her. Her cousin had abused her. And now her favorite person, aside from her sister, was going away to die. The flight academy was her sanest choice.

"So you're leaving me too," Nedrra said. She kept her eyes down and clung to Grrifa like an infant.

"Come with me. The star ships need medicals."

Nedrra shook her head. She still would not look up. "I can't help enough people on a ship. I would feel useless."

Grrifa hugged them both tightly. Ledrra felt the frail thinness of her bones, and she smelled the impending sickness on her breath. She wanted to howl.

"You two have known nothing but terrible separations. But it doesn't have to be terrible every time. I'm going away to live my last days with peace and dignity. Ledrra is going away to see the universe for all Garouean kind. Nedrra is going to—"

"To discover a cure for old age," Nedrra interrupted.

"Oh darling, you can do better than that. Discover something that will do your people good."

"It would do you good."

"Oh darling." Grrifa nuzzled Nedrra's ear. "You are so young."

Year 178: Kuvrro

It was a warm afternoon in late summer when Kuvrro saw the ancestor train for the first time. It rumbled past his small, spare cottage as he sat among the furry pink flowers and practiced catching the many-legged winged flyers that fluttered in and out of the blossoms. He looked up at the four ungula as they plodded past, nodding their furry heads and swishing their thin tails. Their thick hooves left prints in the dusty road that he would examine later. The enclosed wagon was painted dark blue and dotted with white splotches that resembled stars. Through the open window several white muzzles poked out, tasting the flowery breeze.

Kuvrro's father came to stand behind him, and he also watched the ancestor train pass. When it was out of sight he asked Pop, "Where is it going?"

Pop's warm hand squeezed his shoulder. "They're going into the woods."

"Why?"

"It's what ancestors do when they're too sick to hunt."

Kuvrro was barely two and had no concept of death as an abstract. But that image stayed in his mind: the slow-moving wagon, painted to look like deep space, carrying away the tired, sick hunters who could no longer hunt. It didn't frighten him, but it haunted him somehow. So a month later when Mum told him that his grandmother was going away on the ancestor train, he refused to believe her.

"Her life is almost over, Kuvrro," Mum said. She held him firmly on her lap while he stared resolutely elsewhere. His body was stiff and he refused to give in to her gentle caresses.

She touched his pointed ear, and he growled. The touch became a painful pinch, reminding the cub of his manners. Until he could summon the wolf and hunt his own food Mum was alpha. He licked his nose in apology.

"Grrana is old, and her life is almost over," Mum repeated. "Her body is so worn and tired that she can't even change anymore."

"I can't change yet either. But you aren't sending me away to die in the woods." Kuvrro forgot his resolution to keep silent.

"But you are young and healthy. You have a long life in front of you. Grrana's life was long, and now it is over. Everything ends, Kuvrro."

"It shouldn't have to!" Kuvrro's eyes burned with tears.

Mum nuzzled his hair. Her face was salty and damp. Against his resolve, Kuvrro melted into her hug. He realized then that she was hurting as much as him.

Grrana had been an engineer for the deep-space exploring ships, the largest, most expensive, most intricate machines the Garouean people had ever invented. She'd spent the last several years creating designs that would make life onboard the star ships easier and healthier. Confinement during the change was risky; without proper exertion the wolf could go rogue. But Grrana had created sound and smell systems that would refresh the senses and soothe the anxious wolf. She'd learned from the medical researchers in the South-eastern Territory that the smells of fresh grass and flowers would calm a rapid heartbeat, and the smell of running prey sharpened the senses. She'd incorporated this knowledge into the ventilation systems she designed for travelers' sleeping caves. It would be more expensive to build separate systems for different caves or different parts of the ship, but Grrana had argued in its favor. Just last week Kuvrro's father had told the family that preliminary tests were already indicating a significant improvement in morale and productivity.

She had also begun design work on an exercise cave, a radical concept in a field that prized conservation of living space. This cave, she'd suggested, could be spherical and maintained at the very center of the ship. Surrounded by the gravitational field, every inch could be used as running space. Stacking cubes, tunnels, and ropes could be added, optimizing every inch so that the wolf could run and play during the change instead of taking sleeping drugs and spending the change in a drugged haze.

The Garouean hunters were poised to travel farther than ever into the depths of unknown space, and they had Grrana to thank for it. And now she was to be shipped off to die, like a useless bit of gristle. Kuvrro's hackles rose at the unfairness of it.

"But it does. You'll learn to accept it in time. You'll never like it, but you will accept it."

Remembering the pinch and his smarting ear, Kuvrro did not argue. But that night, Mum and Pop went out hunting and left Kuvrro alone in the house. Kuvrro watched them leave, then he went to his sleeping cave and opened the window. The night sky was clear and cool, the stars sharp as teeth. A glowing dot passed overhead like a falling meteorite. But it did not burn out; it moved on steadily across the sky and out of sight. A star ship no doubt, possibly the one that would test Grrana's famous exercise cave. He spoke to it in the cold silence of the early autumn night.

"I won't."

Year 180: Drrak

Drrak woke up first. The family nest was warm and comfortable, and he lay dozing in the warmth of three bodies curled together. His mother and father slept curled up facing each other, with himself in the middle. He smelled their warm breath and listened to their heartbeats. Rruc's heartbeat was heavy and slow, and Mrraska's was a little faster. Drrak watched her face twitch and her ears flick. She was dreaming.

Drrak sat up, and Mrraska awoke. "Good morning, son," she murmured. "Ready for the big day?"

Drrak frowned. He wasn't ready, and he didn't like being reminded of what was going to happen.

Mrraska saw his expression. "Never mind. Let's watch some video stories."

There was an elevated control panel next to the nest, and Mrraska tapped a few keys. The adjacent wall lit up with a burst of color and music, and despite himself Drrak felt a prickle of excitement. Mrraska patted the cushions, and Drrak lay back down next to her. He couldn't resist video stories, and she knew it. They settled down to watch the wall eye together.

Rruc yawned and rolled over sleepily. Mrraska leaned over and stroked his furry shoulder, and Drrak sighed. The family wasn't broken, not yet. The nest puffed pleasant scents of blooming flowers and running prey, capturing Drrak's attention.

The first story was about a little boy who rescued his sister from a rogue wolf. The sister was partial to the color red, and her nickname was Little Rred. Drrak knew the story well and loved it. He clapped his hands at the finale, and he hugged his mother tightly.

"If any rogue tries to eat you, I'll eat him first," he said.

"I'm sure you will." She nuzzled his hair.

"I'll always stay with you, even after he's gone." Drrak looked at his father, still sleeping like a dead one.

Mrraska sighed and squeezed him close. "He's not leaving us, you know. He's going back to his lone cottage, which is just a short run down the road from here. It's what all males do."

"Cavrra's parents mated for life."

"Cavrra's parents are the exception, not the rule. We are not a monogamous species. We don't need his support and protection anymore. You're going to primary academy when the next session starts, and I'm going back to my job."

Drrak didn't want to talk about it anymore. "Let's watch another story."

Rruc woke up about halfway through the second story. He snuggled with Drrak and his mother, and they held each other for what was likely to be the last time.

After breakfast—grain-porridge and yellowfruit, Drrak's favorite—Drrak had to get dressed before he could go out. This was another annoyance. Adults and older children rarely wore clothing outside of ceremonial occasions; they were able to grow out their wolf pelts for warmth and modesty. But Drrak was only six years old. He had not yet started the life-change that meant adulthood and the awakening of the wolf. That would not happen for at least three more years, when he was near graduation from primary academy.

There were several streets filled with the one-hunter homes. They were closely stacked together, and they all shared water and power. Rruc guided his family to his lone cottage, a neat grey box with a bright red door.

Drrak sniffed at the door and the dirt path leading to it. He memorized every scent and every step, and he knew that he would always be able to find his way here. This was reassuring.

Rruc opened the front door, and Drrak was further relieved. There was a family nest here, smaller than the one at home, but still large enough for him and his father to sleep together if he came to visit. Pop wasn't abandoning him at all.

"And look." He led Drrak into a small cave adjacent to the toileting closet. "This room is yours. If you ever need to come stay with me, for any reason. You'll always have a room of your own and a spot in my nest."

Rruc picked up his son and hugged him, and Drrak hugged him back.

*****

The cottage felt empty when Drrak and Mrraska returned. Despite her cheerful chatter, Mrraska felt it too, and she curled up in the family nest and turned on the wall eye. About halfway through the story, the screen froze and a message appeared. YOU OKAY?

Mrraska snorted. "My sister worries too much," she said. She typed on the control pad, FINE. SLEEPING.

HUNTING TONIGHT?

Mrraska hesitated. Then she typed, YES. BRINGING DRRAK. HIS FIRST TIME.

WONDERFUL!

"Drrak," Mrraska said, "do you want to go hunting with me and my sister tonight?"

"Hunting!" Drrak threw back his head and howled at the ceiling. "I'm going hunting tonight for the first time ever! With Mum and Aunt Cyrra!"

Mrraska laughed. "This is going to be quite a night, I think."

Mrraska rested and watched video stories while Drrak ran and played outside. The younger females Cavrra and Nexrra came over and ran with him, and he pretended they were prey and chased them up and down the dirt road. They all stopped and touched their throats when the ancestor train rolled by, pulled by four large ungula. The ancestors inside peered out and waved at the children as they passed, but only Drrak had the courage to wave back.

After the others left, Drrak went on practicing his running and pouncing in the dirt. Mum was taking him hunting, and he wanted to make her proud of him. He would catch his own dinner tonight.

Near sunset, Mum came out to play. She chased him around, prancing and laughing, until he tripped on a rock and stumbled. Mum pounced on him and mock-bit his throat while he shrieked with laughter.

"Come on," she said. "Cyrra will be waiting for us."

The night was cool and breezy. Drrak heard other hunters around them, laughing and talking among themselves, all going to the paradises for dinner. Even when the moon was not full, the wolf instinct to kill fresh food was constant, and the best place to do that was at a paradise, a local hunting ground where game was bred and stocked. There were a few howls, but not many. The full moon had just passed, so most hunters were still tired from the change. Turning wolf was physically taxing, so few hunters changed when they didn't have to.

Mrraska ran down the dirt road to the paradise, and Drrak ran after her. He was hungry, and his hunger made him feel fierce. He couldn't wait until he was old enough to turn wolf. He wanted so badly to run on all fours.

The paradise was a heavily wooded area that smelled of soil and growth and fat, plump animals. Drrak salivated. He was so hungry.

There were already a few hunters there, mostly young adults looking for mates. "I met your father here," Mrraska commented. She watched a female chase a young male around in circles, and she smiled. Drrak frowned up at her. He didn't want to think about his father now. He wanted to eat.

Since they were hunting in two-legged form, they would need tools. Mrraska led her son to the wooden rack and looked them over. Nearby, an attendant sat on the ground beneath a tree and played with his wrist eye. Lively music emitted from the device strapped to his forearm, and Drrak caught the scents of fresh flowers and springtime. The attendant smirked when he saw Mrraska. "Looking to mate again already?"

"Teaching my son to hunt." Mrraska gave the younger male a look Drrak was familiar with—the cold, disappointed look she reserved for moments of unparalleled stupidity.

It worked on the tools attendant as well as it had ever worked on Drrak. He lowered his head and touched his throat. Mrraska ignored him and turned to study the selection of hunting tools.

For herself she selected a double-edged knife with a saw-toothed blade on one side and a smooth razor's edge on the other. Drrak reached for a pointed blade as long as his leg, but Mrraska cuffed his hand. "That's a fighting tool for taking down dangerous game," she said. "Have this instead."

Drrak sighed and accepted the tiny knife she handed him. He hated to admit it, but the knife felt comfortable in his hand, as natural as his own teeth. It had been designed especially for children like him who were just beginning, and the craftsmanship was excellent.

"Cyrra's not here," Mrraska said. "She'll catch up. I'm hungry. Off we go."

Drrak followed her into the woods. She sniffed around and set off in a direction that did not smell of other hunters. Drrak followed her footsteps perfectly, stepping only where she stepped. He did this instinctively without wondering why. Mrraska moved into the breeze and kept her steps short. They walked without making a sound and without disturbing the thick dead leaves that covered the ground.

The soil smelled wonderful to Drrak, like life and death mingled together. The soil was where all life came from, and within it they would find their life-giving meal. Drrak swallowed saliva and held his knife tighter.

Mrraska stopped walking and crouched down. Drrak mimicked her, and they waited in the dark for several minutes. A cool breeze ruffled Drrak's hair, and with it came the smell of living meat. He suppressed a hungry whimper.

He heard a rustle, then another. Their dinner was moving around out there, unaware of their presence. Drrak wanted to charge in and catch them all, but he followed his mother's lead. And still she waited.

As he crouched in the darkness, Drrak's eyes adapted to the night. Now he understood why she had waited. It took a few minutes, but eventually he was able to see what she saw—three small, furry burrowers that scuttled a few arm lengths away. His moonlit eyes marked their progress, watched the pattern of their movement, and as he watched he could pick out the pattern in their scurrying. He felt that he could predict where each of the burrowers would go just before they moved.

Then Mrraska leaped. She swung the saw-toothed side of her blade, and two burrowers fell dead before they could squeal. The third tried to run, but she nicked it across the back and its spine was severed. The burrower scrambled desperately, but it could not drag its useless hindquarters.

"That one is yours, Drrak. End its pain."

Drrak leaped exactly the way he had seen her do, and he swung his tiny, fist-sized knife. He cut its throat open with a single slice, and the creature died instantly.

"Excellent." Mrraska ruffled his hair. "Now I'll teach you how to clean your kill. You must always remove the bowel if you intend to eat it two-legged. Your wolf is immune to the bacteria, but your two-legged body is not."

"Why is that?"

Mrraska did not answer right away. She showed Drrak how to cut and gut his burrower, and he followed her lead a bit clumsily. The meat looked a bit chopped up, but Mrraska nodded approval.

Finally she said, "I don't know. Nobody does. The Science Council is working on it."

"Mum." Drrak hesitated, not sure how to phrase the question. "When I turn wolf, am I—will I be the same person? My body will change, and so will my brain. But how much of that is me?"

Mrraska thought about it. She dropped the cleaned burrowers into the carrying sack she wore on her hip, zipped it closed, and stood up.

"Your brain changes, but your mind does not. You keep all of your memories and all of your feelings. Those don't change. But your emotions become dominant over your thinking mind, and while you're the wolf, you forget how to put reason ahead of feeling."

"Is the wolf dangerous?"

"Yes." Mrraska believed in honesty. "But only when your mind is not healthy. If you are full of rage when you walk on two legs, that rage will create a rogue when the wolf takes over."

"You didn't wait for me!"

Mrraska turned quickly, and she grinned when she saw Cyrra running toward them. "You're too slow, and we were hungry!"

The sisters embraced and nuzzled noses. "How did your little hunter do?" Cyrra asked. She smiled down at her nephew.

"As fine a killer as his father," Mrraska said. "Perfect form and a perfect kill. He'll be hunting independently by the time he graduates from primary. Even feral ungula will be no match for him."

"Speaking of feral ungula—" Cyrra held up a long blade, the one Drrak had coveted at the tools rack. "How hungry are you?"

Mrraska licked her lips. "You're the pack leader tonight. Let's show my son some real hunting."

Ungula were large and hooved, and they tended to prefer open spaces. Mrraska and Drrak followed Cyrra out of the woods and into a cleaning where ungula had been spotted before. Then they settled down at the trees' edge and waited.

Drrak dozed, jerking awake whenever someone shifted or sighed. He was getting tired, but he didn't want to miss the kill. He had seen domesticated ungula of course; they were common pack beasts. But he'd heard that wild ungula were different, leaner and meaner, and he wanted to see for himself.

Mrraska nudged him, and he came fully awake. The females were crouched low to the ground, watching a trio of ungula venture into the moonlit clearing. Drrak stared. They were different.

The ungula he saw pulling carts and caravans were fat and slow, with large, sleepy eyes. These beasts were thin and muscular, and their eyes and ears were constantly moving. The dominant male looked all around, sniffing at the air. The smallest, presumably the offspring, was spindly and a bit clumsy, but it too twitched and flicked constantly. These beasts would not be easy to catch.

"The buck," Cyrra whispered, so quietly that Drrak could barely hear her.

"The fawn would be easier," Mrraska breathed. "The buck is large and dangerous."

"No sport in a fawn. And the doe is still lactating; look at her dugs. Separate the buck."

Mrraska touched her throat. "You are pack leader."

Then she charged. She was a magnificent sight, running out into the night so fast that Drrak could scarcely track her motion. She was a faint grey blur in the night, taking after the little herd with single-minded determination.

The ungula turned as a unit and started back for the woods. The fawn and the mother made it first, while the male lagged behind. Mrraska ran between him and his family, separating them further. The male stopped and backed up, and the rest disappeared into the darkness.

Cyrra joined her sister, and the two circled the confused male, slashing at it with their knives. Mrraska managed to hamstring it with the razor edge of her knife, and Cyrra poked its hide full of holes with the tip of hers. The ungula bleated and lashed out with hooves and teeth, but the hunters were able to stay just out of reach. Cyrra threw back her head and howled with delight, and Mrraska joined her in song.

Drrak felt a howl bubbling up in his chest, and he joined his voice with theirs. They sang together of the joy of the hunt, the smell of blood, and the love of family.

The ungula slowed. Its kicks were more halfhearted, and its head hung lower. Cyrra leaped onto its back and wrapped one arm around the beast's neck. Mrraska hung back and waited.

The beast lashed out with renewed vigor, thrashing and kicking madly. But it was bleeding heavily and hobbling on three limbs, and its strength was almost gone.

Mrraska moved in for the kill. She swung her saw-toothed blade upward and across the beast's throat. But the buck jerked back at the last moment, and the cut was bloody but superficial.

Then the buck did something unexpected. Instead of bucking and trying again to escape, it lunged forward and attacked Mrraska. It slammed into her, knocked the knife out of her hand, and Drrak screamed as he watched his mother collapse under its trampling hooves.

Cyrra also screamed, a scream of rage. She jumped off the ungula's back, swung her blade, and gutted the beast where it stood. Wet coils of intestine fell out onto the cold earth, and it bleated. Then Cyrra swung again, at the throat this time, and its suffering was over.

Drrak was already running to his mother, but even he could see that it was too late. Her skull had been crushed, and she wasn't moving. He knelt by her side and touched her motionless chest. The ribs were caved in, and her heart was not beating. His mother was gone.

Cyrra was crying. She stroked Drrak's back and rubbed his hair and sobbed, "I'm sorry, I'm so sorry, ohh Mrraska I'm so sorry. Drrak, Drrak, I'm so sorry."

"You should be!" Drrak snarled. "You were pack leader; you were supposed to protect your pack! You told her to attack the male, and it killed her!"

Cyrra snuffled and slowly withdrew, chastened by her nephew's rage. Drrak would not look at her, but he knew she was still crying silently. Good.

His teeth felt sharp and pointed, and he felt a little like biting something. Instead, he curled up on the ground next to his mother's body and waited for the next thing to happen.

*****

The medicals came to take Mrraska's body away, and they took Drrak to his father's cottage. Rruc hugged him tightly, and Drrak hugged him back. They slept together that night in the tiny, cozy nest in his father's front room.

"I'm sorry," his sire whispered as Drrak dozed off in his arms. "I know this isn't how you wanted us to stay together."

"When I find a female," Drrak said sleepily, "I'm going to mate for life."

Year 187: Kuvrro and Nexrra

Kuvrro and Nexrra were half-siblings and grew up as neighbors. Their mothers were good friends, and they took care of each other's children. Kuvrro adored his younger sister, but in the manner of all older brothers, he couldn't let her know.

"Why are leap gates only used on other worlds?" Nexrra asked once as they walked to primary academy together. This would be Kuvrro's last year in primary. After the next school session he would graduate to the three-year secondary academy, and after that he would go on to a specialist school. He was considering Flight Academy. Most males left their home territories when it came time to attend a specialist academy, but Kuvrro didn't think he wanted to. He wanted to explore the stars, and that meant flight academy.

"Why?" she repeated. "Why can't we use the gates to go to school and the paradises and all those other places? It's so boring to walk."

"Because I'm older and smarter, that's why," Kuvrro said. He slapped her on the shoulder and ran off down the road a little. Nexrra yelped and ran after him, but she was weighed down by her bag of books. After watching her struggle for a bit, Kuvrro finally pitied her and let her catch up. He took Nexrra's bag and threw it over his other shoulder.

"Why?" she said again. She flexed her shoulders.

"I told you. Because I'm older and smarter!"

Nexrra bared her teeth and snapped at him. Kuvrro started, jumped back, and almost fell over under the weight of two book bags. Nexrra's incisors had grown almost to her lower lip. They receded quickly, but Kuvrro knew what he'd seen. Nexrra's wolf was waking up. She was about to become a woman.

The thought was uncomfortable enough to make Kuvrro forget about teasing her. "Because leap gems are rare, and it's a waste of technology to use them instead of walking. And also because getting fat and lazy makes the wolf turn mean."

"Why?" Nexrra had heard the same thing at school, but she didn't understand it.

"I don't really know. It's got something to do with our brain chemistry. Too much of one hormone and not enough of another or something. But that's why the ungula trains are only for ancestors and for medical emergencies. We walk and run everywhere to keep the wolf happy."

Nexrra was glad that it made somebody happy. She hated walking, especially during the cold season when she had to bundle up in extra clothes. When her wolf awoke she could grow her pelt out to keep warm, like Kuvrro. Since his wolf had awoken two years ago, he could keep warm and modest with his own body fur.

They reached the primary academy, and Kuvrro took off running to find his friends. Nexrra growled. He was her best friend when they were at home, but at school she was invisible to him. Mum said that it had to do with his hormones. "He's starting to notice females now, and he's leaving us behind. It's normal."

"But I'm a female!"

Mum had licked her nose affectionately. "You're a different sort of female. You'll understand all this when your wolf awakens."

Nexrra sighed. That was Mum's answer for everything.

She entered the building and went to the main gymnasium, where the different age groups gathered to socialize before class time started. Kuvrro was already there, laughing and flirting with two females. Nexrra knew very little about the rituals of adolescent courtship, but it was plain to her that they were humoring him. Kuvrro's jokes and antics amused them, but Nexrra could tell by their posture that they were not romantically responsive. Surely Kuvrro noticed, but maybe he was too busy making them laugh. Or maybe he thought he could change their minds.

"Nexrra!" Cavrra bounded over, swinging her book bag over her head. "Mum had her baby!"

Nexrra squealed and hugged her friend. Cavrra's mother had been overdue with the baby sibling, and Cavrra had been gloomy and sullen for days. Now her friend would go back to normal and they could start having fun again.

"Male or female?" Nexrra asked. She didn't really care, but it was polite to ask.

"Male."

"Have the medicals been to see him yet?"

"Not yet. Mum said they'd probably come today."

"But he looks healthy?"

"Healthy and nursing and big around as a ball. Mum says she doesn't ever want to do that again."

"That's good. That's just wonderful. So what do you think Rrusa's going to teach us in Numbers today?"

"Something boring." Cavrra smiled, and Nexrra grinned back. It was good to be best friends again.

Rrusa's Numbers class was boring as ever; Nexrra was far more interested in math's applications than the process itself. She didn't care how one calculated the distance between leap gems stationed on orbiting moons; she only wanted to visit those moons and see the gates for herself. But if she wanted to join the elite star explorers, she had to start studying now.

Cavrra and Nexrra lay together in their group nest at the back of the classroom. There were seven other nests scattered around the room, which was carpeted with green fluff that smelled like grass and purple-fur flowers. The last several years had brought new strides in the technology of smells, and researchers had discovered that certain combinations were conducive to a state of attentive calm, even among growing young hunters.

Rrun lay in the grass among the nests and controlled the wall eye with his wrist. Clusters of yellow balls floated across the screen, illustrating the formula they needed to learn in order to calculate the velocity of a class-G planet around a dark yellow star. Nexrra tried her best to pay attention, but her mind kept wandering away from the math and instead toward the planet itself. Was a class-G more or less likely to have liquid life? It wouldn't be gaseous, not at that distance. A dark yellow star would be on the small side. What if--?

"Nexrra!" Rrun said. "What are you thinking about right now?"

Cavrra's hand tightened on hers. Nexrra licked her nose and answered honestly. "I was wondering about the properties of the average class-G planet."

"Numbers are not your strongest area." Rrun wrinkled his nose at her.

"No." Nexrra touched her throat. Cavrra's hand was starting to hurt.

But Rrun surprised them both. "Numbers are not for everyone, and it's not a failing in character." He jumped to his feet and turned off the wall eye. "Not all of you will absorb every lesson with ease. Not all of you have the neurological aptitude for it. That does not make you a less intelligent hunter, so you must never let anyone think that of you."

Nexrra's heart beat a little faster, and she felt her muscles go limp with relief. That was not what she had expected him to say. She glanced at Cavrra, whose eyes were wide with surprised delight.

After the class ended, the young females took a few moments' rest time in the paradise to the south of the academy building. There was no time to hunt properly, but it was still fun to run around the trees and chase each other through the brush. Once they were panting and breathless, Nexrra flopped into a patch of flowers and looked up at the bright yellow sun. "Can you believe what Rrun said?" she asked.

"That's the first time I've heard a class alpha say being bad at something doesn't make you stupid," Cavrra said.

"I'm still smart," Nexrra mused. "I can go to the stars."

*****

But their happiness didn't last. When Nexrra found her friend the next day, Cavrra was dark and morose. Her ears were enlarged, a sure sign of stress.

"What happened?" Then Nexrra knew. "It's the baby, isn't it? The medicals found something."

Cavrra nodded. Her voice quavered. "He has the wasting disease. They said—they said he won't live more than a year." Her eyes watered, and Nexrra put her arms around her.

"Did they take him already?" Nexrra squeezed Cavrra's shoulders tightly, as though she might fly away.

Cavrra nodded again. Then she started to sob. Nexrra held her and comforted her as well as she could, which she knew wasn't good enough. It was surprising that Cavrra had even come to academy today; she would have been excused if she'd wanted to stay with her mother.

Nexrra scolded herself for her prior selfishness. Cavrra had been moody and anxious for weeks, and Nexrra had thought only of was how it affected her own fun. When Cavrra had cheered up after the birth, Nexrra had only thought of how much more fun she would have. Nexrra would not let her friend down again.

When Cavrra could finally speak, she said, "Mum was afraid it might happen. When they tested her before, back when she had me, they told her she carried the gene for the wasting disease. But I was normal. I'm not even a carrier. I guess she decided she didn't need to test again when she got pregnant with—with the little one."

Cavrra's brother had never been given a name. Nexrra found that incredibly sad. "Who is the little one's father?"

"We have the same father. That's why Mum thought that since I was all right, the new one would be too."

"Your mother has been with the same male for ten years?"

"Longer. They've been together their entire lives. I don't think Pa will ever move on."

Nexrra was amazed. Garouean females outnumbered males roughly three to one, so it was rare for a couple to stay together longer than the three or four years necessary to raise a baby to childhood. Children were considered community property once they were weaned off mother's milk, so it was not necessary for the male to stay once the female was able to support herself again. But sometimes he did. Interesting. Nexrra wondered if she would want the same male around for the rest of her life.

"What's it like, having Pa in your house for so long?"

Cavrra shrugged. "It's all right. He helps Mum a lot. Right now he's at the medical center with her, saying goodbye to the baby."

"How long will your Mum stay at the medical center?"

"A few days at least. She'll probably keep going back to visit until—it's over. She won't want to leave him for good."

"Will it be nice to have Pa in the house while your Mum is out?"

Cavrra smiled into space. "Yes. I like it."

"I can come stay with you too, if you want."

"I do." She took Nexrra's hand and squeezed.

*****

Shifting class was always held outdoors. Xerrya liked to take them out to the paradise behind the Academy building. She said that the smell of wolf and prey would sharpen their minds and help the lessons

30

stick. Nexrra wasn't sure about that, but it did make her hungry, especially since this session's Shifting class was right before lunch break.

Today there were three students with the teacher, and they strolled down a well-worn path into the heart of the paradise. Nexrra smelled burrower and wolf mark everywhere, and her stomach growled.

"What year is it?" Xerrya asked.

"Year One Eighty-Seven," Jerra said quickly.

"And what does that mean?" Xerrya looked at Cavrra, who hesitated.

"It's been one hundred and eighty-seven years since the Enlightenment," Nexrra said. She bowed her head and touched her throat in apology. It was generally frowned upon for a student to come to another's rescue. But Cavrra had been off her mark all day, and no wonder.

Xerrya turned back to Jerra. "What was the Enlightenment?"

"The end of the cure," Jerra said. "They stopped looking for a cure and started learning how to get along instead."

"What cure?" Back to Cavrra.

Cavrra knew this one. "The cure for the wolf. The wolf is not a disease, and our efforts to cure ourselves of the change were suicidal."

"Why?" Eyes on Nexrra.

Now it was Nexrra's turn to hesitate. She looked down at her hands. The air was chilly, and in response a light grey fur had sprouted on them. This happened more and more nowadays; Mum said that it meant she was about to become a woman. "Because the wolf is us," she said. She held up her hands. "The wolf is part of the hunter psyche, just like my hands are a part of me. If we remove the wolf, we castrate and kill ourselves."

"Very good." Xerrya led them down the path, deeper into the forest. "Does anyone know why the full moon triggers the change?"

Silence. Xerrya nodded. "Nobody does. The hunter brain has not yet been fully mapped, and there are aspects of the wolf that are still undiscovered country. But what do we know?" She looked at Jerra.

"The change is necessary. Hunters who fight the change become ill or go mad."

"Excellent. What else?" Cavrra.

"Keeping our bodies healthy and fit keeps the wolf happy. Hunters who are unhealthy in body may go rogue when the wolf comes."

"My teeth, I don't know why I'm here. You all know so much. Let's have a practical demonstration. Nexrra, turn wolf for us."

Nexrra cocked her head. "What?"

"Show your friends that there is nothing to fear."

"I've never changed before. My body isn't ready."

"I disagree. Touch your ears."

Nexrra did, and she was startled to find them hairy and pointed. "I've never done it before," she repeated.

But then she wondered. During the last full moon, when Kuvrro and their mothers went out, hadn't she felt something that kept her awake all night? A strange tickle in her bones, an odd itch in her teeth? Nexrra thought yes. She thought about that feeling and tried to summon it back.

"Your clothing," Xerrya reminded her. Nexrra shed her robe and undergarments. The fur beneath was thick and grey, and it obscured her bare body. She was ready.

The itch was back in her teeth, and Nexrra concentrated on it, encouraged it. The itch rippled through her muscles and bones until it strengthened into a strange pulling ache. Wake up, wolf, Nexrra thought.

And the wolf awoke. It came over suddenly, like an ocean wave. Her brain caught fire, her face pulled and lengthened into a muzzle, and she fell to all fours. Nexrra cried out with the intensity of it, and her voice sounded like a howl.

Xerrya howled along with her. Nexrra trembled with joy and newfound energy. She felt like running, so she ran. Behind her, she could hear anxious questions being asked of the teacher. They didn't matter. All that mattered was the pure, rippling energy that flowed through her like pouring fire. All that mattered was the wolf. All that mattered was that she run.

Between the trees, over boulders and fallen logs she ran. She ran until her new muscles ached and her lungs burned with exertion. Finally Nexrra slowed to a walk, and she lay down in the shadow of a fallen tree. The wolf slept.

When she awoke, she was back in two-legged form. She got up slowly; her muscles hurt, and her mouth felt dry. She walked slowly back the way she had come. She had no idea how much time had passed. Xerrya and the others must have gone back to the academy by now. Nexrra hoped she hadn't missed lunch.

Someone was coming. Nexrra tensed, and her muscles ached. Then she saw that it was Kuvrro.

"Xerrya told your mum!" he said. "She said that you're dismissed from classes for the rest of the day, so I'm supposed to take you home."

"Why didn't Mum just send a message?" She glanced at her wrist eye, a bit scratched but none the worse for her run through the woods. They were built to withstand a lot of punishment.

"Well maybe I wanted to see for myself. It's not every day my baby sister grows up."

Nexrra looked down at herself. Her body was still covered in grey fur. It had finally happened. She really was becoming a hunter.

"Now the males will start coming. Nexrra, avoid the ones who talk and talk about their hunting exploits. A proper hunter will want to take you out and show you his prowess."

"Yes, Kuvrro." Nexrra barely heard him. Her wolf had awakened. She was becoming a woman. She felt no different in her body—aside from the muscle aches—but her mind felt different, buzzing with ideas and possibilities.

She couldn't wait until the next full moon.

Year 187: Cavrra

Cavrra came home to an empty cottage. This was expected; Mum and Pa would be at the medical center with her baby brother. She wondered if they would name him. Mum had been crying so hard that morning that Cavrra couldn't ask.

She dropped her book bag on the floor near her personal corner of the cottage. Like most family homes, the interior was divided into two large common areas; one for eating, playing, and watching video stories, and the other for resting and sleeping. Each family member had a particular area that they claimed as their own, and Cavrra found hers in the far corner and curled up with a school-book about the quantum properties of leap gems. She couldn't care less about leap gems or the imaginary particles that enabled them to bend space, but anything was better than looking around the empty cottage. All those empty places, everywhere her family wasn't.

The front door slammed open. "I'm sorry," Grrifa said. She was a neighbor from down the road, an ancestor who had no family of her own. Cavrra always wanted to ask why she didn't live with one of her own children like most ancestors, but she felt it might be rude. Mum had always shushed her when she tried to ask about Grrifa's family.

"I was sleeping and lost track of the time. I meant to be here when you got home. You shouldn't be alone." Grrifa sat on the floor next to Cavrra and stroked her hair.

"I'm all right." Cavrra stared at her book.

"Yes, you are. Are you hungry? Did you eat anything when you came home?"

"Not yet."

"Do you want cheese or fruit?"

Cavrra wanted to tell Grrifa that she was fine, she wasn't hungry, but the ancestor was already heading for the kitchen. "Cheese," she called after her.

Grrifa cut a large slice of ungula-cheese off a block she found in the ice box. Cavrra took the dish and pretended to be engrossed in her book as she ate. Grrifa left her alone after that.

The afternoon drained slowly away. Grrifa turned on the wall eye and watched several hours of stories. Then the screen flickered and chimed. A message appeared, obscuring the story. IS CAVRRA ALL RIGHT?

Grrifa looked at her, and Cavrra kept pretending to read. Grrifa tapped at the control panel, and before the words vanished Cavrra read them. YES BUT SHE NEEDS HER PACK.

There was another chime, and the video story came back on.

"That was your father," Grrifa said, as if Cavrra hadn't watched the entire exchange out of the corner of her eye. "I think he'll come home soon."

"He doesn't have to. He should stay with Mum."

Grrifa turned off the story and walked over to Cavrra, who tried not to flinch away. She sat on the floor next to Cavrra's seat cushion. Close, but not actually touching. Her courtesy was soothing.

"My family's gone," Grrifa said.

Cavrra finally looked up from her book. Here it was at last. "What happened to them?"

"My mate was a rogue. He ate our offspring—then he tried to kill me." She touched a white scar near her throat, almost invisible under the lines of age.

"That's so sad," Cavrra whispered. Rogue wolves were rare, but it was said that when a wolf went bad, he went very, very bad.

"I never mated again. He was my first, and he frightened me so badly I thought I could never trust my own judgment. I couldn't risk choosing wrongly again."

"But it wasn't your fault."

"That's what my mother told me. But I didn't believe her—not until it was too late to tell her so."

"You must be so lonely." Cavrra put her book down and hugged Grrifa tightly.

Grrifa hugged her back and nuzzled her hair. "Not anymore. I've learned to take comfort in my outside pack—my friends, and their children. All you little ones—you are my family."

Cavrra held on to her elderly friend, feeling her thin bones, hearing the faint wheeze in her lungs. It frightened her to think of growing so old with no mate and no children.

There were worse things than loss. That was what Grrifa was saying.

When Cavrra's sire came home, he found Cavrra and Grrifa curled up together in Cavrra's corner. They were both asleep.

Years 190-195: Mirra

Mirra was the youngest female to ever graduate from Northern Garou's flight academy. She'd pushed herself harder and faster than any other, taking each obstacle and setback as a personal challenge. Her instructors commented on her drive among themselves, but they said nothing directly to her. They did not want to give her a swelled head. But they marveled at her ambition and drive, and they expected in a few years that they would see great things from her.

Her classmates, on the other hand, saw her as a freak.

Yrra was five years older and two levels behind Mirra. Once she had been among the top ranking students, but Mirra made her—and everyone—look like a lazy cub. Yrra pretended not to care, but everyone knew better. Except perhaps for Mirra herself. She was too busy to think about it.

She watched with the pretense of boredom as Mirra ran flawlessly through a simulation of landing a wounded aircraft on an alien plateau.

"Now what do you do once you've landed safely?" asked the instructor, a grey-whiskered old male named Grrun.

"Send a distress beacon through the nearest gate," Mirra said immediately.

"And what of your crew?"

"Tend to any injuries and keep them calm until help arrives."

"And how would you keep them calm? What is the protocol for controlling panic in your pack?"

Mirra hesitated. Yrra sighed with relief. She wasn't perfect after all.

"That's advanced training," Grrun said. "You'll cover it in next session's alpha leadership class. I don't expect—"

"Give them a job to do. Keep them busy and working toward a common goal. Even if they know it's a useless task, having something to do will reduce stress and calm the wolf."

Grrun asked, "And how do you know that?"

Mirra shrugged. "It seems like a good idea."

Grrun and the entire class were silent for a moment. "Creative thinking is a skill that cannot be taught," he said at last. "You have a natural talent for alpha leadership."

Mirra accepted the compliment with a silent nod, but Yrra growled under her breath. Little show-off. She had probably read ahead in the session files.

The academy students had their evenings free for socializing, but Yrra avoided her usual pack of friends. It was time to find out Mirra's weak spot. Everyone had one. Yrra would not accept that this fluffy-coated female was as perfect as she seemed.

Mirra was in the common study hall, reading. The study hall was adjacent to the library and the eating hall, so it was a comfortable place to eat and read at the same time. Mirra munched on a bowl of dried yellowfruits and did not look up from her book when Yrra approached.

Yrra lifted the book out of Mirra's hand and looked at the cover. Mirra snatched it back so quickly that Yrra barely saw her move. She sat back down, popped another fruit in her mouth, and resumed reading.

Yrra was not perturbed. She would not be the first to lose her cool. "A romantic fiction? Hardly the sort of reading material I would expect from Grrun's star pupil."

"It's my free time." Mirra still did not look up from her book.

"All the same, from such a brilliant student I would expect something more intellectually challenging. Haven't you read the classical love poems of Qrre yet?"

"Qrre is overrated and overexposed."

Yrra growled. Qrre was a cousin of whom she was immensely proud. Mirra would show throat for that insult. Yrra would make it happen.

Mirra chewed on her fruit, pretended to read her book, and waited. Yrra had been watching her for over a month now, ever since Mirra had beaten her on the zero-gee agility course. This confrontation was inevitable, and Mirra was prepared for it.

Then she heard the approach of a third. Mirra tensed. This would change the dynamic of the fight.

It was Seirr, a younger male who was sweet on Yrra. Mirra relaxed. He would not interfere. Males did not fight females.

"I know why she's such a great student," Seirr said.

Mirra tensed again. This was unexpected. She kept her eyes on her book, but Yrra saw the faint twitch of her ear.

"Tell me," Yrra said. "Mirra isn't the only one here with a thirst for knowledge."

"She was rejected by a male in her last year of secondary. She chose a male who preferred a soft, caring female over a metal thinking machine. She came here covered in disgrace."

"So that explains it!" Yrra said brightly. "Poor heartbroken Mirra, all you have left are your studies—and your book-romance." She snatched the book out of her hands again and dropped it on the floor.

Mirra was out of her chair in an eyeblink. Before Yrra could shout or even growl, she was flat on her back and pinned to the floor. Mirra's eyes flickered back and forth between sky-blue and wolf-gold. Her face was dusted with brown fur, and her hands felt like paws.

"I. Rejected. Him." Mirra snarled in Yrra's face. Her words were barely understandable around her mouthful of teeth.

"He was stupid and slow and a bad hunter. I rejected him. That soft and caring female who chose him is too stupid to know that she'll be feeding him by hand along with their young."

Mirra snapped her jaws together in front of Yrra's nose. She yelped involuntarily. Mirra stood up and shook herself, and her wolf features fell away.

The academy security force was standing behind her.

The hearing was quick. Yrra willingly admitted to baiting Mirra, and that together with Mirra's exemplary academic record led to a suspension rather than expulsion. Her grades suffered, and Yrra took the top spot just before the end of the session.

In the next session, Mirra pulled ahead again, and she never lost her lead. But Yrra didn't care. Mirra wasn't perfect. She wasn't a paragon of hunter virtue. She had flaws just like anyone. That was enough to satisfy Yrra, and it even made her like her a little. She spent the next session currying Mirra's favor: offering to help her study, sharing food, and inviting her on hunting trips with her friends. Mirra never warmed up to Yrra, but they were able to finish their respective school careers with no further incidents.

But Mirra swore to herself that she would never lose control like that again. Losing control meant losing power, and in a dangerous mission, it could mean losing lives.

After graduation, Mirra was chosen to captain a small mission to Morteloup, a dead world that hunters often visited for training or to mine its few resources. The trip out was routine, but on the way back the ship suffered minor exterior. One section of the ship's heat shield was slightly corroded, and Mirra's error detection system blared an alarm and insisted that the ship fly no further. She landed quickly on Morteloup's small, bare moon and sent messages via both wrist eye and radio for help. In addition to captaining and landing the craft safely, Mirra kept the four wolves under her command calm until help arrived. She remembered the flying simulators she'd captained in the academy, and she took her own advice by ordering them about at useless but tiring tasks like cleaning the spare biosuits and taking apart the sample collection equipment. They growled about it under their breaths, but it worked; nobody lost their temper or lost control of the wolf. After it was over her crew rubbed their throats and thanked her for her firm leadership.

Or, as one hunter put it, "We appreciate your complete lack of style and humor a lot more than we did.

She was awarded a hunting feast in her honor, and most of her former classmates came to the event to run wild ungula and share in their old friend's glory. Yrra was among them.

The Council for Space Exploration met the following month to discuss a new program. A new ship was being built—bigger and more powerful than any before— and it would cross the galaxy via established leap gates and into the depths of unknown space. It would plant new gems and create new gates, so that the hunters could go further than ever before into the unknown.

Some council members argued for a seasoned crew of experienced explorers. But the council alpha, Childrra, had a different idea. "New, young wolves are what we want for this mission," she said. "Old wolves are best at teaching what they know. This journey calls for hunters who want to learn, not to teach." The rest of the council nodded slowly and touched their throats. Childrra had spoken well, and they were all in agreement. When the topic of crew selection rose, Mirra was the first and most logical choice for a new ship's captain.

Mirra did not pick her first crew. No new captain ever did. It was Council policy to assign first-time alphas a crew they had chosen themselves, using their own expertise and the history records of successful pack dynamics. She was content with that. She had few close friends, and she wasn't sure that any of them measured up to her own expectations.

She was assigned a crew of ten who were roughly her own age, though most had more field experience. There was one male and nine females. Throughout all of Garou the females outnumbered the males, but in interstellar travel and other hazardous occupations, the ratio was astronomical. Males were sensitive and easily stressed, and when stressed they were prone to fight with other males. It was an ancient defense that scientists hoped to someday breed out of the species. In the meantime, males were kept isolated from each other in dangerous and stressful situations.

Mirra met her crew on the bridge of her new ship, the Star Pack. The lone male, Kuvrro, gave her a friendly glance that made her feel a little warm inside. She asked him, "Are you mated?"

"No." He yawned and stretched, showing off his strong physique. His pelt thickened a trifle. "Why do you ask?"

Mirra bared a tooth at his shameless flirting. "I want to know the history of all my crew. Mated wolves tend to be less easily stressed." This was true, but only partially.

Kuvrro straightened his spine and touched his throat. "I am a dedicated and educated security officer. My only wish is to serve the Star Pack and my people. Though I am not yet mated, I will perform my duties with the steadiness of an ancestor."

Mirra admired his quick recovery. He was a joker, but he was also a quick thinker who knew his place in the pack. She decided that she liked him.

Several others she was less impressed with. Ledrra struck her as silly-minded and a bit too eager to please. She stared at Kuvrro hungrily when she thought nobody was looking. When Mirra asked her about her specialty, she took off babbling as though she pleaded for her life.

"I study alien species, especially their paths of evolution and cultural development. It's amazing how so many different planets have so much in common. I've written a thesis for the Council of Alien Affairs on the peculiarities of the Harrenan anal worms. Perhaps some time I could show it to you."

Mirra sighed through her nose and looked at the rest of her crew. Cavrra stared back at her with a fawning expression, and Mirra rolled her eyes. Every pack had at least one belly-roller who licked ass and showed throat to anyone with a backbone. Some alpha types found it charming. Mirra found it irritating. And it was just her luck that she had two on her very first crew.

That evening, she went back to the academy library. As a high honors graduate, she had the run of the place, and sometimes an instructor would ask her to speak to a new class. She liked it here, even when nobody noticed or remembered her. The academy was the home of some of her greatest triumphs. (So far, she thought.) She hurried past the study hall. She did not like to remember what had transpired there, with that combative female Yrra. She'd been provoked, but it hadn't been all of Yrra's fault. In fact, Yrra had turned out to be a pretty decent person once she'd gotten past her insecure feelings. But Mirra didn't like to think about how she'd shamed herself and had been punished.

But she would not despise herself for it either. Every mistake made was a learning opportunity. That day she had learned exactly how unacceptable it was to lose her temper. To lose control.

In the library, she found a book about leap mining. She knew nothing about the gems, only that they enabled the gates that allowed explorers to step through entire solar systems in an instant. Garou was the only known planet to have a healthy supply of the gems.

Mirra decided that she ought to learn as much as she could about leap gems. It wasn't necessary, since they had a leap specialist on the crew—that fawning pup Cavrra. But Mirra felt she ought to learn at least a little more about the mineral that her people depended upon for their mastery of the galaxy.

"Mirra! What are you doing here?"

It was Drrak, who had graduated just below Mirra on the honors totem. Mirra smiled at him. "What are you doing here?" she returned.

"Gloating about my triumphant departure from these hallowed halls, of course. But you don't seem the gloating type."

"I'm not. I'm reading about my future." She held up the book, which was black all over with a gold spine. Black and gold, of course. Like a leap gem.

"You have a crew! Amazing. I wish I was an alpha type. I haven't even found one to join yet."

"What's your specialty?"

"Entertainment officer."

"Entertainment officer?" Mirra tried and failed to keep the contempt out of her voice.

"I know, I know." Drrak looked away. "But all the class choices looked so boring. I wanted to do something fun."

Mirra sighed. "You're going to wind up on pleasure cruises, juggling and singing to amuse the cubs."

"Star ships need entertainment too! There are long and boring stretches of space out there. I'll find a job. Don't worry about me."

Long and boring stretches of space were best used for self-education and preparation for the moments of stress and danger that lay ahead. But Mirra pitied Drrak. He wasn't alpha material, but he was hardworking—and intelligent, in his own way. All he needed was a little guidance.

"Join my crew," she said. "I have no entertainment officer. Prove your worth to me on our first discovery, and you'll be able to take your pick of crews when we come back."

"Or maybe I'll just stay with your crew." Drrak touched her shoulder.

"Maybe."

Year 193: Jarren

Jarren entered the Academy two sessions behind Mirra. As a result, he saw her frequently and heard about her even more. They rarely interacted, however, and years later Mirra would not remember his name.

She was a common source of gossip among the younger males. She was out of their league socially and academically, but they admired her from afar and speculated about her romantic life. Jarren was fascinated by her. To him she was stronger, smarter, and more physically attractive than any female his age.

He had acquaintances all over the academy, and through casual conversation he was able to learn most of Mirra's daily schedule. He found reasons to linger near the eating hall before her lunch break, in the library during her free time, and outside the simulation cave during her advanced class on Dangerous Flight Paths.

"Hello, Mirra," he said as she brushed past him on her way to Math and Engineering.

"Hello," she tossed back over her shoulder. She didn't slow, but Jarren hastened his pace.

"Was it a difficult sim today?"

"No. A narrow stretch of flat ground next to a dropoff. It was no harder than the last one. They all tend to follow the same pattern. The instructor is just plugging in different visuals. He's trying to find something that will frighten me into making a mistake."

"Has he succeeded?"

"Not since the first day. I just need to remember that it's only a sim."

"But what will you do when you're the captain of your own vehicle, and it's not a sim?"

Mirra flashed him a smile. "Tell myself that it's just a sim."

Jarren had to double back so he could make it back to his beginner's programming class. But he barely noticed the long walk or the written warning for his second tardy in three days. That smile lingered like a flash of light behind his vision.

Females fascinated him, but they frightened him as well. Mirra was easy for him to talk to because he knew that she didn't think of him as romance potential; she barely thought of him at all. He could relate to females as friends, but he found it hard to make the leap to expressing sexual interest. They seemed to expect something from him, some body language or behavior that he couldn't quite grasp. Maybe they all wanted alpha types.

Tigrra seemed interested in him. At dinner one evening, she asked him if he wanted to go hunting with her. They talked for a bit and Jarren thought there might be potential here. Then he found out that she was earning poor marks in Dangerous Flights. "It's too frightening," she said. "I look over the edge of the cliff and freeze up every time."

"But it's just a sim."

"Have you taken the class? No, you're too young. It's a very realistic sim. It even mimics the air pressure change when you fall off the edge." She shuddered.

"What will you do if you're the captain of your own vehicle and have to land it in real life?"

Tigrra shrugged. She popped a dried yellowfruit into her mouth. "I'm not an alpha type. I probably won't ever become a captain. My plan after graduation is to get a job as a shuttle driver to one of the colonized worlds. Established leap gates and safe passage routes. Nice easy work with good pay."

Jarren shook his head. Tigrra had no ambition. Wasting intellect, he thought, is worse than being stupid. Tigrra was nothing like Mirra.

When Tigrra asked him again about hunting together, Jarren said no. "I'm behind in my studies and really need to catch up before the end of the session."

He spent the night watching video recordings of the landing sims Mirra had aced. She was magnificent.

Year 193: Ledrra

Flight academy was torture for Ledrra. She wasn't sure if it was the loss of Grrifa or the loss of her sister—who was flying through Medical Academy like a ship through space—but she had a terrible time focusing on her studies. She suddenly couldn't bear being alone, and whenever she was around others she wanted to do something fun with them. Studying alone was impossible; she daydreamed and doodled her time away every time she tried. And studying with friends was even harder. Every time she got together with a group, she would get bored and suggest a break. A trip to the dinner hall for a snack, inevitably turned into a flirting session with any male who happened to be nearby, and her friends would go back to studying without her. Eventually her friends started avoiding her, lest her addiction to socializing affect their grades.

She had almost no female friends, but there were always one or two males hanging around, lonely slackers like herself. As long as she had someone nearby to admire her and flirt with her, Ledrra told herself that she was popular and happy.

She graduated in the bottom half of her class—but, she told herself, at least she was near the top of the bottom half. She did well enough to skate by, but she was disappointed to discover that because of her poor grades and attendance, she would be passed over for the best jobs in the field she wanted. There were decent-paying jobs on Garou that would give her the prestige she craved, but she insisted on seeking a ship job, any ship job. And that was how she found herself on a tiny, ancient research vessel orbiting the desert world Harrena, studying parasitic anal worms.

Her first weeks on board the tiny vessel were torture for her and for her partner, Sorr. He was a little old male, well past breeding age, who would have taken the ancestor train years ago had he stayed on Garou. But here in a sterile, low-gravity environment, he was happy and healthy and more than patient with Ledrra as she suffered weeks of loneliness and depression. He walked her through her daily tasks of observing and recording the worms' behavior, then dissecting them and recording their

46

inner attributes. He showed her how to mix the special acid that took apart living things too small to dissect using the usual instruments. Over and over again they did this, day in and day out. Finally Ledrra became comfortable enough—or numb enough—to come out of her shell and get into her work.

The job really wasn't so bad. Harrena was an interesting planet. It was a desert world with almost no standing water on its surface. Ninety-eight percent of its liquid was deep below, and so was most of its life. This life was very primitive and consisted entirely of worms and arthropods. One of the worms, for reasons known to nobody, was attracted to the digestive systems of visiting hunters.

It was an odd puzzle. With the exception of viruses and some bacteria, aboriginal species instinctively avoided aliens. But this particular worm was attracted to them. They were a sharp-toothed parasite that drilled through the shell of a local arthropod, a scuttling black bug with large claws. But somehow their physiology enabled them to adapt to the hunter body, and their natural tunneling ability made the explorer's protective suits useless.

They were a dangerous nuisance, and Ledrra was doing valuable work as she studied and dissected them. But it wasn't the star-faring job of her dreams. She wanted to see a new galaxy, to travel to the edge of known space and then keep going. She wanted to make a great discovery that would change everything she thought she knew about the universe.

She would not do any of those things while picking apart sharp-toothed parasites.

Sorr knew how she felt, and he sympathized. He himself was old and comfortable; he had raised healthy offspring and provided their mothers with care and affection. But he remembered how it was to be young, to want to see the stars and everything behind them. He tried to cheer her up whenever he could.

"We're a mighty pack of two!" he would say, and Ledrra would laugh and agree.

"We are conquerors of an entire world," she'd reply, and they would bare their teeth and howl together.

Ledrra got an idea one day to test the parasites on other alien species. She requested and received a shipment of animal parts from

Garou—ungula, burrower, and waterfur. She inserted two Harrenan worms into the intestines of each animal. Then she turned on her microscopic viewer and watched.

The worms curled up and died.

Ledrra immediately tested the meat for contamination and infection. She called the source farmer on Garou and verified that the meat had come from young, healthy animals. The tests all came back clean, and the farmer assured her on the honor of his pack that he had cleaned and packed the animal parts himself. But the worms were repelled, just as one would expect them to react to a foreign body.

Ledrra ordered another shipment, then another. Again, the worms all died. Then finally, as a control, she ordered a section of bowel from a Garouean hunter. This time they took to it eagerly, tunneling and reproducing in record numbers. Within days the intestine was a roiling mass of tiny white worms, and Ledrra threw the disgusting thing out of the airlock as soon as she was done recording her observations.

She talked it over with Sorr that night over cooked meat and bluefruit. As she told him about the different test subjects, Sorr suddenly inhaled and almost choked on his meat. He coughed and sputtered and finally recovered enough to speak. "We're doing it backwards," he wheezed.

"Doing what?" Then Ledrra understood. "We're only studying the worms. We have to study what they naturally feed on."

"The black scuttlers."

Gathering a sample of the scuttlers would be unpleasant but easy. There was a sturdy tunnel leading down to a narrow cavern filled with mud and life. It would be a matter of walking through the leap gate, down the tunnel, and picking up as many of the creatures as she wanted. Ledrra pulled on her surface suit and told herself that this would be much easier than the dangerous-landings flight simulator she'd suffered through at the academy.

Her gut did not quite believe her. As soon as Ledrra's suit was on, her skin began to itch. She felt like there were worms crawling on her skin, under the suit. She pulled on her breathing mask and snapped it into the neck of the suit, and right away her nose and eyes itched. She growled, and she felt her ears and teeth lengthen.

"This suit's been reinforced with extra layers of nano-rubber," Sorr said. He put the carrying case in her hand and guided her to the sterilizer, a raised platform between hunter-height panels that emitted a combination of ultraviolet lights and mild toxins. She stood patiently while a low hum emitted from the panels for several minutes. Finally there was a sharp yip that indicated her suit was clean. She would not contaminate the natives of Harrena.

Whether or not those natives contaminated her, however…

"You'll be fine," Sorr said, reading her expression through the glass panel of her mask. "It would take most of a day for the worms to reach your skin, and you'll be back in minutes."

This made Ledrra feel a little better, but she still felt hot and scratchy. She would not spend one moment longer than necessary in this sweaty contraption. Her nose itched, and she had no way to scratch it.

She ran through the gate with her eyes closed, and she barely waited for the vertigo to subside before running down the smooth, sturdy tunnel to the underground cave. She unsnapped the carrying case from her waist belt and opened it. The scuttlers were slow and fairly stupid. She should have no trouble catching at least three, and that was as many as she needed.

She did better than that; half a dozen of the black, many-legged crawlers went into the padded case, and Ledrra snapped it shut and bolted back toward the gate. She remembered what Sorr had said, that her suit would protect her from the worms. But she knew too much about them: their grinding teeth, the acid they used to dissolve their food, the horrible lesions they left on the skin after burrowing in. She ran up the tunnel as though chased by rogues, panting so hard that her ventilator had to double its power to keep her mask unfogged. Sweat rolled down her face, and it felt like crawling worms on her skin.

She stumbled through the gate and landed on the sterilizer, which Sorr turned on immediately. A dozen tiny white worms dropped off her suit and curled up on the floor. Ledrra almost wept at the sight of them. The worms weren't frightening under a microscope or in a glass box. But when they were climbing on her, trying to get at her—that was entirely different.

She pulled off the suit, and Sorr came and took the box of scuttlers from her. When she had composed herself (and inspected every inch of her skin for lesions), she joined Sorr in the lab.

"So far they are giving up no secrets," he said without looking up from the glass case where he'd put them. "We'll observe them for a few days, then start euthanizing and dissecting them. There has to be a reason why the worms that feed on these also feed on us. But so far, I don't see it."

Ledrra believed him. She believed in him so completely that she stayed in the lab around the clock, observing and writing down notes about the scuttlers. They didn't look like much; they crawled aimlessly around the case and on each other. Once or twice they tried to climb the sides of the case, but they didn't make it more than an inch or two before falling down again. They had evolved to climb rocks, and their tiny claws could not manage on the smooth glass.

She slept on a cot in the lab, and Sorr brought her food and ate with her. One day, bored, she sat down to watch some old video footage she'd missed by falling asleep. Then she saw it.

She backed up the video and watched it again, then again. "Sorr!" she shouted. "I found it!"

Sorr hobbled in as quickly as he was able. He was red-faced and out of breath. "What?"

"Watch." Ledrra pointed to a single scuttler. "Watch what it does."

Another scuttler thrust itself at the first one, threatening it. The first scuttler curled up—and changed into a small, grey rock.

Sorr's jaw dropped. "They're—"

"Skin-changers. Like us." Ledrra reversed the video and watched it yet again. The scuttler was threatened, and it changed. Its legs pulled in and disappeared. This was not camouflage. Its legs and feelers were completely gone, and Ledrra could even see small cracks in its surface. Then, as the other scuttler wandered off, it changed back and resumed its aimless crawling.

"Prepare two of them for euthanasia," Sorr said. "We'll dissect one physically, the other chemically. Contact the Science Council on Garou and ask them to send us everything they know about the chemical and physical attributes of skin-changers. There must be a protein or enzyme that we share, something that the worms are attracted to. Perhaps it's a necessary nutrient, which is why the worms died when they tried to feed on the other animals."

"Just think, Sorr," Ledrra said. "Those bugs are our cousins! We have family elsewhere in the galaxy."

"This discovery will deliver you from obscurity. You'll be able to leave this research vessel and take a job on any star ship you choose."

"I'm not sure I want to leave now." Ledrra smiled at her elderly friend.

"Oh, you must. The galaxy won't conquer itself."

"But what about you?"

Sorr sighed. "I'm for the ancestor train, my dear. These old bones are finally worn out. I tried to change last month and couldn't. I can't handle the pain anymore, even in low gravity. It's my time."

Ledrra began to cry, and she hugged him tightly. "It's not fair! Why does everyone always leave me?"

Sorr hugged her back. "What's not fair is that I'm not fifty years younger," he said. He stroked her hair. "But never mind fair. Snap your fangs at fairness. Go find your ship, and be happy."

Year 196: Kuvrro

Kuvrro graduated from the Northern Garou Flight Academy as a security specialist. Kuvrro applied for the usual positions as a security guard and pack enforcement officer, but none of those jobs were available. Kuvrro had had too much fun at the academy, and his grades put him near the bottom of the waiting list. His advisor contacted him in person with the bad news, and with the news of the job he was considered suitable for.

Instead of escorting star freighters or hunting rogue wolves here at home, he would be driving the ancestor train through the northeast Territory here on Garou. It would be his job to take the sickly and dying to their final paradise.

The train came once a year to collect those who were ready to go. Kuvrro understood that in other parts of the world the train came more frequently. But the northeast territory of Garou was home to the Flight Academy, where students went on to careers in space travel and astronomy. Space travelers tended to live longer, healthier lives because of the stringent requirements of their profession, and their superior intellect kept mental breakdown at bay.

Kuvrro stood in the doorway of his dormitory unit, which he had just started to clean despite having graduated three days ago. He was too surprised and disappointed to remember his manners and invite the old man in.

Rruj smiled. "I'm sorry," he said. "I know it's not the job you wanted." But he didn't look sorry.

"How am I going to exercise my skills as a security officer while driving a train full of dying ancestors? I'll just be sitting down the whole way there and back, won't I?" Kuvrro thought briefly of his grandmother, taken when he was two. He shoved the memory away.

"The ancestors can be difficult. Sometimes an ancestor will forget where he is and become frightened and violent. You'll have to protect him and the others—gently."

"The females are all going to laugh at me." Kuvrro finally walked away from the door and let Rruj in. He sat down on the narrow cot, leaving the single chair for his superior.

"Only if you make it seem funny." Rruj leaned forward and looked Kuvrro sternly in the eye. "Driving the ancestor train is honorable work. They need a firm, kind friend in their last days at wolves. Females admire a kind male. It means that you'll be kind to their offspring."

Kuvrro sat up. He hadn't thought of that.

"What does the job include, besides driving the train?" He knew they wouldn't pay him a year's wages for a single ungula ride.

"Before Ancestor's Day, you must acclimate the ungula to your sight and smell. You will feed them and spend time with them as a man and a wolf. They will behave better if you are a familiar and trusted sight."

"Nurture a herd of dumb animals. That is definitely a job for a security specialist."

"You will provide basic care for them in the year of your employment and call the medicals for any signs of serious illness or injury. Mention this to any female who asks what you do."

"They do like to laugh. It might work."

"You're a clever young man, but you don't listen. Mention the care you give the ungula, and also how the experience has prepared your for your future as a kind, caring father."

Kuvrro got the idea. "So this job won't rip out the throat of my social life."

"Not at all. And I think you'll find that caring for the ungula and driving the train will teach you some much-needed patience."

Once he'd gotten the hang of it, Kuvrro found he enjoyed the time he spent with the animals. They were quite stupid compared to wolves, but they were also affectionate and personable. There were six in all, and he got to know them as individuals. One was very physical and loved to be rubbed and scratched behind its floppy ears. Another was more standoffish and preferred a quick, casual caress and then food. Kuvrro genuinely liked them.

The ancestor train only required four ungula to pull it, and part of Kuvrro's job was to decide which four would be best for the trip. After weeks of feeding, playing, and exercising them in the grassy little pasture near the center of town, he decided on Softy (the cuddly one), Whitey (pale fur with red eyes), Ginger (red coat, friendly disposition), and Shelby (jet black and always hungry.) He left Sparks and Sickly. Sparks was likely to be jumpy if the ancestors or their grandchildren wanted to pet the animals, and Sickly was—sickly. Kuvrro had had to call the medical center twice in the last three months over a simple virus that any other beast would have shrugged off in days, but almost killed Sickly. Kuvrro feared that he would be euthanized if his immune system didn't improve.

Best of all, Kuvrro found that Rruj was right. Females smiled and flirted when they found out that he was driving the ancestor train that year, and they loved hearing about the animals in his care.

"My grandfather went on the train last year," said young Tigrra, an academy student around his sister's age. "It was hard. My mother cried. But the driver was so kind to us. It's amazing what you do."

By the time the day came to actually drive the train, Kuvrro had a hunting partner for every free day in the next two months, and he wasn't sure he ever wanted to quit. He liked the ungula, and he liked the attention and prestige the job provided. But now the big day was coming. He hoped it would go well. It was the most important day of the year for him, and for many others.

The day dawned warm and clear. The train was always scheduled for a fine spring day to ease the stress of the transition. Kuvrro hitched up the ungula and guided them down the dirt road. The wagon was equipped with an electronic map that guided his route, but he scarcely needed it. He had walked the ungula down this path many times in preparation.

Kuvrro's eyes wandered, and he watched the little cottages as the train moved past. Here were most of the families with young children, closest to the academies and the center of town. The cottages were small, built to accommodate a mother, one or two offspring, and their father if the children were too young to leave. It was customary for a male to move on once the child he'd sired was old enough to attend academy, while the mother went back to work. Kuvrro tried to imagine what that would be like for him. Siring a child with one of the females he hunted with, caring for her and the baby for three or four years, then going back to the single life before moving on to the next. It was hard to picture. Right now the females were just friends, people to socialize and flirt with. None of them were old enough to settle down and reproduce, including him. He wasn't sure if he would ever feel old enough.

Also—not every male moved on. Nexrra's childhood friend Cavrra had a father who still lived in her mother's house, though they were both past childbearing years. Kuvrro found that sort of life even harder to picture.

As he passed the rows of family cottages, a young male came out and waved. Kuvrro halted the ungula; this was his first stop. He growled at himself for letting his mind wander; he had almost missed the cottage completely.

He jumped to the ground. The youngster touched his throat and ran back into the cottage. Kuvrro opened the side door and pulled down the auxiliary steps. Moments later, an attractive older female with ginger-red hair came out, leading an ancestor of incredible frailty. Her eyes were milky white. Blind.

He ran to the old female and took her hands in his. "Can you change, ancestor?" he asked.

She shook her head. "Too tired," she wheezed.

Poor old thing. "I'll help you. You'll be more comfortable in your wolf body." She would also move more easily with her keen wolf nose to guide her.

Kuvrro held her hands and changed, very slowly. It hurt more than usual, a drawn-out creaking and snapping of joints. But he closed his eyes and bore the pain, because she needed his contact to help her own body remember what to do. Finally it was over, and a white-eyed she-wolf lay in the dust before him. She panted, exposing worn teeth.

Kuvrro licked her face and walked slowly to the train. The blind female was able to follow her nose, and she boarded the train with only a little effort. Kuvrro shifted back to his two-legged form and smiled at the mother and her child. He tried to put as much kindness and reassurance as he could into that smile.

It must have helped, because they both smiled back. "Take care of her," the woman said.

"With my life and my honor," Kuvrro said, touching his throat.

So it went through the Northeastern Territory. Kuvrro collected the ancestors, reassured them, and helped them board the train. One male was completely disoriented and terrified. Kuvrro had to pretend to be the ancestor's long-dead brother to get him on board. Once he was safely settled into his seat, Kuvrro turned to the ancestor's daughter with a reproving look.

"He came over very suddenly," she said defensively. "Just this last month or two."

Kuvrro doubted that. In addition to the dementia, the ancestor's body was in an advanced state of age-decay. Kuvrro had had to change twice before the ancestor could join him in wolf form. The old man should have gone on the train last year, and they both knew it. It was cruel of her to have kept him alive past his time.

Kuvrro felt as though his muscles had been torn apart and slapped back together, and he was grumpy and out of sorts. But he bit his tongue. No doubt the daughter already felt terrible about neglecting her ancestor's needs in favor of her own selfish desire to keep him close. She knew now that she had done him no favors. All Kuvrro could do was make her feel worse.

He thought again of Grrana. As a small child, he had wanted nothing more than to have her next to him, all the time. When she was taken away, he had been angry at the world, especially at his mother for letting her go. Now he knew better. And so did this female.

So he just nodded and climbed back into his seat. He started the ungula forward with a word, and in his rearview mirror he saw her staring after him. She held her fingers tightly to her throat.

The train was silent; all of its passengers were in wolf form and most were sleeping. The few that were awake just stared out the open windows, enjoying the warm breeze and new sights and smells. Kuvrro closed his eyes briefly and pretended that he was one of them.

I'm so old, so tired. They're taking me away, taking me someplace new. Am I afraid? Not really. Death is an old friend to me. My parents are gone. My last mate is gone. Now I'm going too. There will be fresh water and cool green grass. Cozy dens to sleep in and burrowers to chase. I won't die hooked to machines and watching my children suffer for me. I'll run—until I can't anymore.

When Kuvrro opened his eyes, they were blurred with tears.

Year 199: Kuvrro

Kuvrro kept his job for three more years. He was starting to think he might keep it for life. The job paid well, and he had enough tender saved that he could afford to mate and sire offspring. Tigrra, who had recently graduated from the academy and didn't yet have a steady job, had expressed an interest.

The problem was that he wasn't sure he wanted to mate or sire offspring. He was content in his job with the ungula, but he felt sort of stuck, like he wanted to run faster but couldn't quite find the muscle. Still, Tigrra was a fine female who would make a good mother. He could easily see himself raising a child with her.

But then Kuvrro got a message from his sister. It came through his wrist eye, which was odd. Nexrra hated using the messaging system to communicate. When she wanted to talk, she usually just came and found him.

But the message itself was odd. COME NOW—AMAZING OPPORTUNITY. Nothing else. Kuvrro tapped the screen and his window went dark. Better find out what she wanted. He ran to the stable to check on the ungula, and then he went back to his mother's cottage to find his sister.

Nexrra was waiting outside for him. "Come now, you have to come now, the spaces are filling up and this is our big chance!"

She could only be babbling about one thing. "A new job? I don't know. I like the one I have now."

"Kuvrro, this is the opportunity of a lifetime! It's a brand-new star ship with a brand-new captain! They're looking for crew members who know each other, for better cohesion. I can get an application because of Cavrra, and I also worked with Ledrra on that cellular analysis project our last year at the academy. It won an award, remember? And you can apply because you're my brother! They're looking for people to fly it who are comfortable together and won't show fang. Be very friendly when you come apply with me."

Kuvrro's curiosity prickled. A new star ship with a new captain. This was a rare opportunity. It was a chance to bond and form a pack with someone new and green, someone who would have no personal prejudices. It was a chance to try new things, take risks, and make a name for himself. He loved the ancestor train, and he loved the ungula. But now that Nexrra had dropped this in his lap, he knew that he was not cut out for a lifetime of planet-side dwelling. He wanted to see the stars.

Kuvrro and Nexrra ran together to the space center, which was just a few minutes' fast run from the Flight Academy. Nexrra led him into the large building and down the shiny, cool hallway to a large office crammed to the ears with hopeful graduates. Kuvrro wasn't sure they'd made it in time.

"Don't worry, I already put our names down," Nexrra said. "It shouldn't be too long."

"But what if they called for us while you were fetching me?"

"They didn't."

"How do you know?"

Nexrra looked at him. Her eyes were dilated, and the irises were golden. "Because this is it!" she said fiercely.

Kuvrro thought he should tell her that just wanting something badly was no guarantee that it would happen. But he didn't want to fight with her, not while she was so excited and nervous. She might bite.

And it turned out she was right. After just a few minutes they were called together by a grey-haired female with round shoulders and enormous breasts. "Kuvrro and Nexrra," she said. "Brother and sister pair. You'll follow me."

Kuvrro squeezed through the shuffling crowd after his sister. The grey female led them through another door and into another hallway. This one was painted red. It made Kuvrro nervous. "That door," the grey female said to him. "Nexrra, you come with me." Nexrra had to trot after her; the female was fast on her feet. Then they were both gone.

Kuvrro opened the door in front of him. The interviewer was a burly male with a strong resemblance to the grey female.

"Sit down," he said. He did not offer his name or attempt any social niceties. But he carried himself like an alpha, so Kuvrro touched his throat and sat down. This was no time to be prickly about manners.

The interview was long, thorough, and deeply embarrassing. "How frequently do you hunt? Have you mated? Have you sired? How frequently do you pass a bowel movement?" Kuvrro had to close his eyes and pretend that he was talking to a machine so he could answer without getting flustered.

At last the questions stopped, and Kuvrro could breathe again. "You'll do," the grey alpha said. "Your sister was already accepted, so the Council will be pleased with this dynamic for the new crew."

"The Council?"

"The Starship Council. They're in charge of staffing and organizing the shuttle programs and space missions."

"So—I'm in? Just like that?"

"Yes. We already checked your academy and employment records before we called you in. Barring any surprises from your physical exam, you'll report to the Star Pack tomorrow to meet your captain. Good luck, Security Officer Kuvrro."

Nexrra met him outside. She bounced like a puppy and grabbed his arms. "I knew it!" she said. "Come on, let's get our med exams now before they change their minds!"

"So tell me about this new captain," Kuvrro said. They left the building arm in arm and headed for the road leading to the medical center. "And everything you know about the ship, the Star Pack."

"What do you want to know first?"

"The captain."

"Her name is Mirra. She's young. Younger than you. The Starship Council thinks that if she does well on the Star Pack's shuttle missions, the local assignments to Tetran and Kissmee, they may send us on an exploration within the year."

"It takes years to earn an exploration."

"Mirra's different. She's driven. She finished flight academy at the top of her class, almost a full year early, and she only got in trouble once. She's a legend."

"Is she nice?"

"Oh no. She's very cold. She has almost no friends. Nothing at all like your other—friends."

"Humm."

Nexrra thought she'd dissuaded him. But Kuvrro was thinking he liked a challenge.

Year 193: Grrifa

Grrifa was old, and her eyesight was bad. Her limbs creaked and ached, and she hurt so badly when she made her monthly change that the wolf just lay on her bedroom floor and whined the entire night. The ancestor train would come for her soon, and Grrifa was ready to go.

One beautiful spring morning, when the flowers smelled as sweet as anything Grrifa had ever known, an enormous grey wagon pulled up outside her cottage. The hooved ungula were calm and gentle, waiting patiently with nary a flick of their floppy ears or tails. The attendant who came to Grrifa's door was a handsome young male with a kind smile.

"It is time, Grandmother," he said. He touched his throat with three fingers, the gesture of respect reserved for the old and loved.

"I'm ready," Grrifa said, touching her own throat with a single finger. The youngster's eyes glistened; she had honored him with the gesture. Grrifa truly felt honored by him. Driving the ancestor train was a difficult and heartbreaking job.

The attendant held her hands and encouraged her to change to wolf. Grrifa tried, but her head ached and her joints burned with age and pain. "Try," he said. "You'll feel better."

The attendant's hands curled and slowly shifted into paws. Grrifa felt the chemical change in him, and it gave her the boost she needed to coax the wolf out of hiding. This would be the last time, she felt. It hurt so much.

Once down on all fours, Grrifa allowed herself to be led onto the train. It was an enormous carriage filled with comfortable seats designed for both two-legged and four-legged people. Grrifa climbed into a low cushion and looked out the window to her right. Her cottage was empty now, and before long it would be turned over to another single hunter like herself. Grrifa felt sad and tired.

The attendant took his place at the front of the train and called to the ungula. The big beasts took off at a gentle trot. They were intelligent creatures and knew the way. The attendant's job now was to watch for obstacles in the road and keep the old ones calm. Sometimes one or two would panic and want to go home. Grrifa couldn't imagine wanting to go home and continue her existence as a burden on her friends, in constant pain. But of course not everyone here was clear-headed. It was part of getting old.

Grrifa watched the scenery flow past. The trees were so pretty in the spring, with blue-green leaves and brilliant flowers of every shade imaginable. She leaned out through the open window, and her nose brushed the petals of a magnificent yellow blossom with a red stamen. Heart's blood, that one was called. The blossom shrank from her touch, and Grrifa breathed deeply. The red-dust pollen smelled like sweetness and life.

All too soon the journey was over. The elders slowly rose from their seats and exited the train. A few were confused, staring around in fear. The attendant watched them; if necessary he would coax them out of the train and into their new life. But the rest were smiling and content. This was the end they had all been promised. It was now time for them to die like wolves.

As they exited the train, the wolves blinked and sniffed around. Their coats were patchy, and their teeth were worn. The game here was fat and plentiful, but even so they would not live long. But that was all right. They were at the end of their lives, and they would die like wolves.

Grrifa took a few steps and stumbled. Her legs felt all different lengths, and the ground came rushing up at her. She yipped with pain and moaned a little as she lay panting on the cool grass.

"It's all right," the attendant said. "You're just disoriented. Let me help you."

He wrapped his arms around her torso and carefully lifted her back onto her feet. Grrifa licked his arm with gratitude, and he nuzzled the top of her head. Then he went back to the train and called to the ungula. It was time for him to go back.

Grunting a little, she limped away from the train in search of a den. There were caves and burrows nearby, and Grrifa smelled rain coming.

The burrow she found was small but deep, and Grrifa slept comfortably as the storm howled above her head. The fresh air and warm burrow felt marvelous around her, and she thought tomorrow she might try to hunt.

In the morning, their numbers were fewer. Out of twenty wolves, six had already passed away peacefully in the night. It was as if they had been waiting for just the right place to do it.

Grrifa met another female, an old friend she had once worked with in a repair shop for computer systems. She sniffed the other in greeting, and as she inhaled the familiar scent she remembered her name. Trresna. A good worker and mother of many offspring.

Grrifa and Trresna trotted through the forest together. Grrifa's nose was weaker than it had once been, but she could still smell burrowers nearby, fat and plump. There would be litters of young this time of year, slow and stupid and tender. Hungry Grrifa broke into a lope, ignoring the ache in her legs and hips.

She found the warren of burrowers and stopped just out of sight of their holes. She looked around for Trresna, but the other female was nowhere to be found.

Grrifa lay down on the cool ground and waited. The wind was blowing her way, carrying her wolf-scent away from the warren. As she watched and waited, several burrowers poked their heads out of the holes, sniffed the air, and hopped out onto the grass.

Grrifa still waited. She was tired from her brief run, and she wanted Trresna to catch up. Trresna would want to catch one herself if she still could.

More burrowers emerged. There was now half a dozen of them, and as expected many of them were half-grown. They would be the slowest and easiest to catch. They would also be the tastiest. Grrifa salivated. She decided that Trresna would forgive her for going ahead with the hunt as long as Grrifa saved her one.

Swift and silent, the old wolf charged into the warren. She snapped and bit and broke the necks of three burrowers before the rest had the sense to run for the safety. It felt good to help the burrowers this way; the survivors would be stronger and faster. Compassion was all well and good for the individual, but it did no good for the species as a whole.

But now Grrifa was completely exhausted, and the pain in her hips burned like fire. She lay down while she ate the first two, then very slowly she picked up the third and went back in search of Trresna.

There was no sign of her at all. Grrifa dropped the burrower and sniffed deeply at the soil. There was the wolf's scent; she'd been following Grrifa closely. But as Grrifa investigated, she got confused. The trail just ended next to the trunk of an enormous tree. Grrifa sniffed all around it. Trresna's trail led right to it and then stopped. This wasn't possible.

Grrifa sighed and picked up the burrower. Her nose was failing her too. Perhaps Trresna had gotten confused and wandered off, or perhaps she had felt her death approaching and wanted to be alone. Either way, Trresna was gone, and Grrifa was apparently too old herself to track her down.

Grrifa carried the burrower back to her new home, feeling sad and alone.

Part Two:
The People of the Star Pack

Chapter One

The voyaging ship, Star Pack, was a silver needle piercing the velvet depths of space. Outside all was cold emptiness, but the central hub of the Star Pack was warm and alive. The hub was a silver island of life, bringing the superior species through the galaxy in search of knowledge and power.

Most of the ship was propulsion and energy systems. Even with the use of leap gates, the ship had to travel far distances on natural power, and such power took up enormous space. The body was sleek and shining, long and silver like the body of an ancient wolf. At the center of the needle was a spinning ball, small compared to the rest of the ship but larger than any such habitat had ever been built by the people of Garou.

The living hub of the Star Pack was a globe, a miniature version of the world they'd left behind. The inhabitants felt at home here; surrounded by the oceans that provided food and energy to its people.

The Star Pack neared its destination: a small blue planet thought to be habitable. As the ship crossed the solar system's asteroid belt, the long needle detached from the bulb and fell away to join the interplanetary wreckage. There it would drift peacefully until the voyagers called it back to reattach for the voyage home. The thick, round bulb puttered on, passing a small red planet and settling into orbit behind the blue planet's single moon. It was not yet known if this planet contained life intelligent enough to spot the ship or fearful enough to see it as a threat. Until the hunters knew exactly what they were about to conquer, they would exercise every caution.

*****

"Where's Drrak?" Mirra asked.

Kuvrro's ears twitched. "He had to change," he said.

"Now? Is he insane?" Mira growled to herself. They had just reached orbit, and the scout ship would be touching down in ten hours. This was no time to change.

"He lost track of time and put it off too long. He had no choice." Kuvrro's tone was sympathetic, but his nose wrinkled in amusement. And no wonder. Drrak would be confined to the exercise cave for at least the next twenty-four hours, leaving a spot on the scout party for Kuvrro. Only one male was allowed to go; that was the rule.

Captain Mirra dismissed Kuvrro and went to the exercise room. As she walked down the hall, the ventilation system activated, filling her nose with pleasant scents meant to calm and soothe. Fresh grass, soil, flowers. All specially designed and chemically formulated to keep the crew happy and well-adjusted on long flights.

The door to the exercise room was locked. Mirra bared her teeth. Kuvrro was right. She'd been hoping it was one of his jokes.

Mirra punched a button, and a wall eye lit up. The digitally enhanced image from within was that of a huge, shaggy wolf. Larger and heavier than Mirra herself, it paced back and forth, baring and relaxing its muzzle. Mirra slapped the eye and cursed. It was Drrak, all right.

Mirra pushed the intercom button and said, "You're an idiot, Drrak."

The wolf stopped pacing and turned toward the ear. It growled.

"We were going to howl on the planet together. Now Kuvrro is my choice."

The wolf charged with teeth bared. Despite herself, Mirra flinched and stepped back as the beast bit and clawed at the eye, which was safe behind a layer of glass. Then the eye went dark. There was a faint beep, signifying the start of the security cycle. A gentle tranquilizer was being pumped into the cave, which would put the wolf into deep sleep. When he awoke, the wolf would be gone. Drrak would wake up calm, refreshed, and man-shaped.

And alone.

*****

Mirra was captain of the Star Pack, and as such she had the right to lay claim to the planet they had discovered. She would name it, lead the scouting parties to explore it, and if their people agreed to colonize it she would be the alpha female of the colony. The planet below them showed every sign of being habitable, so that was a possibility she looked forward to.

She had also decided that now was a good time to choose a mate. Kuvrro and Drrak were both strong males with good genes and healthy temperaments. She had chosen Drrak during the long voyage to this solar system, but now she was having second thoughts. She wasn't sure that his good qualities outweighed his flaws.

Mirra went back to her cave and settled down in a comfortable chair. She considered Kuvrro. Strong, healthy, even-tempered—bit of a joker, but that was no detriment to his qualities as a mate and father. Then she considered Drrak.

If she really wanted to choose him as her mate over Kuvrro, she could postpone the landing by a few hours until he had recovered. But she wasn't sure she wanted to do that. He had put off the necessary change for too long, no doubt wrapped up in anticipation of their discovery. That sort of poor planning was not a trait Mira wished to pass on to her offspring. Even worse: he'd shown aggression towards her, his alpha. Even under the stress of the change, such lack of control could not be ignored.

Reaching the stars had been a blessing for her people; as spacefarers they were no longer at the mercy of their planet's moon. They could choose their time to change, instead of changing involuntarily when the full moon reached the sky.

But it was still a biological need. Centuries ago scientists had developed treatments that would suppress the wolf, but each time the cure was worse than the malady. Madness, depression, and ultimately death were the results. The wolf was a necessary part of the hunter, tied deeply to his biochemistry. The hunters had learned to accept it and to live within the wolf's framework.

But Drrak had failed, and Mirra did not trust his judgment anymore. Kuvrro would make a better leader and mate. He always planned out his days of change months in advance.

Spontaneity was not a blessing when it could cause an injury or death.

Mirra turned on her wall eye and scrolled down to a popular entertainment. She focused on the mindless story and tried hard not to think about Drrak, sleeping in the exercise cave alone.

*****

Drrak slept deeply, but in his mind the wolf ran fast and free. The wolf pounded through the forest, muzzle to the ground, seeking its prey.

A trace of scent, warm and delicious, tickled his nose. The wolf slowed down to a silent creep as he approached his quarry. It was a young female ungula, new and stupid. The wolf's jaws gaped open in a panting grin, and saliva dripped from his muzzle. It would not live long enough to gain wisdom.

He crouched, waited. The leaves rustled as the ungula pulled and nibbled at the leaves.

He charged.

The ungula startled and bolted, but too late. The wolf's jaws clamped down on the ungula's hind leg, laming her. The bone shattered under his jaws. The ungula squealed and thrashed. The wolf let go and circled around. The grazer tried to rise on three legs, but before she could gain purchase the wolf rushed again. This time he went for her throat.

As his jaws closed, the ungula changed. It wasn't a grazer; it was another wolf. A female.

Drrak awoke with a pounding heart. He was human again; the change was over for another month. He sat up on the floor and rubbed his sweaty face.

He remembered Mirra coming to see him yesterday, and she had told him that she would choose Kuvrro to howl on the planet with her. That and the sleep drug must have triggered his nightmare. Ugh, he didn't want to ever experience something like that again.

He found the control panel near the door and punched in the intricate code that proved he walked on two legs. Mirra, Kuvrro, and the rest of the scouting party would have left already, dropped down to the surface in the scout ship. Drrak had missed his chance at becoming alpha male of the Star Pack.

Drrak had no appetite for breakfast, but he forced himself to eat. The changed burned stored energy, and he didn't want to give Mirra further evidence of his foolishness by making himself sick.

The irony was that it was the anticipation of going to the surface with Mirra that made him lose track of time. But Mirra wasn't one to accept that as a valid excuse. Drrak knew that about her. She hadn't become the captain of her own ship at her age by being easygoing or lenient. Kuvrro had commented once that she was equally cutthroat as a woman and as a wolf. Today, Drrak agreed with him.

A slice of dried fruit and bowl of water were all he could stomach at the moment. Drrak choked them down without tasting them and wandered back to his quarters. Ledrra was lingering next to his door, very obviously trying to look like she was busy with something else and just happened to cross his path. Drrak sighed. He should have seen this coming.

"Oh—hello, Drrak," Ledrra said. "Feeling better?"

"Much, thanks." Normally the change left him feeling refreshed and energized. That was not the case this time. From the concerned expression in Ledrra's eyes, she knew it. Of course, she was a biologist.

"I'm sorry about Mirra," she said. "The party just left an hour ago. Jerra's expecting to hear from them any minute now."

You don't look sorry, Drrak thought, but he said, "Thank you. I suppose it was for the best."

"You will have more freedom now than you would have as a captain's mate. With Mirra, you would be tied to the Star Pack for life, and at the whim of her duties."

Drrak nodded. It was hard to maintain his end of the conversation; there was too much in his head that social convention would not allow him to say.

"Will you choose a different mate soon?" she asked.

Drrak considered his answer. If he said yes, she would put every effort into attracting him. That would be flattering, but he wasn't sure he wanted that kind of attention. He still felt raw from Mirra's rejection, and the idea of a lesser female throwing herself at him was exhausting rather than exciting.

But Mirra might be jealous if she saw how easily she'd been replaced.

"Yes," he said. "I believe I will. There are over half a dozen competent and attractive females here, and it makes no sense to waste time over what I've lost, instead of enjoy what I might find."

Ledrra's smile was like a flame in the dark. "Join me for breakfast?"

And suddenly, Drrak's appetite was back.

Chapter Two

Mirra and Kuvrro were the first to enter the tiny scout-ship, followed by four lesser females. The central cave was equipped with body-hugging seats and restraint harnesses, and Mirra waited until the rest of her pack was properly buckled and fastened in before fastening her own. The air was a little musty; the ship's ventilation system had not been running long enough to clear the dust and oil. Mirra made a mental note to give the mechanic, Jerra, a black mark for not getting everything up and running sooner. What if something had been wrong with the scout? They would have had to delay planet-fall and throw everything off schedule.

The timer on the console at the center of the scout blinked and started beeping. After twenty beeps, the autopilot system would disengage the scout from the main craft, and they would drop out of orbit and into the planet's atmosphere. And then—they would land on Mirra's planet. She had to think of a name for it.

The beeping stopped, and seconds later came the heavy grind and thump of moving machinery. Then they floated free.

Mirra's stomach rolled into her throat, and she swallowed. Next to her, Kuvrro looked pale and nauseated. Brown fur sprouted on the backs of Mirra's hands, and tickled across her cheeks—she was bristling. Most of the others were doing the same. As the scout tilted, Mirra saw Karra's face lengthen slightly, and her incisors slipped past her lips. That, Mirra thought, was going too far.

"Do you need to be sedated?" Mirra asked her sharply.

Karra jumped, and her face shifted back to full woman-form. She even lost her bristle. "No, alpha," she said. "I have complete control."

"Keep it that way," Mirra said. Karra looked down at her lap and nodded. If she had to be sedated in order to keep the wolf inside, that would go into her permanent record and count against her on future missions.

"So Ledrra was saying that this planet is likely to be inhabited," Kuvrro said, trying to distract everyone from the discomfort of the drop. The scout's jets growled distantly.

"Of course it's inhabited," Mirra said. "Water, land, oxygen—why would there be no life?"

"By intelligent life," Kuvrro said. "Ledrra said she found unnatural structures on the surface."

"Why was this not brought to my attention before?" Mirra asked. She wasn't sick anymore. Now she was angry.

"Ledrra said she told you two days ago."

Now Mirra remembered. The silly little female was always getting excited over random details, and she had said something to Mirra about electrical currents and tool-made structures. Mirra had told her she already knew all about it and that everything was under control. Maybe she should have paid closer attention. The one time the silly thing had something useful to say...

"Oh, of course," Mirra said. "I do remember now. Yes, Ledrra and I went over the details when she made the report two days ago. Intelligent life, tool-made structures. They use electricity too."

"Will this interfere with our howling on the planet?" Kuvrro asked.

"No, of course not. We won't interfere with the other life forms in any way. They won't even know we're there."

The scout slowed, and Mirra's stomach dropped from her throat to her bowels. The brown hair on her hands and face thickened, but Mirra gritted her teeth and pushed the wolf back. Her teeth sharpened a trifle, then subsided. It would not do to show loss of control in front of her pack. Especially after she chided Karra.

Then, with a final bone-rattling thump, the scout came to rest. There was a moment of dull, disoriented silence as the party's respective digestive systems settled back into their proper places.

"Suit up," Mirra ordered. The air had proven to be breathable, but the planet teemed with foreign bacteria against which they would have no natural immunity. It was Karra's job to collect samples of soil and air so that they could begin creating cultures and developing vaccines as necessary.

The party suited up, and once again Mirra waited until everyone else was ready before turning on her own bio-suit and donning it. She smelled dust again; its vents hadn't been cleared yet. Another black mark for Jerra.

The suits were comfortable and fit like a second skin. Mirra looked around, checking one last time to make sure that all helmets were buckled and suits properly fastened and operational. Nothing but green lights all the way around. She strode to the hatchway and hit the switch that would open the inner doors.

She and Kuvrro stood together in the mini-sterilizing cave and waiting for the cleaning cycle to run its course. In less than three minutes they could open the outer doors and be the first to leave footprints on the surface of their new planet. Mirra corrected herself. The first to leave hunter footprints.

So there was already intelligent life on this planet. That meant the Council for Alien Affairs would rule against colonization. Mirra was disappointed, but that was all right. She would still lay claim to all the riches they found here, be it new technology, medicines, or a delicious new food source. Every habitable planet had secret treasures to find, and Mirra was thrilled to discover what this new planet would yield. If the intelligent beings here were friendly, they might share their knowledge of the planet with them.

If they weren't—well, that was a tree Mirra would piss on when she smelled it.

The hissing of the sterilizer stopped, and the white light over the outer hatch flicked on, indicating that it was safe to open. Kuvrro reached the switch, but then he stopped. Mirra nodded. He knew that this honor belonged to her. Slowly, and staring at Kuvrro the whole time, she reached out and flipped the switch open.

The scout had landed on an uneven surface, and the hatchway slammed against the ground before it was fully opened. Mirra had to hunker down and crawl out, which was less dignified then she liked. Kuvrro followed, his eyes wide with amusement at her awkward pose.

"This part does not need to go into the official report," Mirra whispered.

"Duly noted." But she could still hear the humor in his voice.

Mirra crawled out onto the planet's surface and stood up. She looked around and took a deep breath, pretending that she was inhaling fresh air from her new home. Kuvrro did the same.

"Does it have a name?" he asked.

She looked around. It was sunrise, and the sky was a lovely blend of pink and blue. The planet's single moon was a pale sliver overhead. Only one moon: that was a blessing. History told that the hunters had once tried to colonize a larger planet with six moons, and that had not gone well. They'd been forced to vacate when the constant changing had interfered with their ability to colonize.

"Otsanda," Mirra said. The grass was so green. This place was like home. She could see mountains in the distance. She ached to take her helmet off and breathe deep of the fresh, clean air.

The rest of the scouting pack wiggled through the scout's half-open hatch and stood straight beside Mirra and Kuvrro. The little pack stood together, a cluster of familiar strength in a sea of newness. This was the epitome of Garou spirit: to stand together as a single pack and face the unknown with absolute strength and absolute loyalty.

Mirra put her hand on Kuvrro's shoulder. Kuvrro put one hand on her shoulder and the other on Karra's. Karra put one hand on Cavrra's and the other on Mirra's. Nexrra and Dumrra joined the chain, one hand on a packmate and the other on their leader. Mirra felt the strength of six wolves across her arms and shoulders, and she reveled in the sensation.

"Otsanda," Mirra repeated. "This world is Otsanda, and she is our friend. She will guide us and shelter us, and her moon will give us strength. We will protect her and learn from her, and we will grow in mutual respect."

Then she raised her face to the dawning sky and howled. Kuvrro's voice joined hers, then the rest of the pack joined them. They sang together, their strength and their voice baptizing the new planet.

*****

After howling together, Mirra and Kuvrro got to work setting up the leap gate. Travel between the Star Pack and the surface of Otsanda would be much easier once the gate was up. Not exactly easy—passing through was physically unpleasant—but much easier than launching the pod twice a day.

They buried the posts deep in the ground a safe distance from the scout. Kuvrro tested the distance by running from the scout to the spot where Mirra intended the gate to go. If he got winded and had to slow down, the rule of thumb and paw went, then the gate was far enough away that a malfunction would not ignite the scout. Mirra viewed the steam on the inside of the visor of his bio-suit with satisfaction. Without pausing for a rest, Kuvrro set to work helping her set up the gate.

It resembled a doorway, but a doorway unlike any other. Any stranger who walked through that door would find nothing on the other side but more Otsanda. It could only be activated by a member of Mirra's pack. The alpha opened a side compartment in her bio-suit and removed the leap gem, the single great discovery of the hunter race. It was miraculous, it was amazing, and it had given them the stars.

The gem was jet black, but when the sunlight hit the stone it gleamed like purest gold. Mirra bared her teeth and held the stone up, and Kuvrro growled. She growled with him, and the others moved closer, drawn by its power. Leap gems were one of the strangest things in the galaxy, and even scientists who made a life's work out of using them weren't completely sure how they worked. All they knew for certain was that they were attracted to each other like magnets, except magnets didn't bend space to reach their attractants. The hunters had harnessed the power of the leap gems and used them to conquer the stars. Just like Mirra would conquer Otsanda.

Mirra snapped the jewel into its place over the doorway, then she called, "Line up to be identified!"

The pack formed a straight line in front of the doorway. Cavrra, the beta explorer who specialized in alien flora, was first. She took a deep breath and stepped into the center of the doorway. The fabric of space rippled around her, and Mirra's stomach rolled at the uneasy sight. She removed her glove and placed her forefinger into a specially made hole in the side of the gate. A thin needle scraped her skin and extracted a few cells. Cavrra flinched, though she had barely felt it, and Mirra frowned. The needle withdrew, and she replaced her glove. Avoiding Mirra's stare, she scuttled away from the gate. She had no tail at the moment, but still she moved as though it were between her legs. Mirra had that effect.

Nexrra joined her after a moment, and the two stepped away from the rest of the pack. The beta females' eyes met, and Cavrra felt better. Nexrra understood her as well as any litter-mate, and they communed silently together.

That's just Mirra's way, Nexrra's eyes said. She is alpha.

Her eyes are sharper than her teeth, Cavrra's eyes responded.

Nexrra bumped Cavrra's shoulder with her own and ran away a few paces. Cavrra laughed and gave chase.

"Stay within sight of the gate!" Mirra called after them, but for once Cavrra did not cringe at her tone. She ran after Nexrra across the grassy hill and clambered over the top. Then she stopped. Nexrra stood like a stone, staring across a low valley at another hilltop just ahead. Standing at the top, silhouetted against the sky, was a wolf.

"Who is that?" Nexrra asked.

"He's not one of us," Cavrra said.

Another wolf joined the first, and the two stared at them without blinking.

"Kuvrro said there are intelligent creatures here. He didn't say they were wolves."

Then a third wolf appeared. It was an entire pack. They made no move to advance or retreat; they stared at the strange females with what could only be astonishment. They know we don't belong here, Cavrra thought.

"I don't think so," Cavrra said, finally answering her question. "The signs of intelligence are far from here. There are no buildings here, no straight lines or artificial constructs."

"Perhaps those folk are hermits or travelers."

"Perhaps you are projecting your own species prejudice onto beings that probably bear no resemblance to us under the skin. Remember the first law of observation."

Nexrra nodded. The first law of observation was the only law of observation. Record only what you see and smell, not what you think, feel, or believe. What she saw were three furry natives that resembled wolves. And that was all she saw. Interpretation was to be left up to experts like Ledrra.

Cavrra held up her left wrist and pushed a button. A digital image scanner snapped a picture of the "wolves," and another press of the button uploaded the image to the Star Pack and Ledrra's waiting computer.

"Come on," Nexrra said. "Mirra will have instructions for us."

Cavrra followed, but slowly. She could not take her eyes off the creatures still standing at the top of the rocky hill and stared at them as though they were the most interesting creatures on the planet.

*****

Drrak and Ledrra enjoyed a hearty breakfast together, and Drrak felt a hundred times better once his belly was truly full. It also didn't hurt that Ledrra gave him her full attention, staring at his eyes as though drinking him in.

After breakfast, Ledrra showed Drrak her office, a tiny cube adjacent to her sleeping cave. Only a select few of the pack had her own office, and Ledrra was justifiably proud of hers. The floor was just wide enough to accommodate one hunter sitting in the lone chair, and Drrak had to press himself against the far wall to fit in. Ledrra turned on her wall eye and her computer, which she'd used to scan the topography of the planet. She told Drrak about her hypothesis of intelligent life, and he admired her intuition. "Mirra didn't seem impressed," Ledrra said, her voice full of hurt surprise.

"Mirra's not impressed by anything that's not part of the planned schedule," Drrak said.

This cheered Ledrra up, and she was almost bouncing as she showed Drrak the images the Star Pack had scanned as it had entered the planet's orbit. "See those lines? They're all perfectly straight. I think they're roads—paths used for traveling. Look how they connect in those symmetrical angles. And those square shapes are buildings. There are lines all around them, connecting them to each other. It's a city—a big one, full of life."

"Do you have any pictures of the creatures themselves? Do you know what they look like?"

Ledrra shook her head. "Not yet. Once we've been here a while I can calibrate the camera resolution and get some clearer pictures. I'm also looking forward to the samples that the scout pack brings. The air and soil quality will tell us a lot about the evolutionary state of the beings down there."

"How's that?" Drrak was genuinely curious now.

"Intelligent species in the beginning stages of technological development usually go through a 'messy stage.' They go to war with each other and pollute their homes until their only choice for survival is to advance to the next technological stage. It seems like a natural evolutionary process. I can tell where these creatures are on the development scale by the levels of carbon in the air and poison in the soil."

"We never went through a messy stage." Drrak studied the images. This was his first close look at an intelligent alien race. It felt strange, odd and new and wonderful all at once.

"Yes we did. Remember primary academy? The struggle for the cure."

Drrak remembered the history lessons. For hundreds of years scientists and researchers had wasted countless lives trying to 'cure' the wolf. Most of them had worked, but all of them had been worse than useless.

"So we destroyed ourselves instead of our planet," Drrak said.

"That's about right."

Drrak put one hand over Ledrra's. "You're really something."

Ledrra smiled at him.

Chapter Three

"I still can't believe it," Ledrra said. "What do you think, Nexrra?"

Nexrra didn't know what to think, so she said nothing. They were in Ledrra's office, studying the images that her computer had called up. Ledrra tapped the screen and scrolled up and down, up and down, looking at each image carefully and taking assiduous notes. Nexrra was getting dizzy from the up-and-down motion on the wall-sized screen. She closed her eyes.

"What do you think?" Ledrra asked again.

"I don't know." Nexrra kept her eyes closed. "I'm a botanist. Alien species are not my specialty."

"But are they alien?" Ledrra's voice was soft. "Look at them. Just look at them."

Nexrra opened her eyes and looked. It wasn't just the motion of the screen that made her dizzy. It was them.

They were identical to hunters in every way. The pelts, the teeth, the muzzles. Their muscles and bones moved the same way. They were wolves.

Then Nexrra looked at the other images, the two-legged ones. They, too, were almost identical to hunters. Their variations in skin color were slightly different; their darker-skinned races had more brown and less grey in their skin. And they were largely fur-less. Their naked bodies were like pubescent hunters just beginning to grow their pelts. They seemed to always wear clothes when out in public.

But the facial features. The body types. Even some of their expressions. It was like they had taken the single species and split it in two parts.

"Why are they baring their teeth?" Nexrra asked.

"They're smiling. It's an expression of friendliness."

"Are you sure?"

"Look at this one's eyes. He's looking at an attractive female with desire. His showing of teeth is a friendly gesture, like the pricking of ears."

"Good."

"What's good?"

"That there is at least one significant difference between us and them. This new species is raising my hackles.""They frown and cry just like we do," Ledrra said. "Look at their young." She scrolled down to a picture of a naked infant. It was red-faced, screaming, and tears streamed down its face. Nexrra's breasts prickled at the sight. It's not even your species, she told herself. But she still felt her body react.

"I know, I feel it too." Ledrra had read Nexrra's reaction without looking around. "I'll turn this off now. What do I say to the Council?"

"Collinear evolution," Nexrra said. "Call it collinear evolution for now. Two species following similar paths due to similar ecosystems and planetary features."

"I've never seen such a close resemblance on two such distant worlds."

"Neither have I. But the Council won't accept anything else without strong evidence. So just call it collinear evolution until we get that evidence."

*****

The hunter species had spread all across the galaxy. More than a dozen planets were now inhabited by the wolf people, all connected by a network of satellites and leap transmitters. Each planet was a stepping-stone across the river of mystery. It was across these stepping-stones that the information came, moving from planet to planet faster than light. In a matter of days, the news came back to Garou and the Council for Alien Affairs.

"The planet is inhabited by an intelligent species," Councilman Jarren said.

"So colonization is out of the question," said Council Alpha Terra, who sat at the head of the table.

Hrraz nodded. "Mirra must be disappointed. She's always been ambitious."

Terra shrugged. "She still has first howling rights. And who knows—maybe one of Otsanda's neighbors will turn out to be good for terraforming."

"What else do we know about this planet?" Hrraz asked. The fourth Council member, Brrina, said nothing but tapped busily at her wrist eye, taking copious notes.

Jarren tapped at his own screen, calling up Ledrra's reports. "The air and gravity are similar to Garou. The atmosphere is a bit high in carbon, and Ledrra thinks it's a sign that the aliens are in what she calls the 'messy stage' of tech development."

"Are they as aggressive as the other primitives we've encountered?"

"There has been no direct contact yet, but Ledrra is in the process of decoding their system of information transmission. We'll know more in a few days. In the meantime, Mirra is taking every precaution to avoid them. The scout's landing location is deep in a northern wilderness, away from those lights and roads that Ledrra tracked, so it seems unlikely that the aliens will stumble upon them unexpectedly."

"What if the aliens have the technology to detect the Star Pack's orbit?"

"That's Mirra's problem," Terra said. She bared her teeth a trifle.

"You don't like her, do you," Jarren said.

"I admire her drive and her energy."

"But you don't like her."

"No. I do not. She is not a likeable person."

"She has traveled farther than anyone else on the planet her age."

"And that is why I admire her. And I wish her luck on her mission."

"Has she chosen a mate?" Brrina asked, still tapping away at her wrist eye. Terra gave her a stern look, but she ignored that too.

"Kuvrro. The lesser male," Jarren said with a touch of surprise. "I thought she'd decided on Drrak, last time Ledrra reported."

"I thought the leap-relays were for passing important information, not gossip," Terra said with irritation.

"I show my throat." Jarren matched his words with the deed.

"I too," Brrina said. She did not repeat Jarren's gesture. "Jarren— any other important information in Ledrra's latest report?"

"One more item, but I don't know if it qualifies as important information or gossip, as it is currently unsubstantiated."

Terra's face darkened. "As long as it does not pertain to the captain's sex life, I want to know."

"It's just that it's pure speculation," Jarren said rapidly. "We don't know enough about Otsanda to confirm or disprove Ledrra's notion, and she herself says that it's extremely far-fetched. She didn't even want to tell me. She asked me to keep it private for now."

"Tell us."

"She thinks we may have been there before." Jarren still spoke in a rapid voice, staring down at his shaggy hands. The sudden, sharp attention of the other council members did not put him at ease. "Pure speculation, as I said. Idle thoughts. Evolutionary parallels are inevitable among planets with similar aspects. It means nothing."

"It's impossible," Terra said. "Every planet Garou has laid claim to is carefully mapped and catalogued. This planet is farther than we've ever gone."

"Of course you are correct," Jarren mumbled. His face was pale and bristly.

Terra settled back, satisfied that Jarren had been put in his place. "Is that all, then?"

"Just a few notes on the soil and air samples Ledrra is currently studying."

"Anything useful yet?"

"Inconclusive." Jarren was not sticking his neck out again. "It's too soon to tell."

"Very well. We'll re-convene in a half-moon's time. Has everyone made preparations for the change next week?"

Brrina nodded, and Jarren said, "I'll be hunting with my cousin."

The others looked at him, but this time he did not shrink. "My cousin Drroj lives in a single hunter's cottage near the paradise. We'll spend the evening living like our ancestors."

"You're going out?" Brrina's eyes were round. "I thought you preferred sleeping through the change at home."

"Yes, well, you were wrong for once." Jarren rose and headed for the door. "See you all in half a moon."

The other three council members waited, and it took Terra a moment to remember that it was her job to end the meeting. Technically

Jarren had committed a social offense by leaving before she rose from her seat, but she let it go. Jarren had had a rough couple of weeks. She stood up and nodded to each hunter in turn, and they prepared to leave the cave.

"Jarren is going out to change," Hrraz said. "That's not like him. Brrina was rude, but she wasn't wrong. I never would have expected a pup like Jarren to do it."

It was each hunter's choice to decide to go out for the change or stay indoors. Many settled types stayed in, taking sedatives and sleeping through the change. It was considered healthier to go out and run under the moon, but it was also more dangerous. Wolves sometimes fought over game or females, and injuries were common. Death was also a possibility, either in a fight or a hunting accident.

"Jarren made a bid for Mirra," Terra said, "before she left. She rejected him. He's been meeker than usual ever since." She walked out the door, and Hrraz followed her.

"This will be good for him then," Hrraz said. They walked back to their little house, which was close to the main council building. "The fresh hair, the thrill of the hunt. If he fights someone and beats him, that will really raise his spirits."

"Jarren is a clever worker and a strong wolf. He deserves some happiness." Terra took Hrraz's hand in hers. They had met during a change, and Hrraz had fought for her. The memory still sent a shiver down her spine.

Hrraz drew close. "We should go out too," he whispered.

Terra met his eyes, and the air nearly sparkled. "Do you think you can still keep up with me?"

"The question is: can you keep up with me?" Hrraz nipped her ear, and she chased him, howling the rest of the way home.

*****

The full moon came five days later. Jarren was already feeling shaggy; his hair was thicker, his incisors longer, his temper shorter. The weather was clear and cloudless, and the reflected light of the moon was already putting everyone on edge. Jarren considered his plan to go out with Drroj. It would be a bright, clear night, and everyone would be aggressive and in high spirits. It made him nervous. There could be fighting; someone could be hurt. Probably not killed; hardly anyone killed as the wolf anymore. But Drroj's co-worker had lost an eye in a fight over a female. The idea of losing part of his sight and damaging himself made Jarren feel a little sick.

But that was exactly why he needed to do this. Mirra had rejected him for impulsive Drrak, who went out hunting whenever he pleased and feared no one. That was the sort of male that females were attracted to, not cautious little pups who feared getting scratched. He knew he would never be an alpha, but he wanted to at least shed some of his fear. Females could smell the fear, he was sure of it.

He spent his last hours as a man poring over Ledrra's newest report. She was no fool; she was aware of the common phenomenon known as collinear evolution. Jarren knew that there had to be more than that going on here. She would not have suggested what she had without strong evidence, whatever Terra thought.

Ledrra had sent images of local plant life and wildlife, and Jarren saw it too. The blue flowers they used as a sedative for the wolf grew on Otsanda—or so it appeared. The distinctive scent and leaf shape were the same. Ledrra was currently running tests on its chemical properties.

And they had wolves.

So far they had only been glimpsed from a distance. Ledrra didn't know if they were skin-changers or not; she wanted badly to run on the surface without her suit so that she could get closer and possibly interact with them. Every day Cavrra the microbiologist was developing more vaccines for the various infections and viruses that existed on Otsanda's surface, and she hoped that soon they would be protected enough that Mirra would give them permission to run naked. Maybe by the next full moon. Maybe.

Actual wolves. Jarren put the paper work away and settled into his favorite chair to ponder. It could not be a coincidence. The odds against it were astronomical. Other planets had four-legged carnivores, some of them quite wolf-like. But these animals were identical in almost every way. They even howled like wolves.

A knock came at the door, and Jarren felt a thrill of frightened anticipation. "Let's go!" Drroj called. "Moonrise is here, and I'm hungry!"

Jarren headed out the door and slapped his cousin on the back in greeting. Drroj was a huge, hearty male, hairy in the face even when the moon was shadowed. This evening Jarren could scarcely see his eyes through the black fur. Drroj slapped him back, and Jarren bared his teeth mockingly. If Drroj noticed the slight tremble in Jarren's lips, he was too kind to comment.

The moon was a heavy, pregnant sphere peeking over the horizon. The silvery light fell on them both, and Jarren felt the change ripple through him. A sense of this is it, of inevitability, of falling over the edge of a cliff overtook him. It was thrilling and terrifying, like a first orgasm. No hunter ever got used to that feeling.

His joints cracked and popped, and Jarren breathed through the pain. He was aware of Drroj nearby doing the same. The air smelled of fear and excitement and wolf musk.

His face lengthened, and his jaws ached as his incisors and canines lengthened and pushed past his lips. A thick grey pelt sprouted over his body as his limbs warped and shrank and dropped him to the ground. Jarren snapped his jaws, enjoying the definite clap of powerful wolf teeth. He raised his muzzle to the glorious moon and howled for joy. Drroj's voice joined his, and all over the village they could hear wolves, some confined and some free, singing along. They were wolves, they were one, they were all part of the Great Pack that encompassed all the world and all the stars. Someday their greatness would spread across the entire galaxy, and the universe would sing their song.

Drroj ended his song and took off into the forest, and Jarren followed. They loped silently through the night woods, noses low to the ground, seeking their prey.

For a while Jarren followed his cousin and just took in the sights and smells of the forest. The air was fresh and clean, and the trees were heavy with moving sap. Jarren had been out here before, but it was different as a wolf. Everything was sharper and brighter, and Jarren felt marvelously alive. He pissed on one tree after another, honoring the forest and at the same time laying claim to her. Then Jarren caught the scent of prey, and he trotted away to investigate, leaving Drroj alone.

It was a nest of ground-dwelling creepfurs, long-eared and tasty. The younglings were just starting to leave the nest, scurrying about and exploring the night under the watchful eye of their mother. Nestlings were poor sport but good eating, and Jarren was hungry. He crouched downwind and waited for them to scatter a bit, growing in confidence. Then he charged.

The first barely had time to squeal with fear before dying. The wolf dropped the first nestling and went for a second, chasing it a short distance before catching and crushing the soft, delicious body. Yum.

He ate the second nestling on the stop, then he found the first he'd dropped. This one he'd take to Drroj. He stopped and listened for his cousin. From the west, he heard Drroj call for him with a friendly yip. Jarren headed off in that direction with a prickle of excitement. Drroj was right; this was exactly what he'd needed. Fresh air, fresh meat, no more hiding in a locked room waiting for the curse to be over. How had he ever thought it was a curse? Being a wolf was fun!

Then he heard the snarl.

It was deep and ugly. It was a fighting growl, a killing growl. It wasn't Drroj. It wasn't anyone Jarren recognized.

Jarren dropped the nestling and flung himself into an all-out run. There was another snarl, then he heard Drroj respond.

Then the fight began.

Jarren tried to shout, forgetting his current shape. All that came from his wolf throat was a strangled, yelping whine. He heard his cousin thrashing around in the leaves, biting and struggling against an unknown assailant.

Jarren felt a snarl bubbling up in his chest, and he burst onto a horrific scene. Drroj was bleeding from a deep track of wounds across his throat, and his assailant—wasn't a wolf.

Jarren wasn't sure what it was, but he wasn't about to stop long enough to find out. His teeth flashed in the moonlight as he charged at the dark creature that was trying to kill his cousin. He snapped and bit and tasted blood, and the monster ducked away. Drroj rallied and joined in, fighting as well as he could in spite of his wounds.

The dark creature hissed and retreated. The two wolves chased after it, but it flowed away over the ground and deep into the forest. It moved like a black river.

Drroj collapsed onto the ground, panting and bleeding. Jarren laid down next to him. He intended to stay awake in case the creature came back, but the hunt and the fight had exhausted him. Curled up next to his cousin, Jarren fell asleep.

Chapter Four

In the morning, Jarren and his cousin were both two-legged again. Drroj was pale and disoriented, but his wounds were no longer bleeding. Jarren blearily lifted his arm and pushed the yellow HELP button on his wrist eye. Then he settled down on the dirt path to wait for the medical service to arrive. Drroj opened his eyes and mumbled, "Something bit me."

"I know." Jarren touched his own arm where the creature had tagged him. It was barely a scratch, but it ached like an infected tooth. Drroj had those wounds all over; he must be in agony.

"You fought it off."

"We are pack." Jarren touched Drroj's throat, then his own. "We are one."

Drroj's eyes closed again as the emergency vehicle pulled up. It was a heavy rectangular box on wheels, drawn by four ungula. The vehicle opened in the back, and two females jumped out. "Rival fight?" one asked, a petite, red-haired little thing who smelled like an alpha.

"It wasn't a wolf," Jarren said.

The other looked at him curiously. "Then what was it?" She had dark hair, grey freckles across her nose, and a respectably large bosom.

"I'm not sure." Jarren tried to remember what it had looked and smelled like. Rather like a wolf, but larger and black all over. Huge claws like those of a burrower. But the claws were so sharp, they were like hunting knives on its feet. It hadn't smelled anything like a wolf. It had smelled like nothing familiar. Definitely a carnivore, but that was all Jarren knew.

"You'll have to make a report," the red-haired alpha said. She touched a button on her wrist eye, and it lit up blue. Jarren sighed. His day was ruined now. He was about to spend the next twelve hours speaking to the Dangerous Animals Unit. The DAU would ask him the same questions over and over again, and if he were really unlucky they'd decide that the situation was serious enough to warrant drugging him with memory serum.

Then he looked at Drroj, who had slipped into unconsciousness. However his day was about to go, his cousin's day would be so much worse. The two medical attendants worked him over expertly, washing his wounds and stitching them closed.

The red-haired alpha pried open Drroj's mouth and felt around inside. "I found material!" she announced, and with one gloved hand she pulled a short black hair out of his mouth. The black-haired beta took the hair and put it in a plastic envelope.

"We'll know soon enough what attacked you and your cousin," she said. Jarren felt relieved. If the medical assistants could figure out what the creature was by analyzing its genetic material, maybe he wouldn't be subjected to the memory serum. He'd been "requested" to take it before his appointment to the Council for Alien Affairs, to ascertain that his interview was truthful and accurate. He'd had a thumping headache for two days and a strong sense of having been violated.

"Are you injured?" the alpha asked.

Jarren paused before speaking. If he said yes, he would be brought to the medical center for evaluation and treatment, and it might be days before he was allowed to go home. If he said no, they might think that he was a coward who had let Drroj do all the fighting.

"Yes." He showed them the wound on his shoulder.

"You'll have to go as well," the alpha said. Jarren nodded humbly. He sensed them both studying him, evaluating him, and he hoped he made a good impression.

They had Drroj stabilized and secured on a stretcher, and Jarren followed them into the medical unit. The beta smiled at him as she settled him into a seat. She cleaned and dressed the wound while the alpha went up front to guide the ungula.

"What do you think it was?" she asked.

Jarren looked at her. The dark-haired female was looking up at him shyly, head cocked slightly. This wasn't an official question; she was making small talk.

She was making small talk; that meant she liked him. Maybe she thought he was brave for going out like a real hunter instead of hiding in his locked bedroom.

Maybe he should hurry up and answer her question, because she was still looking at him and waiting. "I didn't get a good look at it," he said. "It didn't smell like anything I've ever fought before." As if he'd done battle against a hundred foes.

"Only another wolf could do so much damage to your cousin." She looked round at Drroj, who slept comfortably in the stretcher. The medical unit swayed slightly as the ungula took a gentle curve.

"It was no wolf." That was one thing Jarren was certain of. "It didn't smell like one at all. And that hair was much too short."

"That cut on your shoulder doesn't look like a bite, either. It's more like a scratch, but it's too deep and thin."

"Almost like a knife wound," Jarren agreed. "What sort of animal has knives for claws?"

"Nothing that lives around here." The female tossed it off as a casual remark, but it stuck in Jarren's mind like a bone in the throat.

"Do you have a mate?" Jarren asked quickly, before he lost his nerve.

"No. My name is Nedrra."

"Good to meet you." Jarren touched her hand.

*****

Ledrra sat at her desk and toyed with a small dark jewel. The leap gem. Garou's most valuable resource and prized possession. The black crystal glinted gold in the bright artificial light of her office. Ledrra bared her teeth slightly. Though this one was inactive, its energy used up long ago, something about the golden spray of glitter made her feel fierce.

She put the gem back on her desk and turned to her wall eye. She still couldn't come to terms with what they'd found here on Otsanda. They'd encountered bipedal life forms before, some very similar to themselves. But these folk—were identical.

Ledrra had figured out how to break into the aliens' own communications system, and the information had come flooding in. Anything she wanted to know was just humming around in the sky; she knew all about their population (astronomically high), their weaponry (terrifying), and their space exploration status (deplorable). It was shocking how much loose information the natives had drifting around for anyone to pick up. Their communication technology was advanced, but so unsecure.

But the simple creatures had barely made it to their own moon. Entire tribes got excited over a simple probe reaching their neighboring

90

planet, which told Leda that planetary security simply hadn't occurred to them. Some of the aliens even thought themselves alone in the universe. The ignorance was saddening.

"They're experts at killing each other," Ledrra said aloud, taking notes on a satellite image of a bomb-dropping aircraft, "but they're yapping puppies compared to the rest of the galaxy."

"We should invade them!"

Ledrra jumped at the voice behind her. "Drrak, you idiot," she said affectionately.

"We should invade them," Drrak repeated. "We could probably conquer the entire planet in a matter of weeks, if they're so blind."

"We don't have the resources for a full-scale invasion," Ledrra said. "And Mirra wouldn't approve it anyway."

"We don't need resources. All we need is the illusion of superior numbers. Holographic projections, special effects, a few leap-transfers to impress them with our superior technology. The whole planet will show its throat."

The fool was actually serious. "Drrak, you really are an idiot." This time there was no affection in her voice. "Have you watched their video entertainments? Every single picture story I've studied had the same theme: conquering impossible odds. They idealize doing what can't be done. Their entire culture is built around the concept of fighting and dying in the service of freedom. We might conquer one pack, maybe two. But the whole planet? It can't be done. We'd have to kill them all."

"You can't mean that."

"Shut up and sit down. Watch this." Ledrra tapped at the wall eye, and the picture changed.

The story was about planetary invaders with vastly superior weaponry and technology. Native after native gave his life and went down fighting when a more sensible creature would have shown throat and survived. In the end, the natives found a loophole in the invaders' defenses and conquered them by sheer luck and grit. Ledrra looked at Drrak, eyebrows raised.

"That's just fiction, though. That never happened." But Drrak was already deflating.

"That's exactly my point!" Ledrra tapped at the eye again, and it went blank. "Over and over again this happens in their fiction. Impossible odds, death, and honor. Their cubs are weaned on these stories. Every one yearns to fight and die for something great and impossible. If we show our muzzles to these people, they will fling themselves into our teeth."

"And we will bite!"

"For how long? There are billions of them. They would smother us with their dead."

"All right." Drrak sat back in his chair. "No invasion, then. So what are we doing here?"

"That's up to Mirra. And I think she'll have an idea what to do after our meeting this afternoon."

"You've got a meeting with Mirra? Can I sit in?" Drrak perked up, and Ledrra showed her teeth.

"This is a private meeting, and a very important one. I have information for Mirra of a sensitive nature, and it is for nobody's ears but hers."

"Oh, of course." Drrak rose and headed for the door. He knew that mood, and he knew that a strategic retreat was his safest course of action. "I'll go—catalog that new fungus that Nexrra found."

Ledrra watched him go. She was angry and hurt by the way he'd perked up at the mention of Mirra's name, but that wasn't why she was glad to see the tail of him. She was not prepared to discuss the upcoming meeting, and she did not want Drrak asking questions she was not ready to answer. Explaining things to Mirra would be difficult enough.

Ledrra stroked her wall eye, as though she could manipulate its content with her fingers.

The hunters had been here before. She was certain of it now.

*****

"The moon is full tomorrow," Mirra said. She sat down at the table across from Ledrra. "How much longer until we're fully acclimatized to Otsanda's atmosphere?"

"Not in time for this change, I'm afraid." Ledrra rummaged through her packet of notes. Now that the moment was here, she felt flustered and uncertain. What she had to say was so bizarre, so improbable.

Ledrra didn't like impossible odds. She was nothing at all like the aliens she studied.

"Pity. Kuvrro and Drrak are both anxious to run on all fours on the surface."

"They'll have to wait. And not just because of the risk of disease. You see—" Ledrra stopped. Her mouth felt dry; her skin was hot.

"Yes?" Mirra looked impatient. Ledrra knew that Mirra thought her a silly female, prone to overreaction. She had to make this moment count. She had to make sure Mirra took her seriously and understood the implications of her discovery. But she had trouble speaking. The very importance of her statement made her feel small and silent.

"Remember how I said I think we share a common ancestor with the natives?"

"Of course. And I explained that collinear evolution is a common trait in planets with similar features."

"Mirra, we're part of their mythology!" Ledrra blurted out the words, shoving them in her commander's face. They fell like rocks into the space between them.

Mirra slowly cocked her head. "What?"

"Just watch." Ledrra tapped at her wrist eye, and a moving picture appeared on the tiny screen. Mirra leaned forward and watched it all in silence. She said nothing, but her face went pale. By the time the story had finished, her eyes were hollow and dark.

Finally, Mirra spoke. Her voice sounded very young. "They make up stories about us? These horrible stories?"

Ledrra nodded. "They're all like this. Bloody, gruesome, out of control animals. And we're everywhere. Their wall eye stories, their books... They even write songs about us."

"How is this possible?"

"It's not just collinear evolution. It can't be. Mirra, we've been here before."

"It's so horrible." Mirra closed her eyes. Once again she saw the flashing teeth and heard the dying screams. "If we show ourselves to these people, they'll think we're monsters."

"I know."

"We're not like that. Not anymore."

"I know. But Mirra—is it possible that we crossed paths with these folks centuries ago, before we learned how to control the wolf?"

"We lived in caves and holes in the ground then. And these folk can't even put one of their people on their brother-planet. How could we have met before?"

"I don't know. I'm just trying to think of everything."

"Keep thinking. Write down every idea that occurs to you, no matter how silly. I'm going to my cave to forget all about this for a few hours."

*****

Nexrra sighed. It was so beautiful here—the green trees, the tall, snowy mountains. It made her painfully homesick. She hated her bio-suit with all her guts and wanted so badly to take off her helmet and breathe fresh Otsandan air.

But even if she survived the experience, Mirra would make her wish she hadn't. Ledrra had catalogued dozens of bacteria and viruses in the first twenty-four hours they'd been here. Many were similar enough to Garouean microbes that they were probably immune already, and a few others Cavrra had already developed vaccines for. But Mirra was one for following procedure, and the procedure for planetary acclimatization did not involve opening one's helmet and gulping foreign air on a whim. The Star Pack was slowly being infused with native air via the leap gate, just a few particles a day so that the hunters could get used to breathing the air at a safe pace. So far there had been no adverse effects, unless one counted being jabbed with a needle every other day or so.

Nexrra followed her wrist eye to the dense forest she'd found yesterday. Rumor had it Ledrra was a little spooked by the aliens' physical resemblance to themselves, and Nexrra couldn't blame her. This was the twelfth planet Garou had discovered, and it was the fourth that held intelligent life. Nowhere else had the intelligent natives so closely resembled the Garouean hunters. Even their technology was similar— similar enough that it had only taken Ledrra two days to tap into their satellite and computer networks.

Ledrra found it frightening. Nexrra supposed she ought to feel the same way, but it was so damn convenient. It was hard to be frightened by hypotheticals when things like the Internet and global positioning satellites made Nexrra's job as easy as strolling in the woods.

And speaking of woods, there they were. Dense and deep, probably loaded with edible game. Nexrra's mouth watered and she felt her hair thicken. Her bio-suit beeped, detecting the slip, and Nexrra sighed and pushed the wolf down.

She jogged toward the forest, sublimating her instincts in exercise. Wear out the wolf, that was the hunter motto, and it worked. Don't walk when you can run. Her project these days was edible plants and fungi; a mind-numbing task. The wolf would be restless all day if Nexrra didn't tire her out somehow.

Her bio-suit beeped another warning, and Nexrra jogged to a halt. It wasn't the wolf this time; the map on her wrist eye indicated a large moving mass. Something big was coming her way.

In a moment she saw it. Huge and shaggy brown, with a long muzzle and heavy paws. It resembled a wolf, but it was bigger than any wolf she had ever seen. Nexrra placed it after a moment. The natives called it a bear. It was considered largely harmless, living mostly on fish and berries.

Apparently this one didn't know that, because it was charging straight toward her. Its eyes were dark and fixed. Was it protecting offspring, or was it just hungry? Nexrra didn't know and didn't care. She turned and bolted in the other direction.

Thankfully the bio-suit was light and easy to carry, and Nexrra easily outdistanced the beast. The leap gate was just ahead, and then she'd be safe. She risked a glance back and felt reassured by the distance between her and it.

Then she heard the howling.

It was a deep bay, the call of a wolf rallying his fellows. Nexrra looked all around, wondering who'd had the nerve to change on the surface against Mirra's orders.

The wolves charging at the bear were nobody that Nexrra recognized. She stopped and turned around, staring aghast, until she had the sense to lift her wrist eye and start snapping pictures. They bit and worried at the bear, jumping and biting and dodging faster than Nexrra could track them. The bear snarled and swung at them, but it could not score. After being bitten and bloodied four or five times, it decided that the odds were not in its favor and rambled off, growling. The wolves did not follow.

Now she remembered the creatures she and Cavrra had seen on their first day here. In addition to the physical resemblance, apparently they howled and fought like wolves as well.

The largest wolf—clearly the pack leader—walked straight up to Nexrra and sat down. The wolf and the woman regarded each other.

Nexrra clicked on her speaker and said, "Why did you do that? I'm not of your pack."

The wolf blinked at her. His gaze was calm and friendly, and he looked as though he expected something. Of course, Nexrra thought. He wants to sniff tails.

Unfortunately, Nexrra was not allowed to remove her suit, let along change to wolf. But the wolves had risked injury to rescue her from the bear, and it would be rude to just walk through the gate and leave them.

Mirra would understand if Nexrra bent the rules just a little. Well she wouldn't but hopefully she would never find out. Slowly she removed her right glove and extended her bare hand to the wolf. Her bio-suit beeped anxiously at the contamination, but she ignored it.

The wolf bared his teeth, then he relaxed and sniffed her hand. His cool, damp muzzle felt wonderful on her skin. The rest of the pack hung back. They looked confused.

Quickly Nexrra re-fastened her glove and hurried to the leap gate. Before she stepped through, she glanced back at the pack leader. His golden eyes seemed more than animal; he seemed almost intelligent in the way he watched her. She could never tell Mirra what had happened here. The captain wouldn't understand any of it.

But Ledrra—Ledrra might understand.

Nexrra stepped through the gate, and before the nothingness of the gate engulfed her senses, she heard once more the howl of the Otsandan wolves.

Chapter Five

Jarren lay in his tiny but comfortable nest in the medical center. All around him were deep, soothing colors meant to comfort the patient. The color green dominated, with traces of brown and blue as well. On the wall in front of him a wall eye played scenes of wolves running, hunting, and sleeping. Jarren watched the video and tried to be soothed by its message, "We are pack. We are strong. You will run again."

But he remembered the creature that had attacked him and Drroj, and he shivered. Nedrra had stopped by to tell him that they were still analyzing the hair as well as traces of saliva they'd taken from Drroj's wounds.

"How long does that usually take?" Jarren had asked.

Nedrra did not meet his eyes. "It usually doesn't take this long."

"What do you think it could be? Personally, off the record?"

Nedrra shook her head. "You must not tell my alpha I said this— but I don't think it's a natural creature. Some scientist's experiment, or something they brought back from another world perhaps. Its genetic markers are unlike anything I've ever seen."

"Gene manipulation has been illegal since they outlawed the cure. Taking an alien species away from its home planet is illegal, too."

"I know. That's why you must not say anything. I don't want to make a report until I have enough evidence to justify accusing someone."

Jarren wasn't about to say a word. Apart from simply liking Nedrra, if he made such a suggestion he'd be off the Council before he could sneeze. They'd had little enough patience for Ledrra's suggestion about the life they'd found on Otsanda. He would keep Nedrra's hypothesis a secret for as long as she wished.

Meanwhile, he lay on his cot, stared at the video screen, and tried to concentrate on other things. His shoulder would have been cleaned and disinfected, and as a precaution they had injected antibiotics into his bloodstream to stave off any infection the animal might have carried. His stomach was queasy from the effects of the medicine, but the deep ache in his shoulder was gone. He would be allowed to go home tomorrow if he showed no signs of deeper illness.

Drroj, unfortunately, would be here for a few days more. His wounds were deeper and more serious, and he had lost a lot of blood. He was currently being kept unconscious while they pumped painkillers and antibiotics into him through a tube. Jarren's guilt made his stomach hurt worse. He should have stayed closer to Drroj while hunting.

Someone was coming; someone was at the door. Jarren tensed, feeling vulnerable here on his cot. His brain knew the medical center was staffed by efficient fighters—it was more secure than his own home—but his gut was still reacting to last night's fight.

The door opened, and Jarren saw the red-haired alpha who had treated them and brought them here. She was followed by a physically-imposing male who looked a little older than Jarren himself. He was an alpha, a security chief of some type. Jarren could smell power and force on him. He was here to question Jarren about the monster, no doubt.

"I'm Kerr," he said. "Tell me everything you know about the creature you fought last night."

Jarren took a deep breath and told Kerr as much as he could remember. He hoped it would be enough; that memory serum was awful stuff. The red-haired female watched Jarren as he spoke, occasionally flicking her eyes to Kerr's face as though checking for a reaction. Kerr's face was like stone, his eyes like blades.

"What do you think, Lyrra?" Kerr asked the female. She was his mate, Jarren realized. It was in the way he looked at her. Jarren was glad that he'd taken to Nedrra instead. Hardly anyone died in a rival fight these days, but he thought Kerr had it in him to kill.

"I think we need to make a report to the Rogue Council. Nedrra is a good scientist, and I trust her judgment."

"Should I file the report now?"

"No. We'll have definite proof of her suspicions once the animal is in custody."

"Good." Kerr stroked her shoulder with a heavy, possessive hand, and Lyrra moved into his touch.

They started to leave, and Jarren said, "Wait!" At Kerr's pause and inquiring glance, he said, "You have hunters out looking for it?"

Kerr nodded, and Jarren said quickly, "I want to help. I know what it smells like, and I know the country around Drroj's house. I can track it."

"You're not due to be released until tomorrow," Lyrra said. "By then we may have caught it."

"But I'm already healing, and the extra day is only for observation. I want to help. It may attack someone else while I'm lying here. Please let me help."

Lyrra looked at Kerr, who shrugged. "All right," she said. "I'll have a word with the center staff, and if they agree I'll let you join the hunters."

"Thank you."

"Nedrra will be impressed," Lyrra added. Then she and Kerr left before Jarren could embarrass himself with his reaction.

*****

Everyone stayed on the Star Pack for their changes that month, spacing their nights out so that they could take turns with the exercise cave. Nobody wanted to be confined to their own personal quarters as the wolf; the space was far too small and was likely to make the wolf fearful. They went on gathering information and vaccinating themselves. Nexrra kept quiet about her brief encounter with the alien wolves, and it appeared that her transgression had gone unnoticed. And so life went, until the following month.

The Star Pack rested on the farthest side of Otsanda's single moon. Nexrra and Ledrra tossed Ledrra's dead leap gem back and forth and discussed the coming wolf-change. The gem was played out; its surface was cracked, and it no longer held the energy necessary to bend space around it. Even so, if Mirra saw them playing with it, she would go rogue. Ledrra wasn't sure that Mirra even knew that she had it. It had been a gift from Grrifa years ago, and she'd brought it along among her personal possessions.

"We still don't understand it, do we?" Nexrra said.

"No." Ledrra leaned back in her chair and held the jewel up to the light. As always, its golden glint danced in her eyed and made her feel a little vicious. Part of it was the effect of the jewel's energy, a source they understood even less than the wolf. Even with its fatal flaw the gem had a rippling effect on the space around it. But part of her fierceness came from knowing what the gem represented. Garou had conquered the stars because of these gems. In the universal pack where all living things belonged, Garou led them all. Ledrra's canines lengthened and she licked them reflectively.

"We're sitting on the moon, and it doesn't affect us. But down on the surface, the sight of the full moon turns us into animals. Will we ever understand why?"

Ledrra tossed the gem back to Nexrra. "We understand enough. We know how far we can push the wolf, and we know when to leave well enough alone."

"Do you think it's all psychological, like Jarren says?"

Ledrra spared a thought for Jarren, that simple cub Mirra had rejected. She had considered taking Jarren for herself; he was a sweet male with a kind disposition. She missed him a little. But she was finally making progress with Drrak, and she pushed Jarren out of her mind.

"It doesn't matter," she said finally. "We wasted too much time and technology trying to control what we could not. Better to ride the ocean and survive than dive to the bottom and drown."

She set the leap gem down on her desk. Nexrra chewed on her thumb as she studied it.

"I'm going down to the surface tonight," she said.

Ledrra sat up straight. "The moon is full."

"I know."

"We have not been approved to run on the surface. You aren't allowed to change down there."

"That's what Mirra says. What do you say?"

Nexrra was still chewing her thumb, and it was turning red. The two females regarded each other.

"We have been breathing Otsanda air for weeks now," Ledrra said. "There have been no adverse reactions, and there have been no serious illnesses."

"Do you think it's safe?"

Ledrra shook her head. "It doesn't matter what I think. Mirra is pack leader. And if you do this, I must report you."

"I understand." Nexrra touched her throat briefly, acknowledging Ledrra's superior wisdom. Then she said, "I'll see you tomorrow. Maybe."

Ledrra nodded as Nexrra trotted out the door with her head down. Then Ledrra picked up the gem and studied it again.

She would have to report this conversation to Mirra. But she thought she'd give Nexrra a head start first.

Jenrra ran the sonic cleanser through the wide breezeway that housed the three leap gates. One led to the small dead planet they'd passed through to get here, the first link in a chain of gates that would eventually take them back to Garou. One led to the surface of Otsanda. And the third was dead and dark, containing no gem. An extra gate in case of damage to one of the other two.

It was important to keep this passage exceptionally clean, since there was likely to be debris and contaminated air from the other worlds. Jenrra liked working here; it made her feel useful. And she liked looking at the gates and watching the explorers pass through them. She hadn't been off the Star Pack yet, but she still waited and hoped.

There was a scuffle in the hallway behind her. Jenrra backed up into an alcove, out of the way. The explorer Nexrra brushed past her without seeing her, which was normal. Jenrra was near the bottom of the pack hierarchy and went almost universally ignored. She didn't mind. She overheard a lot of good conversations this way. She knew, for example, that Drrak was trying to use Ledrra to make Mirra jealous, except only a complete fool would think that Mirra was stoop to such an immature reaction. Jenrra hoped that Ledrra wouldn't be hurt by the backlash, but maybe she was using Drrak a little bit too.

Nexrra stood at the gate that led to Otsanda. Odd. It was nighttime down there, according to Jenrra's wrist eye. Was she going to change? That couldn't possibly be an authorized excursion. Jenrra watched and waited. This was better than a video story.

The explorer tapped a complicated series of symbols into the paw pad, and the leap gem glowed. After Nexrra had gone and the gate closed again, Jenrra approached it slowly. She was not authorized to pass through the gates under any circumstances, but she wanted to see what Nexrra had done. She reached out with a single finger and tapped the paw pad. It flashed red, then green. Then the words CONCEALMENT DISABLED appeared.

Jenrra considered. She wasn't the quickest mind in the pack, but she did get there eventually. Nexrra had done something to the gate to conceal her departure, and apparently Jenrra had accidentally disabled it. Well, there was no way to fix it now. Jenrra went back to polishing the floor. If Nexrra got in trouble, it was probably her own fault anyway.

******

Mirra considered her options. Since she was off-planet, the moon's effect was weaker. She was not yet compelled to change. She could put it off another day or two, though not forever. But if she wanted Otsanda to become home, she had to adapt to the planet's rhythms. That meant she ought to change tonight.

But there was so much to do! Ledrra had told her that the atmosphere was as safe for them as it ever would be. Mirra wanted to go over the scientist's work a few more times to make sure. It was better to keep everyone in bio-suits a while longer than to lose someone to an accident or infection. Such an incident could reflect badly on her, as pack leader. Otsanda would still be there next month.

An alert message on Mirra's wall eye beeped. Someone in the main corridor was using a leap gate. Curious, Mirra tapped the blue alert symbol on the screen to see which gate was being used.

It was the gate to Otsanda's surface.

Mirra frowned. There was a small pavilion on the surface that was used as shelter for scouts, and of course there was the scout craft they had ridden down initially. But there were no structures large or comfortable enough to use as a change cave. And anyone who set foot on the surface would be subject to the Otsandan moon.

Mirra's canines lengthened, and her hackles bristled down her back. Someone was defying her direct order and going to the surface to run as the wolf. She tapped the alert message several times in a pattern designed to call up specific information. Who was the renegade?

Nexrra's name flashed on the screen. Mirra growled aloud. Of course.

"Problem?" Kuvrro stood in the doorway. His pleasant expression vanished when Mirra turned her golden eyes on him and bared her teeth.

102

"How can I help?" Kuvrro said. He strode into the cave with his head up, trying to exude an aura of confidence. It wasn't easy. Inside, the wolf was whimpering and tucking his tail.

Mirra pointed wordlessly at the screen. Nexrra's name was flashing over the gold symbol that signified the Otsandan leap gate.

"I'll go fetch her for you," he said. He'd been planning to change tonight anyway, and this would be a great opportunity to do what he'd wanted ever since they'd landed here. This way he could keep an eye on his sister, keep her safe, and do Mirra a service at the same time.

Mirra growled at him again. Kuvrro stared. She was furious, completely out of temper, and he needed to tread carefully. Alpha males were replaceable.

"I will catch her, and I will force her to return for punishment." He spoke in a deep but careful voice, trying to sound authoritarian and humble at the same time. "Even as the wolf I have excellent control; you know that. I can follow her and bring her back. You should stay here and gather your thoughts."

Mirra swallowed, and her yellow eyes turned blue again. "Thank you," she said. "I would go myself—" She stopped.

"Don't give it another thought," he said. He stroked her arms soothingly and led her out of the office to the exercise room. He knew what she was afraid to admit. She had never been defied like this before, and she was hurt and frightened as well as angry. In the skin of the wolf, those emotions would dominate. Nexrra would be badly hurt if Mirra caught up to her, possibly killed.

And alphas who killed their own pack did not stay alpha.

Kuvrro ran as fast as he could on two legs to the Otsandan leap gate. Mirra was safely locked in the cave and already in wolf-form. When she awoke tomorrow, she would be exhausted and calm, and hopefully grateful to Kuvrro for his intervention.

The leap gem over the gate still glowed, meaning that Nexrra had passed not too long ago. Kuvrro regarded the golden radiance that emitted from the black gem. Some superstitious folk thought that the gems had a mind and soul of their own, though of course this was nonsense. All the same, the black jewel that glowed with such eerie golden light was like an eye. The eye of the wolf.

He placed his palm on the paw pad, pressed the power key, held his breath, and stepped through.

He hated these gates. If it wasn't such a horrendous waste of resources, he would be in favor of old-fashioned nuclear fusion for all travel. Kuvrro's stomach roiled, his eyes burned, and his head pounded as though he'd been struck between the eyes. Then he was through, gasping and heaving and trying not to vomit all over his new planet. With his eyes still closed, he knelt and touched it with bare hands for the first time.

The grass was thick and damp under his hands, and the air was heavy with moisture. But the sky was clear, and the full moon stared down at him like a keen, passionless eye.

Kuvrro bared his teeth at the moon. His teeth lengthened and sharpened, and the wolf took over.

His joints snapped and popped as two legs became four. His spine lengthened, and a bushy grey tail sprouted from his backside with an audible crack. Kuvrro grimaced and growled through the discomfort. It only became pain if he fought it, but Kuvrro was tense and frightened. It was hard to relax this time.

Finally it was over. Kuvrro released a full-throated howl of relief, and he lowered his muzzle to the ground. His sister's scent was as plain as the moon, and he took off after her.

Nexrra ran through the moonlit night, breathing the life-giving scent of trees and flowers. This was how the wolf was meant to run. It was all well and good to keep the wolf locked up on a ship, out there in the emptiness of space, but it made no sense at all to keep her caged when there was a full, beautiful planet that loved and welcomed her paw prints.

She became aware of pursuit and slowed. Was it the wolf pack that had helped her before? No, it was a solitary wolf, and it smelled familiar.

Oh no. It was her brother. Which meant that Mirra knew she was here. Kuvrro must have been sent to fetch her, like an errant cub.

Nexrra bared her teeth and ran. Kuvrro was larger and faster, and he would catch her eventually. But Nexrra would make him work for it. She ducked in and out of trees, circled them several times to confuse the scent. She found a small stream and ran through it a few times, then waded downstream a while. The faint sound of Kuvrro's pursuit vanished. He was slowing down.

Now she could actually have some fun. She slowed to a trot and sniffed the ground. Otsanda was alive with creatures that each told a sweet, simple story. Here a fox had rolled in the grass, leaving its musk for a mate. There a bird had crash-landed after leaving the nest for the first time. Just a few paces away a trace of blood signified the bird's meeting with the fox. All over creatures were living their lives and dying their deaths, and the traces they left behind blended to create a symphony that played in the wolf's nose. Nexrra reveled in it. One could only learn so much from gathering plants and taking pictures. In order to really learn about a planet, one had to press her nose into the dirt.

Nexrra climbed a small hill, looked around, and breathed deeply. So much to learn, so much to discover, so much life here that begged to be lived. Nexrra didn't want this night to end.

But end it must, and all too soon. Kuvrro appeared at her left shoulder and sat down. He was huge, shaggy and black, and Nexrra was aware of how strong he was. He looked down at her with deep amber eyes. Nexrra looked away, but she refused to cower. Kuvrro was her superior, but he was not pack leader.

They sat at the top of the hill as the moon rolled across the sky. Neither moved, and neither spoke. The moon was bright, and it cast silver ghosts over the hill and valley. All around, they could hear the chirps, creaks, and growls of nighttime living. But neither wolf made a sound.

When the moon set, Nexrra yawned. The wolf was getting tired, and in a few more hours she would go back to sleep. Kuvrro sighed and lay down. Nexrra hesitated, then joined him on the ground.

She bolted upright. Down at the bottom of the hill and padding their way was the wolf pack. The leader walked with his head lowered and his tail stiff. There was a look of determination in his pale blue eyes.

Kuvrro leapt to his feet. Nexrra turned to him and touched his nose with hers. These wolves were no threat to them, and she did not want a fight. There was a lot they could learn from the pack if they stayed friendly.

Kuvrro sat back down, acknowledging her wisdom. Nexrra was relieved. Kuvrro was impulsive and self-centered, but he was not a fool.

The alien pack leader drew close, and Nexrra approached to sniff noses. He smelled of Otsanda and wildness. He also smelled of fleas, and Nexrra tried not to cringe. They were wild animals, subject to the parasites of a natural environment. It did not mean they were inferior beings. But smelling the natural world on the other wolf still made her feel itchy.

The rest of the pack gathered around, and they all sniffed the newcomers. Nexrra smelled caution, curiosity, and only a trace of fear. Finally the pack leader sat down and howled at the lightening sky.

Nexrra and Kuvrro joined in, and the wolves sang together as the night faded to pink and blue dawn. As the sun's rays reclaimed the sky, Nexrra felt the wolf inside relax and go back to sleep. Her pelt receded, her muzzle shortened, and her paws lengthened into hands. Her back cracked, and Nexrra stood up and stretched. Kuvrro did the same.

The Otsandan wolves sat still and watched. Nexrra's nose was less than it had been, but she could still smell curiosity and just a bit more fear. They had seen her in two-legged form before, but perhaps they hadn't realized that she was the same creature.

"Mirra's going to punish us both," Kuvrro said. "I was supposed to bring you back hours ago."

Nexrra did not take her eyes off the pack leader. "I'll be back," she told the wolf, and he sneezed.

"Not if Mirra has anything to say," Kuvrro said. He followed her back down the hill and toward the leap gate. "She'll see to it that you never walk on the surface again. I hope this was worth it."

Nexrra knelt at the stream and dipped her hand in for a drink. Then she splashed water on her face and neck, reveling in the chill. "It was."

Chapter Six

Drrak and Ledrra ate breakfast together. It had become a tradition between the two of them since Ledrra had noticed Drrak tended to have a poor appetite the morning after a change. So she had taken it upon herself to take charge and force food into him.

Drrak appreciated her efforts. He enjoyed the attention, and he was grateful for the distraction from the real reason for his post-change malaise. Ledrra thought it was exhaustion and hormone drop, and that was part of it. The other part was Mirra.

Logically, he knew that things had turned out for the best. Mirra was happy with Kuvrro, a bigger and stronger wolf than himself. And Ledrra was loving and beautiful. She was far more devoted to Drrak than Mirra ever could have been—Mirra, who loved order and control and authority above all else. But Drrak was still wistful over what might have been.

Or maybe he was just disappointed that he'd never be alpha male.

Drrak frowned and shoved a strip of yellowfruit into his mouth, and Ledrra smiled.

"You're getting better," she said.

Drrak swallowed and grinned. He felt like a liar. "So tell me about your work. What's new on the beautiful surface of Otsanda?"

Ledrra looked down at her fingers. They flexed anxiously, and thin grey fur sprouted along her knuckles.

Drrak frowned again. "Something wrong?"

Ledrra did not know what to say. She'd waited a while before going to look for Mirra to make a report about Nexrra's insubordination. By the time she'd found the captain, Mirra was already in the exercise cave. Ledrra swallowed, remembering how she'd looked. Ledrra had seen the captain in wolf skin before, but never like this. She'd been slavering and snarling, biting the rubber exercise shapes and rending them like prey.

She'd looked like the images from the Otsandan video stories. Like a "werewolf."

Bad enough that Nexrra had disobeyed a direct order from the captain. But Ledrra heard from Jerra that Kuvrro had gone after her. He was supposed to arrest her for insubordination, but Ledrra knew that Nexrra was Kuvrro's sister, and that he was not known for following orders. So far this morning, neither had yet been seen.

Ledrra thought that it would be best to avoid Mirra for the time being, even after the change was over.

Drrak reached out and touched her hand. "Anything I can do?"

Ledrra smiled and sipped her fruit juice. "It's just work," she said. "You want to come back to my cave? We can watch Otsandan video stories."

"Are they interesting?"

"Some are. I found a 'web-site' that details their mating rituals. They're very noisy."

That sounded good to Drrak. He swallowed the last of his yellowfruit and followed.

*****

Ledrra transmitted daily reports to the Council of Alien Affairs. They were filled with facts and numbers—pollen count, indigenous species, the presence or absence of edible plant life. As she learned more and more about the intelligent natives, the reports got longer and longer, and more interesting.

One such report left the Council completely flabbergasted. Head Councilwoman Terra sent back several requests for clarification, confused by what she was reading.

The Otsandans have a system of morality based on the approval of an invisible being that lives in the sky. He has many names, but most of them translate to a word that means "All-Knowing Alpha." Their young call him Santa Claus. He is seen as the giver of gifts and life, and every good deed the Otsandans do for each other moves through him, like some sort of conduit.

The Otsandans have gone to war and murdered each other by the thousands over perceived slights to their version of All-Knowing Alpha. They bicker constantly over what they think the Alpha wants of them. Their pack leaders use the Alpha as a threat and a promise in order to keep the pack subordinate. I believe that this is a ploy by ambitious betas to attract females and attain the illusion of alpha status.

There is a minority among them who believe that the Alpha is imaginary, and they seek to end injustices carried out in his name. These people are frequently shunned and banished from their packs for their lack of belief.

"Jarren, have you ever heard of such a thing?" Terra asked.

"I've heard of it," Jarren said. "It's called religion." He read Ledrra's report again. Amazing.

"I call it madness," Brrina said. "We should instruct Mirra to leave the place at once."

"Calm down, Brrina," Terra said. "Mirra and her crew are perfectly safe. Not one of them has even seen one of them in the flesh."

"But what if they do?"

Terra ignored that. "Jarren, I want you to visit the Academy library. Learn all you can about 'religion.' It has to have appeared in other races before. Find out how we handled it the last time we encountered it."

"Certainly." Jarren touched his throat as he left.

*****

The library was indeed helpful. Jarren found a number of books and portable computer files about religion, and what he found was interesting. It didn't completely solve the mystery of the Otsandans and their Alpha, though.

Religion was a natural stage in the evolution of an intelligent species. It was a by-product of curiosity in a species that had not yet developed the technological capacity to answer the questions they asked themselves. Usually by the time a species developed space travel, their religion evolved into a comfortable morality and no longer governed ugly behavior like war and murder.

Odd. The Otsandans had space travel. Stumbling and slow, true, but they had reached their own moon and were sending robotic probes to their nearest neighbors. According to Jarren's reading, their religion should not be so aggressive by now.

The Otsandans were either very stubborn, or completely mad like Brrina thought. Jarren was glad that he was nowhere near the place.

*****

It had been two weeks, and there was no sign of the creature that had attacked Jarren and Drroj. Jarren was frustrated. Drroj was home again and fully healed, but he was still jumpy and out of sorts. He'd decided to stay inside for the next change. That told Jarren all he needed to know about his cousin's state of mind.

Jarren returned to the site of the attack several times, searching for a trail. It had rained since that night, but his nose still detected traces of the creature's spoor. He should have been able to trace the creature back to its lair—or cage, he thought grimly. He wanted to find the creature and be a hero in Nedrra's eyes. He also wanted to put his cousin's mind to rest so that they could go out again as wolves. He'd only done it once, but he already missed it. He wanted that freedom back.

Nedrra came to see him early one afternoon, just as he was preparing to go a Council meeting. Ledrra had sent a message: there had been some sort of incident on Otsanda's surface, and the Council was convening to discuss the matter. Jarren was not looking forward to it. Whenever an incident involved Mirra, they always acted as though he was personally responsible, just because he knew her. He hoped that she was just the messenger this time and not actually involved.

Jarren was just leaving his little house and starting the short walk to the meeting hall when Nedrra trotted up. "Oh good, you're still here," she said.

Jarren's heart thumped an extra beat. "I'm on my way to a meeting. What can I help you with?"

"Is it about the creature?" Nedrra walked with him. Her hands were folded in front of her, and she seemed worried and a little pale.

"No, it's the alien affairs Council. It's about Otsanda."

"Oh." Nedrra kicked a pebble. They moved out of the way of an ungula-drawn wagon. Out of the windows peered a dozen white, aged muzzles. Another generation was going to the forests to rejoin the warriors of the past.

Nedrra walked backward and watched them go. "Do you ever think that's cruel?"

"What's cruel?" Jarren's mind was on the meeting.

"Taking our oldest out to the wilderness and leaving them to fend for themselves. I feel bad for them."

110

"Have your parents gone yet?"

Nedrra shook her head. "They died years ago. But Grrifa—a family friend went. She's the reason I went to Medical Academy. I wanted to find a way to fix her, so she could stay with us."

"Ah." That explained her concern. "Well, if you've seen an ancestor in the end stages of life, you know that it's not cruel. The forest where they're going is full of game and clean water. They'll be comfortable for as long as they're able to hunt. And when they can't, their deaths will be quick and painless."

"Death by starvation?"

"Oh no. Most of them die from accidents while hunting, or from heart failure while running. They are also provided with syringes if they wish to take their own lives."

Nedrra shuddered. "It seems wrong to abandon them like that."

"It's wolf nature." Jarren touched her shoulder. "When a wolf feels that his time has come, he will move away from the pack to die alone. If we didn't drive them out there, they would go by themselves. This way, they still have the company of their own kind."

"I suppose you're right."

"Think of Grrifa and how she was in the last year of her life. Was she forgetful and slow? Did she sometimes wander away from her home, and someone had to go find her?"

Nedrra's face darkened, and she took a ragged breath. Then she changed the subject.

"Can we meet after the meeting? I'd like to go hunting tonight. I want to clear out my cluttered mind."

"Certainly. I don't know how long the meeting will last, though."

"I'll wait."

"All right." As he spoke, Nedrra stopped and turned back the way they had come. Her hair thickened, and she broke into a wolf-like run. She's following the ancestor train, Jarren thought.

The Council was already assembled and waiting when Jarren entered. "You're late," Terra said.

"My apologies. One of the medical staff wanted to talk to me about the creature that attacked my cousin."

"Have they found it yet?"

"Not yet, but Nedrra thinks she has found a trail."

"Hrraz, please read the transcript from alien specialist Ledrra," Terra said.

Ledrra… Nedrra. Jarren hadn't noticed the similarity of names before. They were probably sisters.

Hrraz picked up his personal view screen and read, "Explorer-Scout Nexrra disobeyed a direct order from Alpha Captain Mirra and ran wolf-skinned on Otsanda's surface. Alpha male Kuvrro also went to the surface and did not return with the rogue until morning. He was also unsuited and wolf-skinned. Mirra is beside herself. She has imprisoned them both until further notice. Repeat: Mirra is beside herself. Please advise." Hrraz put the screen down and folded his hands.

Well. "What does Mirra want to do with them?" Jarren asked.

"I imagine she wants to skin them both alive," Terra said. Her lips were tightly pressed, and Jarren though she might be suppressing anger. Or amusement.

"Is the message from Ledrra herself, or is it on behalf of Mirra?" If it was Mirra asking for help, Jarren would chew his own leg off.

"It comes directly from Ledrra," Hrraz said. Jarren's leg was safe.

"This isn't good," Terra said. "When Mirra discovers that Ledrra has come to us, she'll accuse Ledrra of going over her head and undermining her status. An unstable situation will de-stabilize further."

"Tell Ledrra to advise a quarantine on the two offenders until further notice," Jarren suggested. "If their imprisonment is seen as a health precaution rather than a punishment, the rest of the pack will accept it. And it may help Mirra calm down and see it from a more rational perspective."

"Mirra was too young to travel so far." Terra shook her head. "We should have kept her on local scouting missions for a few more years."

"She is an excellent alpha," Hrraz said. "So far her mission has been a success."

"It's too soon to know if the mission is a success or not," Jarren said. "We should save our analyses for a few more moons."

*****

Nedrra was waiting for him as promised. She jumped from foot to foot when she saw him, and Jarren's stomach made a funny little jump. "Are you ready to hunt?" he asked.

"Actually I found something you should see. I think it explains where that monster came from."

"What do you mean? Where is this?"

"It's in the woods not far from where you were attacked. I don't want to tell you; I'd rather show you."

Jarren was curious. Nedrra had been distant and a little stressed this morning. Now she was sparkling and alive, and incredibly attractive. Perhaps she had followed the ancestor train and something about what she'd seen had rested her mind about her old friend Grrifa.

"Turn wolf with me," she said. "I want to run."

Jarren felt strange about changing in broad daylight. It wasn't something he normally did. But Nedrra's pelt was already sprouting, so he followed suit and summoned the wolf from its sleep. He bared his teeth and breathed through the familiar pain, which was more intense now that the moon was not full. When it was over Nedrra was already running. Jarren took off after her, spurred by physical desire as much as curiosity. His intellectual brain still remembered the mystery of the creature in the woods, but the wolf was awake now and in pursuit of an attractive female who smelled of health and sex. The wolf nose never lied, and it was plain that she wanted him as much as he wanted her.

Nedrra slowed down a little, letting him catch up, then took off running at top speed. Jarren chased after her joyfully, lolling his tongue out. She slowed down again, and Jarren caught up to her and bit her furry neck. She yipped and snapped back playfully, catching him on the ear. Pleasure and pain.

Jarren mounted her then, and they mated cheerfully under the spreading branches of the trees. Jarren smelled the delightful furry body under him and felt that all was right with the world. This was wolf nature at its finest.

When they were finished, the two wolves curled up and rested together. Slowly they shifted back to two-legged form, drowsing and comfortable. Finally Nedrra tapped his chest. "Come on. It's not too far now."

Jarren yawned. He was tired and a little sore, and he really wanted to sleep the rest of the day away. But he dragged himself up and followed

Nedrra deeper into the forest, where the shadows were longer and the air cooler. He shivered a little.

"There," she said. Jarren looked up at the tree. It looked normal, just a huge old tree with a thick trunk and wide-spread branches. The trunk was big enough that a grown hunter could hide behind it.

Then he saw it. A leap gem, black and gleaming, was embedded in the bark.

"How did that get there?" It was impossible. Leap gems were mined under strict supervision and regulation. They were controlled entirely by the ruling Councils and used almost exclusively for star travel. There was no way one could just be left lying around, and it was almost certainly illegal for this one to be here.

Nedrra stroked it with her fingertips. "It's partially buried in the tree; the bark is growing over it. It's been here a very long time. Maybe hundreds of years."

"There's no gate. There's no structure here. It's just the gem—and the tree."

"But it works. Look." Nedrra touched the bark of the tree. It was solid. Then she pulled back and thrust her fist into the tree as hard as she could—and her arm disappeared up to the elbow.

"The tree is there, and it's still alive. But there's a gate too, sort of. It's like a cloud. It comes and goes." Nedrra withdrew her arm, unharmed.

"Where does it lead?" Jarren touched her arm. It was slightly cool.

"I don't know. I want to go through and see."

Jarren took a step back. "We should tell the Council. It might not be safe." But he was just mouthing words. He wanted to know as badly as she did where the rogue gate led, and he wanted to find out with her.

Nedrra saw the truth in his eyes and grinned. Her incisors were already growing.

As Jarren watched her slowly change back to wolf-skin, he felt a helpless sort of agonizing pleasure. It felt like falling.

Is this what falling in love is like? he wondered.

Then Jarren joined her in wolf form. The wolf came more slowly this time, tired from the unseasonal exertion.

He followed the irresistible, irrepressible she-wolf into the tree and into the jaws of their fate.

Chapter Seven

The air was thick, and it was hard for Jarren to breathe. He pushed through the tree step by step behind Nedrra. It felt like swimming down, pushing against his natural buoyancy. For a moment all four paws lost touch with solid ground, and Jarren panicked. He flailed, striking out with his forelegs as if trying to swim.

Nedrra's jaws clamped on his ear, and with the pain reason returned. It was a wild gate, unmanned and uncontrolled. Jarren needed to keep his head and keep moving forward, and he would soon find himself on solid ground again.

Unless the other leap gem was floating through the vacuum of space. Jarren shuddered. They hadn't thought this through at all.

The air thinned and cooled, and Jarren took a deep, grateful breath. His feet touched solid ground, cold and comforting solid ground. He let out a yip and Nedrra turned to face him.

She sat down and panted at him. Then they looked around themselves. It was daunting—at least to Jarren—to realize that they could be almost anywhere at all in the universe.

The sky was blue, the grass was green, and the sun was setting in a brilliant display of orange and red. So far it looked like Garou. But there was something different about it. The ground felt different, more spongy, and the air smelled different. It was heavier, moister, more animal-laden. And there was something underneath it all. It was a sort of burning smell, like lightning and burning leaves.

The land around them was grassy⌐—and round. The tree they'd come out of was next to an enormous hill, like a half-circle jutting out of the soil. It was bigger than a cottage and covered in grass and brush. There was no way that this could be a natural occurrence, and Jarren sniffed at it cautiously. But there was no time to investigate; his companion was interested in other things. Nedrra put her muzzle to the ground and stalked away, into the trees. Jarren followed her lead.

The scents were amazing. Nothing at all was familiar; they truly were on an alien planet. He smelled life, death, and animals. But none of the life he smelled resembled the creatures indigenous to Garou. Nedrra was deeply absorbed in exploring, and her eyes were closed in rapture. Jarren sniffed around as well, taking a moment here and there to glance over and enjoy the beauty of her pleasure. So they went, as the sky darkened from blue to black.

The moon overhead was not their moon. Garou's moon was large and orange; this one was small and silver. The stars were also different. Jarren was not an expert on constellations, but he was familiar with several. These stars were a meaningless scatter, like spilled drops of water. Jarren could make neither head nor tail of them.

Somehow they were on one of the domesticated alien planets. But which one? Jarren was not familiar enough with the flora of each planet to guess by the evidence around them.

Nedrra started back toward the unnatural hill, and Jarren followed. Apparently she had had enough adventure for now, and Jarren was happy to follow her lead. Now they would go home and tell the Council what they had found. Which branch would be best able to handle this? Probably Alien Affairs, Jarren's own branch. Or the Council for Pack Health. They would have to cut down the tree and deactivate the gem on the Garou side. Jarren didn't know the process for deactivation; there was a team of scientists who did that sort of thing. He had once known a female who had known how, but she had never shared the process with him. But he had never been too interested either, which might be why she'd rejected his advances.

A hot explosion right next to his ear interrupted Jarren's ramble of thought. He froze and looked for Nedrra.

She lay on her side just a little ways off, panting weakly. Her midsection was a bloody mess. Jarren smelled blood and metal—and something else. He smelled death.

He ran to her side, and she looked up at him. Her beautiful golden eyes were glazed with agony.

There was a shout from behind him. It was in no language Jarren recognized, but the tone was aggressive. There was another explosion, and Jarren's hackles stung. His heart burned inside of him—he didn't want to leave Nedrra—but his wolf instincts took over and he ran.

He ran around the side of the mound and peeked behind him. A pair of large two-legged beings hunkered around Nedra's dying body. They were clothed in patches of green and brown, and their faces looked Garouean.

Nedrra let out a low moan that sounded like a howl, and slowly she shifted to woman-form. The creatures were surprised; they jumped back and shouted very loudly. Jarren smelled their fear and growled.

One stood up and looked around. It held a long black tool in both hands, and its body language was aggressive. That tool was what had killed Nedrra. Jarren was certain of it. His lip raised in a snarl.

They were still talking, chattering back and forth at each other in loud, urgent voices. They were frightened and confused, and looked like hunters in every way, but hunters would not have taken fright at the sight of a change. Nor would a hunter take the life of a stranger for no reason. Perhaps these creatures had some sort of disease or mental illness.

But that tool was not Garouean. Not at all. No one on Garou had invented a weapon that killed from a distance. It wasn't right to kill like that. Good strong teeth were the proper tools for hunting, or blades when one was in two-legged form.

Nedrra was surely dead by now; Jarren could not see her moving at all. All the creatures did was chatter and look around, chatter and look around. The one was holding its black tool, but it no longer seemed so aggressive. It seemed more fearful now, more timid.

Their fear fed Jarren's anger. Those creatures had taken the life of Jarren's mate, but they seemed more frightened by the fact than triumphant. They didn't act like killers. They acted like prey.

It was against the law of Garou to kill if one was not hungry. But Jarren was not on Garou anymore. And apparently on this planet, different laws applied.

Nedrra lay still and pale in the weird grass of an alien planet. She had died light-years from home, shivering from fear and pain. Jarren thought it was time for these creatures to learn about fear and pain.

He padded closer to the strangers. He made no attempt to keep silent, but all the same neither creature seemed to notice. They were scared prey, completely blind to their surroundings. The idiots deserved to die.

He went for the one carrying the tool first. The creature's blood was hot and stung his mouth. The creature tried to push him off with the tool, but it was physically weak. It was like fighting a cub compared to the black-furred creature Jarren had fought before. He tore its throat open and went for the second creature while the blood from the first still poured.

This one looked him in the face. Moisture welled in its eyes, and it uttered something in a whining, cringing voice. Weak and stupid. It knew how to kill but not how to defend itself. Jarren mauled the creature's face and neck, chewing and biting with pleasure. The alien beat at his furry flanks with its fists, but not for long.

Jarren lapped at the blood that dripped onto the ground. It was stinging-salty, but it was fresh and good. He had never killed anything so big before. He felt strong and alive.

Then he looked down at Nedrra, lovely Nedrra who would never run or kill again. He growled to himself. What sort of beings were these that killed intelligent creatures for no reason? Useless, stupid things. If Jarren came across any more on his way back to the leap gate, he would kill them too.

But he met no one, and the gem stared at him with its glinting gold pupil. Jarren stared back at it for a moment, searching his conscience and daring the gem to accuse him. But the gem was just a gem. It saw nothing, and it did not judge.

He tapped the tree with his muzzle. Solid and cool and smelling of soil and health. Jarren licked the smell of blood off his muzzle, closed his eyes, and leaped through the gate.

The dizziness seemed less this time. Maybe he'd gotten used to it, or maybe the disorientation in his body was less than that in his heart.

*****

Kuvrro and Nexrra stared at each other across the cave where they'd both been imprisoned. Mirra hadn't listened to a word of Kuvrro's explanation, hadn't said a word to either of them. She'd pointed to Dumrra, Kuvrro's second in command, and walked away silently. Dumrra was equally silent but full of sympathetic glances. She had led them to the change cave and locked them both in. There was no point in fighting it or arguing with the security chief. Mirra was pack leader. Sympathetic or not, Dumrra would obey.

"I'm sorry you got in trouble too," Nexrra said.

Kuvrro looked down. "It wasn't your fault. I could have caught you. I could have forced you back. I was as excited as you were to run on the surface in wolf skin."

"The moon was full. Your wolf was in control, bending your mind. Mirra has to know that."

"She knows the truth."

Kuvrro had never intended to follow Mirra's wishes to the letter. He'd offered to bring his renegade sister back with every intention of enjoying himself on Otsanda along the way. He'd gambled that Mirra would make the same assumption as Nexrra, that the wolf had taken over and he'd forgotten his task in innocence.

He had gambled and lost. And now his future as alpha male was in doubt.

They sat together in silence, twin victims of impulse.

Mirra stood outside the cave and watched them on the wall eye. She told herself that she was watching for signs of illness. Their health screens had come back in perfect form, but one never knew. There might be some invisible parasite in them, a microbe that the Garouean scanners might not recognize because of its alien nature. Such a thing was nearly impossible. But one never knew.

Jealousy was a weak emotion, and Mirra would not condone it in herself or others. She was not jealous, and she would not stoop to admitting to such weakness. But Mirra was Kuvrro's mate, and his first loyalty should be to her, especially as chief of security. Any bond he felt with his sister should have atrophied years ago. It was the way of things. Mirra was observing them out of concern for the security of the pack. And to watch for signs of infection.

Others passed by as they went about their day. Mirra ignored them. Nobody asked why she was standing there, so straight and so still. Her blank face and dilated pupils suggested that such a question would not be well received.

An hour later, Mirra was satisfied. There was no lethargy, coughing, discolor, or any other signs of infection in either of them. Kuvrro was probably angry at his sister for getting him in trouble, and ashamed of his impulse. She could go back to work now and ponder what to do with the criminals.

Ledrra found her in her office. "Captain, what are your plans for Nexrra and Kuvrro?"

"They both disobeyed direct orders from their alpha. I could have them executed." Mirra would do no such thing of course, but it was a pleasure to see the fluffy-headed female cringe.

"Is that your plan?"

"Of course not. I'm just reminding you that anything I do isn't the worst I could do. I know you and Nexrra are friends."

"I have a suggestion, if you'd like to hear it."

"I'll always listen to suggestions from my inferiors."

Ledrra's incisors sharpened a bit, but she kept her lips closed over them. "Too strict a punishment will cause discontent among the rest of the wolves, since no harm was done by their actions. Imprison them, but don't call it a punishment. Call it a quarantine. They'll understand that they're being punished, but the rest of the pack will think you're being overly cautious rather than overly punitive."

Mirra considered. She didn't want Ledrra to think that she was more clever than her alpha, or that her ideas had any merit, but this one was pretty good. "I'll consider it."

"Thirty days seems fair."

Mirra bared her teeth. "Sixty."

Ledrra left quickly.

*****

Drrak was waiting for her when she got back to her office. "You told the Council about this, didn't you?"

Ledrra growled at him, and he took a step back. "Shut your mouth," she said. "I don't want the whole pack to know. If Mirra finds out she'll rip out my throat."

Drrak followed her into the office with his nonexistent tail tucked between his legs. Ledrra closed and locked the door. Then she said, "Yes, I wanted the Council to know how things are going here. In case matters get worse."

"Mirra's a good alpha. It's normal for her to be upset by insubordination."

"Normal for her, yes."

"What does that mean?"

"Exactly how it sounds." Ledrra sat down in a chair and turned on her wall eye. The Otsandan "Internet" appeared on the screen, and she tapped at pictures and keys randomly, trying to keep her hands busy. Drrak was still infatuated with Mirra, and anything she said against the captain would count against her in his eyes. But she couldn't stop talking. "Normal for Mirra and normal for a mature, seasoned captain are two very different things."

"Are you criticizing our pack leader?"

"Now you sound like her. Why is it wrong to comment on her personality?"

Drrak was silent. Ledrra's heart was quickening. "Let's watch a video together," she said. "It will take our minds off all of this."

"Perhaps another time." Drrak unlocked the door and left the office without looking back. Ledrra bit her own hand in frustration. She never should have gotten involved with him. If he went to Mirra with this information, she would soon be joining Nexrra and Kuvrro in "quarantine."

She turned back to the Internet and searched for a video about Otsandan mating rituals. They were fascinating creatures.

But first she clicked on a few news stories. For weeks she'd been trying to understand the motivation behind their unnatural levels of aggression. Their news was full of rogues, and their methods for dealing with them were criminally aggressive. She wanted to understand.

What she found made her completely forget about mating rituals or any other mild entertainment. Ledrra's heart shattered in her chest.

Chapter Eight

That night, Drrak moped in his bedcave. It was self-indulgent and pitiful, ill-befitting a strong male like himself. But he could not help it. He'd thought that Mirra would be friendlier now that Kuvrro had disappointed her. Hadn't she once thought him worthy of being named alpha? What had he done to change her mind so thoroughly that she was willing to forgive Kuvrro and still prefer him to Drrak?

Drrak had thought that telling Mirra about Ledrra's betrayal would bring him back into her good graces. He'd been mistaken. Mirra had been irritated by the news, but she considered Drrak's betrayal of Ledrra far more serious. He had not anticipated that.

Her rebuke still rang in his ears like a clanging bell. "Put it out of your mind. Stay with Ledrra, a female worthy of you. You and I are done." Clipped, final words. There would be no changing her mind.

There was a commotion outside. Someone ran past his door, shouting for the captain. Drrak perked up. It sounded like Ledrra. What was she shouting about?

One way to find out. He ought to make amends with Ledrra, and this was a way to do it. He'd treated her pretty shabbily last time they met.

*****

In her time on the Internet, Ledrra had learned that not every news item was true. Some were exaggerated for emotional effect, while others were outright lies told for entertainment. But this story had been repeated on several news sites, and the details were consistent.

Then they'd showed the photograph, and that was when the Ledrra knew that this was real.

"Mirra! Captain!" she shouted as she ran toward the alpha's office. She stopped outside the door, hesitated, then banged on it with the flat of her hand. "Captain, I need to talk to you! You need to watch the news!"

Mirra opened the door and studied Ledrra coolly. "Have you spoken to the Council about it yet? I understand that your first loyalty is to them, rather than to me."

"I will apologize and show throat for that misstep as soon as I have shown you this." Ledrra barged past Mirra and went straight for her wall eye. Her behavior was so unusual that Mirra pushed her anger away in place of curiosity. The female had to be on to something.

Ledrra turned on the Internet and after a few taps at the screen she found the first broadcast video. Mirra was impressed. The biologist really knew her way around the Otsandan information system.

But all emotions, save fear were erased in about thirty seconds as Mirra watched the news clip about the "animal attack." Ledrra stood next to her, pale and silent, and watched it all happen again.

Two Otsandan men had been found dead in the land of Wisconsin, a territory many days' run south of here. The Otsandan alphas believed that they had been poaching: hunting without permission on land deemed sacred by an ancient people called Native Americans. They had been carrying firearms, weapons used to kill from a distance. Both their throats had been torn out. With them was a naked woman who had been shot through the chest. The firearm that had killed her had belonged to one of the men.

It was thought by authorities that they'd killed the female in a rape attempt, and some animal—perhaps the woman's dog—had attacked them. The woman had no clothing and no identification, and no one had reported a woman missing in that area. They were scanning missing-persons reports from across the country, but in the mean time they were posting photos of the woman's face in case someone knew her. The face Mirra saw bore an eerie resemblance to the hunter at her side.

"That's Nedrra," Ledrra whispered. "That's my sister. She was going to cure old age." Then she burst into tears.

All anger, spite, and fear drained out of Mirra instantly. She threw her arms around Ledrra and held her tight as the other woman wept. It was impossible that Nedrra could have come to Otsanda with them and even more impossible that she could have come any other way. But all of that was irrelevant. One of Mirra's pack was in pain. That was all that mattered.

Mirra held her crying packmate and nuzzled her, soothing her tears. She helped Ledrra into Mirra's own nest and encouraged her to tuck up into a ball for comfort. "We are pack," she whispered. "We are one. Your pain is my pain, and we will howl for Nedrra together."

Ledrra was drowsy-eyed and dozing. It had clearly taken all her energy to hold herself together long enough to tell Mirra what she'd found. Now she was exhausted and near sleep. Mirra found a blanket in the closet and covered Ledrra up with it.

She left her there to rest while she headed for the change cave to release Kuvrro and Nexrra. The time for pettiness was gone. She needed the entire pack for this, especially those with the most experience on Otsanda's surface.

Just outside her office she came nose to nose with Drrak. He was flushed, his eyes lowered, and he stunk of shame. Mirra's nose wrinkled. "Comfort your mate," she growled, showing her sharpening incisors. Then she walked past him without a backward glance.

*****

Terra listened with a pale face to the message from Captain Mirra. Ledrra was usually the Star Pack's liaison to the Council, but she had been given an indefinite leave of duty. Under the circumstances, it was the only sane decision Mirra could have made.

Cavrra, one of the beta scouts, would take Ledrra's position as alien analyst. She knew the languages and the Internet well enough to continue organizing and documenting information about Otsanda. Ledrra had already done the hardest parts: learning the computer languages and hacking into the planet's information systems. All Cavrra had to do was read, listen, and document.

Kuvrro and Nexrra had been released from quarantine. All visits to the surface had been suspended, and under the circumstances Mirra felt they could be trusted to stay where they belonged. They were both filling out reports about everything they'd learned from the surface, especially the native wolves.

"A hunter was killed on the Otsandan surface, but we do not know who killed the Otsandan males. Given what Nexrra told us about the pack she interacted with, it's possible that Otsandan wolves might have come to Nedrra's aid. Until we understand how Nedrra came to be on the surface, I won't know which is the more plausible conclusion." And that was it.

The Council sat in silence. All of them were slightly shaggy, and Jarren's ears were pointed and tufted. They twitched constantly, whether from fear or something else was unclear.

Terra decided that she'd try to find out. "Jarren, what are your thoughts?"

Jarren had initially planned to go to the Council himself to report what had happened. Technically they should not have entered the rogue gate, but aside from that he had done nothing wrong. It was no crime to kill in defense of one's mate.

But now he reconsidered. He wasn't sure he wanted anyone to know about the gate. The Council would come and take it away, and that would be the end of it. Walking on the surface of a different planet had been an exhilarating experience, like his hunting night with Drroj. He didn't want that taken away.

And he was still angry about what had happened to Nedrra. What if she'd been carrying his cub? He would never know now. The vicious aliens needed to pay for what they'd done.

Jarren did not look up from his hands, which were clenching and unclenching. His fingernails were thick and black. "It's complete nonsense to think that Nedrra could have reached the surface of Otsanda. Ledrra must be mistaken. Perhaps the dead female is an Otsandan who resembles Nedrra. Ledrra's loneliness for her sister caused her to make a mistake."

"Nedrra and Ledrra have been separated for years by their lives and their jobs," Hrraz said. "Why would Ledrra make such a mistake now?"

"I'm sure I don't know." Jarren pressed his lips together over his teeth. "Perhaps she has an Otsandan illness. But she must be mistaken. It is the only logical conclusion. I saw Nedrra myself only recently, so she cannot have gone to Otsanda."

"When did you last see her?" Hrraz leaned forward.

Jarren hesitated. Nedrra had died two days ago. "Last night," he said. "We turned wolf and hunted together."

"The moon is not full until next week."

Jarren shrugged. "She didn't want to wait. I don't argue with females."

Neither Hrraz nor Terra responded to the attempt at humor. They stared at him in stony silence, which Brrina tapped relentlessly at her wrist eye. She never seemed to look up from the device, but she was even more invested in taking notes and messages down during times of stress in the council cave.

Nobody really understood what was going on yet, but they all had the sense that something big was about to happen. A proper hunter could always read the weather.

*****

Kuvrro stayed close to Mirra, so close that she could hear his heartbeat. While she recorded her report to the Council, he stood just behind her, his breath warm in her hair.

Part of it was concern, Mirra knew, and part of it was a demonstration of his loyalty to her. He would not give her reason to doubt him again. She didn't mind his insecurity. The extra attention was pleasant.

After ending the message, Kuvrro said, "That wasn't all true."

"I know."

"Ledrra has studied Otsandan wolves. They fear Otsandan men like nothing else. They would never attack one to protect a stranger. Especially if one of them was carrying a kill-stick."

"They're called guns. And I know. I don't want the Council to know everything we do."

"You think the Council cannot be trusted?"

"I think that something very improbable is going on, and I think I want to keep information close and guarded until I understand more."

"How can I help?"

Mirra said, "The only way Nedrra could have come to Otsanda independently is via a leap gate. Do you agree?"

"Agreed." Kuvrro wanted to ask a dozen questions, but interrupting Mirra during her thought process would likely put him right back into "quarantine."

"Could she have found a way through the chain of gates, through ours here on the Star Pack?"

Kuvrro considered. Technically it was possible to get from Garou to Otsanda via the network of gates they had set up on all the civilized planets. But all of them were monitored and their use recorded. At some point Nedrra surely would have been intercepted and sent back. She had no training and no official business on any other world. It would have meant the end of her career if she were caught.

127

And the last gate in the chain was right here on the Star Pack, which led to an empty paradise in the land of Canada, many days' run from Wisconsin. Even if Nedrra had gotten past Mirra's attention, how had she traveled so far across Otsanda?

"So unlikely that it might as well be impossible," Kuvrro said at last.

"Which is less likely: that Ledrra mistook her sister or that somehow there is a rogue leap gate here on Otsanda?"

Kuvrro rubbed his forehead and crawled into the nest, and Mirra lay down beside him. They both sat in silence for a long time, considering the question together.

Mirra was well-known for holding Ledrra in contempt, but Ledrra was an intelligent and competent analyst. It was understood among the rank and file of the pack that Mirra's animosity was due to a clash in personalities rather than any genuine shortcoming. Kuvrro thought that Mirra knew it too.

Ledrra was not given to leaps of imagination. She gathered information and based her conclusions only on what she could see and smell. If Ledrra thought the murdered female was her sister, Kuvrro believed her.

But there was more going on here than one dead wolf. A rogue gate—or a series of them—could explain the strange coincidences they had observed. Native creatures identical to both sides of hunter nature, evolving side by side as rivals. The mythology of the "werewolf" that permeated every aspect of Otsandan culture. If there was a leap gate here, then there had been crossings before. Perhaps they even shared a common ancestor.

It was all so strange. Kuvrro shook his head. It was the stuff of children's tales. Perhaps it was more likely that Ledrra had made a mistake. Perhaps she was ill.

"Where is Ledrra now?" he asked.

"Sleeping in her cave. I put a portable nose in her room and turned on the sleep-scent. She hasn't moved since Drrak took her there this morning."

"Is he staying with her?"

"I have seen to it." Mirra's eyes were stormy and dark.

"Does anyone else know about this?"

"No. I want to wait until we know what's going on so I can explain things properly to the pack."

"Good. There are others here who have seen and interacted with Nedrra, correct?"

"Nedrra was a medical officer, and most of this pack is from her territory. We all saw her for routine care at least once."

"Summon a picture from the Internet and show it to everyone— individually, so they don't react to each other. See how many identify her as Nedrra."

"What if they assume that it's Nedrra just because it resembles her?"

"Tell them it's an Otsandan woman, and this is an experiment of some kind."

Mirra nodded. "I will take your suggestion. Thank you."

"Can I do anything more?"

"Find Nexrra and learn everything you can about the surface terrain. You may be visiting the surface again soon, and this time for a longer duration."

*****

Jenrra knew that the ship was in distress, but she had no idea what she could do to help. So she did what she did best: she stayed out of everyone's way. She settled down in her nest cave, turned on her wrist eye, and waited for someone to come tell her what to do.

She occupied herself by connecting her ear to the ship's computer system, which was hooked into Otsanda's world-wide communications. The Internet was short on science and fact, but long on entertainment, probably devised to distract people from their miserable status as landbound primitives. Jenrra couldn't imagine living in a world without space travel. She felt claustrophobic just thinking about it. Her role on the Star Pack was subordinate, but at least she was in space.

Apparently some of the aliens felt the same way, because entire swaths of the Internet had been devoted to fantasies about space travel and what lay beyond their solar system. In particular, millions of Otsandans were obsessed with the fictional adventures of a time-traveling medical officer. While studying the lives and stories of this fantastical physician,

Jenrra came across an online journal by an Otsandan male named Bob Garnier. Garnier was apparently a follower of the physician's stories, and he'd made up a number of his own, which he shared online.

Garnier's website was nothing remarkable by itself, but two things caught Jenrra's attention. The first was that Garnier was apparently a police officer, a sort of alpha among his kind. It was unusual for an Otsandan in high authority to make up stories about the outer worlds; generally alpha types were content enough where they were.

The other was that Garnier was part of the pack that lived close to the mound where an Otsandan female had been inexplicably killed. In his "blog," he talked about finding a dead woman who had seemingly come out of nowhere. Details were sparse, as the death was part of an ongoing investigation, but Garnier speculated that the woman was of alien origins.

Jenrra absolutely could not tell Mirra about this. Mirra would only be more angry and afraid, and she would want this Garnier person dead. Jenrra knew that the Internet was full of lies about aliens, and nobody in the real world would take Garnier's speculations seriously. But there was no point in upsetting Mirra further.

All she could do what was she did best: keep her nose to the ground and the ship clean while she waited for more information.

*****

Drrak curled up in the little bed beside Ledrra, who still slept. She'd been asleep when Drrak found her in Mirra's office, and he'd had to carry her back to her own bedcave. He felt calm and sleepy, despite knowing that Mirra hated him and Ledrra might as well. A portable nose hummed from the corner of her cave, and Drrak smelled calmative scent.

Mirra hadn't explained what had happened, and Ledrra was in no condition to do so. So Drrak still didn't know what was going on when Kuvrro summoned him to see Mirra. Drrak swallowed and tried not to show fear. Would Mirra punish him? He hadn't done anything to warrant punishment, but the captain had let her feelings make decisions before.

Thankfully Mirra's office was close, so Drrak was spared a long, silent walk. Kuvrro led him into Mirra's office, and the captain pointed to an image on her computer screen. "Who is that?" she asked.

It was a dark-haired female with a strong resemblance to Ledrra. Her eyes were closed, and her face was very pale under the freckles.

"That's Ledrra's sister, Nedrra," he said.

"Impossible. That's an Otsandan female. She was killed on the surface a few days ago."

Drrak looked more closely. He remembered Nedrra well; she had given him several vaccinations and a vitamin booster before he'd left Garou. There was the fat chin freckle he'd stared at to take his mind off the needle.

"Your files must be mislabeled. That's Nedrra."

Mirra and Kuvrro looked at each other. "Five out of five so far," Mirra said.

"It's her," Kuvrro agreed.

"What's going on?" Drrak asked.

"We have an improbable situation," Kuvrro said.

Chapter Nine

Ledrra had done an amazing job gathering and organizing the information she'd developed from the Otsandan web, so easy that Cavrra didn't even feel like she was working. Ledrra had created virtual databases for the major areas of study: the intelligent Otsandans, the wolves, and other flora and fauna. All Cavrra had to do was read.

The file on the Otsandan wolves was enormous. The two-legged Otsandans had volumes of scientific data about their behavior and habits, and Ledrra had also added Nexrra's observations from her direct contact with them.

Mirra had asked that Cavrra look for any information suggesting that the Otsandan wolves might attack humans, either in self-defense or for other reasons. So far she had found nothing. She had found Ledrra's file of "fairy tales" which portrayed wolves as psychotic eaters of children. But the notes on the file made it plain that these stories were only to entertain Otsandans and frighten their young into obedience. Real wolves, according to Ledrra's research, were shy and preferred smaller game.

Then Cavrra noticed a small black icon in the lower corner of the screen. It read "DOGS." She tapped the icon, and moments later had to re-evaluate her conclusion.

Dogs, according to this new file, were closely related to wolves. They were so closely related that they were capable of interbreeding with them, and their offspring were usually fertile and healthy. But dogs were very different from wolves in temperament. They were obsessively fond of humans and blindly loyal—so loyal that a dog could be trained to attack and kill its own kind at its master's command. Cavrra shuddered. There was something very wrong with these animals. Some sort of mental defect that the Otsandans had exploited for their own gain.

But now she had to reconsider her assumption that the killer had to be a hunter. It was unlikely; the images Cavrra saw of dogs did not look like they could kill two grown males. But it was just as improbable that a hunter female could have turned up out of nowhere on a planet they had only reached a few months ago. The whole situation was improbable. Cavrra could eliminate nothing.

She had nothing substantial to report to the captain. Mirra was not going to be happy.

*****

But Mirra surprised her. "I thought this might be the situation," she said. "The mere appearance of Nedrra is so improbable that all possibilities seem equally likely. To what degree are you able to eliminate Otsandan wolves as suspects?"

Nexrra was sitting on the couch behind Mirra's chair, listening in silence. Mirra turned around slightly as she asked the question, directing it at both of them. Cavrra looked at Nexrra, who had met the wolves herself and had read most of the same material in Ledrra's files.

"It is the least likely of all scenarios," Nexrra said. "The Otsandan men were armed with guns, and their mode of dress suggests that they were experienced killers. A single wolf might attack if it were ill—"

"There is a disease here called 'rabies' that causes a psychotic breakdown," Cavrra interjected. "It is a deadly disease that causes its victims to kill others."

"—but it would have taken a pack of wolves to kill the two men," Nexrra said. She appeared unperturbed by Cavrra's interruption.

"Which means that the killer is probably a different sort of animal, like this 'dog' Cavrra mentions," Mirra said. "Could a single dog have killed them both?"

Cavrra said, "Some types of dog are much larger than wolves, and if the dog were a pet it might have taken them by surprise. According to Ledrra's notes, humans are usually taken by surprise when a dog kills one of them."

"Nexrra," Mirra said, turning around again. "Would you like to revisit the surface?"

"I beg your pardon?"

"We have a very peculiar situation under our muzzles, one that could prove dangerous to both Garou and Otsanda. As much as I would like to continue wallowing in hurt pride, it is no longer safe. You have been to the surface more times than anyone, and you have interacted directly with the wolves. I need your expertise."

"What do you want me to do?" Nexrra straightened.

"Assemble a small pack to travel to the place where Nedrra was killed. Find the leap gate, if one exists. Remove the gem and bring it back to me."

"How could there be a leap gem on a planet we've never visited?" Cavrra asked.

"How could two almost identical species have evolved on different worlds? How could one of those species have myths and fairy tales about the other species throughout their entire planet? You have read Ledrra's file. Every single culture, every single pack on the planet of Otsanda has stories about shape-shifting wolves. And now—here we are. How is that possible? The wolves that Nexrra met recognized her as one of their kind. But she isn't. We aren't even from the same solar system. How is that possible?"

Mirra's face was pale, but her eyes were large and bright. She's enjoying this, Cavrra thought. She's found something she never expected, a true mystery, and she's so excited she can hardly contain herself.

"Five pack mates," Mirra said to Nexrra. "I recommend Kuvrro be one of them. He is an excellent tracker and a quick thinker."

"Yes, captain." Nexrra touched her throat and left the office. Mirra nodded at Cavrra, dismissing her as well.

Cavrra left, her head filled to bursting with questions and confusion. But Mirra was right about one thing. This was rather exciting.

*****

"Currency," Cavrra read from the list she'd printed. "The second item on the list after clothing is currency. The third is identification."

"What sort of identification?" Kuvrro asked.

"A plastic card with a picture and name on it. Otsandans use them to identify each other."

"Why? Have they no sense of smell?"

Cavrra shrugged. "The only time they smell each other is when they're preparing to mate. I don't understand either. Ledrra could probably explain it."

Kuvrro shook his head and looked around the cramped meeting room. His body language was loose, relaxed, and slightly contemptuous.

He hadn't held a high opinion of the Otsandans from the start, and everything he'd learned since only reinforced his opinion.

"Can we use the currency to obtain identification?" he asked.

"Maybe. But I think it would be easier to create our own. The printer-copier can make plastic cards similar to the ones Otsandans use. All I have to do is plug in photographs of us and fill in the necessary information."

"What sort of information?"

"The Internet has images of different types of identification, and most of them have the individual's name, date of birth, and location of their home pack."

"Back to currency," Nexrra said. "What kind of currency do they use? Is it a stone or a metal?"

"This part is trickier," Cavrra said. She tapped the printed sheet. "It's paper, a very special sort of paper. They keep its components closely guarded, and every single piece of it has a tracking number printed on it."

"So we can't duplicate it without being discovered. Could we steal it?"

"It's not advisable. In some packs, theft of currency is punishable by death."

Nexrra said, "We may not need currency at all. Mirra has given us permission to use the second scout pod to drop down to the Otsandan surface. We can go straight to the spot where Nedrra was killed."

"Then why are we bothering with this identification and currency?" Kuvrro asked.

"Because there may still be Otsandans in the area, sniffing at the place of death. If we encounter them, I want to look like a woman, not a wolf."

Cavrra shivered. As much as she wanted to see the surface again and run as the wolf, she was afraid of the Otsandans. The species was still in what Ledrra called the messy stage; they were violent and short-sighted, like children. They were capable of almost anything.

"So we have sufficient identification," she said, trying to focus on another problem. "Nexrra, how do you think we should go about acquiring currency?"

"The easiest way would be what Ledrra called 'identity theft' in her notes." Nexrra ran her fingers through her hair. Cavrra thought she was trying to calm her hackles. It made her feel better to know that she wasn't the only frightened one.

"Theft of identity? What do you mean by that?" Kuvrro's eyes were wide.

"It's in Ledrra's file on Otsandan crimes. The type of currency most often used to purchase items through the Internet is called credit. Ledrra learned how to break into data storage systems so that she could monitor the sorts of things Otsandans buy. We can use her program to steal credit information from Otsandans who have used the Internet."

"That sounds unethical."

"It's a serious crime on Otsanda, especially in the country we'll be visiting. But since we only need currency as a precaution, with luck we won't need to use the cards at all. No harm will be done to the Otsandans."

The door to the meeting room opened, and Drrak entered. Kuvrro growled.

Then Ledrra followed him in, and they all startled. Nobody had expected her to be back on her feet until after the next moon, at the very earliest.

"We're coming too," Ledrra said. "I want to find my sister and howl for her."

"That's not our mission," Cavrra said gently. "Our mission is to find the leap gate, if one exists."

"I know. And I won't ask you to jeopardize our main objective. But there's a chance we could find the place where they are holding her body. I want to try to find her."

"How do you know the body wasn't already destroyed?"

"I am familiar with their death customs. They will keep the body frozen while they search for her pack."

"And you are surviving family," Kuvrro said. "They don't need to know where you're from. They may see that you are her pack and surrender her body to you."

"Can you speak their language well enough to pass as a native?" Cavrra asked.

"No, but that doesn't matter. I can speak it well enough to communicate, and they will assume that I am from a foreign pack on another part of the planet."

"Which would explain, in their minds, why it took so long for you to come." Kuvrro nodded. "This may work."

They all looked at Nexrra, the alpha. She bared her teeth at Drrak. "Why is he coming? We don't need two males."

"I seek to show throat and redeem myself for my recent behavior." Drrak looked down at his feet while he spoke. His cheeks were fuzzy and flushed with shame.

"For mistreating the female who inexplicably cares for you, or for trying to take my place as alpha male?" Kuvrro's face was also red, but not with shame. His ears were pointed and furry.

"Both." Drrak spoke to his feet. "But mostly for what I did to Ledrra."

"Do you really want him along?" Nexrra asked Ledrra.

Ledrra regarded Drrak, who still stared at his feet. If he currently had a tail, it would be tucked between his legs. "Yes. I think we need him. And I'd like him to have the chance to make it up to me."

"It's decided, then." Nexrra looked around at them all. "The five of us are going. Cavrra, when can you have our identification ready?"

"If Ledrra can assist me in finding the proper files and images, they can be ready in a few hours."

"Tomorrow morning, then. Drrak, you get to work cleaning and preparing the second scout pod. I'll give you the coordinates you'll need for the drop."

Drrak nodded. He still had not made eye contact with any of the pack. Good. The fact that he had accepted his task without protest—menial cleaning work was Jerra's job—indicated that he was truly repentant.

Chapter Ten

Jarren stood in front of the huge old tree. The leap gem stared impassively back, glinting gold in the late afternoon sun.

One mystery was solved; this gate led to the new planet, Otsanda. But that answer only raised a dozen more questions. Who had placed the gems? Had the Otsandans done it? But they were too primitive. They hadn't even left their own solar system yet.

That left the possibility of a third race, one more advanced than Garou. But if they were so advanced, why had the gate been placed in such a haphazard fashion? The gems had just been pressed into the ground and left there with no controls and no monitor. If it were an experiment, it was a very sloppy one.

Jarren touched the rough, cool bark. The gate didn't always work. The pack out looking for the animal that had attacked Drroj must have run past this tree again and again, and they had never even seen it. Perhaps it wasn't always visible. Maybe it was a sort of test.

Jarren looked up into the darkening night sky. He thought he might like to go hunting again when the wolf came.

There were new paradises to explore.

Jarren went back to his lone wolf's home, a place Nedrra would never see. His head hurt, and he felt feverish. It made him want to bite something.

*****

Kuvrro growled at his harness-pack. "I'll feel like an ungula in this thing. Why do we all need to carry one?"

"Because we need clothes," Nexrra reminded him. "Otsandan bodies are hairless, so they cover them with clothes. If you try to go among the aliens wearing just your fur, they will call you a monster—or a rapist."

"What's a rapist?"

Nexrra told him, and Kuvrro was horrified. "Let us stay in wolf bodies while we're down there. These people are mad."

"We will stay as wolves as much as possible. But in order to identify and retrieve Nedrra, Ledrra must become a woman."

138

"If those mad folk harm her—"

"She is able to defend herself, and we will be close enough to come to her aid. Calm down, Kuvrro. You're getting musky."

The rest of the pack adjusted the straps on their packs and checked the contents silently. It wasn't just Kuvrro who smelled of anxiety, though as alpha male he had status enough to verbalize his fears without losing face. They had learned enough about the natives to be afraid of them.

Drrak was particularly withdrawn. He kept his eyes down and his hands busy, and none of the others made a move to interact with him, even Ledrra. They thought he was still ashamed, but shame was no longer his dominant emotion.

It was determination. He would redeem himself in the eyes of his pack and in the eyes of his mate. He caught her looking at him occasionally while she adjusted her harness pack. He wondered what she was thinking.

Finally everyone was ready. The harness packs were equipped with clean clothing similar to what Otsandans wore. Nexrra didn't think any natives would get close enough to notice that the fabric was composed of molecules never seen on Otsanda. They also had identification and credit cards with false names on them. Nexrra hoped that they would not be needed, since that would mean attracting the attention of Otsandan authorities. But she wanted to be prepared for anything.

The scout pod was clean and ready, and they all settled into the huge, embracing seats and buckled their harnesses. Their harness packs were secured by special loops on the sides of their seats. The hatch slammed shut, and the engines roared to life. Kuvrro and Nexrra were the only two who had ridden in a scout before; the rest looked pale and a little sick.

Drrak had programmed the coordinates of their landing when he'd prepared the scout, but Nexrra double-checked anyway. Part of her reason was to needle him further, but part of it was simple caution. All readouts were green and healthy. The scout was fully functional and ready to launch. The pack was settled and as ready to go as they could be. Nexrra tried to find a bright spot. She would get to breathe fresh air again, and she would not have to wear a suit.

Then she looked at Ledrra. There was no bright spot anywhere in her future.

Ledrra's face was still and calm, but her eyes shifted from their typical blue-green to wolf-yellow and back again. Nothing else showed; Ledrra's face and hands were hairless, and her teeth were covered. But her eyes could not lie. Ledrra was deeply stressed and needed close supervision.

Nexrra pulled the release lever and leaned back in her seat. Her stomach leaped as the scout dropped away from the Star Pack and out of the minor gravity well of their moon. Its boosters jerked and jolted them on their way to Otsanda. Nexrra shivered. The second scout pod was almost never used. In a typical mission, only one was ever needed to establish a base on the new planet. After that, the leap gates were a faster and more efficient way to get around. The second scout was reserved for emergencies, such as evacuation or rescue.

The pack was silent as they dropped toward Otsanda. The only sound was the steady hum of the scout's propulsion system. They rocked and danced as the scout adjusted its direction to bring them closer to their destination. Nexrra closed her eyes. It made the ache in her stomach worse, but she couldn't look at her mates anymore. She was afraid. She had never been afraid before, even when she had snuck to the surface and fled from Kuvrro. But she was afraid now.

The scout slowed, and Nexrra's stomach dropped from her throat to her bowels. There was the smell of nervous flatulence. Then, with a heavy thump, the scout came to a halt. They had landed.

Everyone was completely still, waiting. Nexrra remembered that she was alpha; they were waiting for her to issue a command. "Unbuckle," she said. "Cavrra, turn on the external eyes."

There was no way to conceal the scout from view as it landed; if Otsandans had seen it there was nothing they could do about that. But Nexrra could at least keep her pack from being spotted as they left it. If there were Otsandans about, the pack would wait inside for them to go away. With luck, the falling scout would be dismissed as one of their own flying machines.

Luck was apparently with them. Nexrra studied all four wall eyes and saw no signs of two-legged life. There were few trees, and she could

140

see a long ways off. In the distance she saw a round hill so uniform in size and shape it had to be artificial. "We'll go there first," Nexrra said, tapping the monitor. "The Otsandan news mentioned that place. Nedrra's body was found in its shadow."

Ledrra growled, and Kuvrro glanced at her. "Do you have complete control?" he asked.

"Mirra isn't here," Nexrra said, touching his arm firmly. "And there is no shame in being upset by what happened to Nedrra."

"If she is full of rage when she turns wolf, her rage will let the wolf take control."

"I am well aware of that." Nexrra's tone was sharp. Kuvrro was alpha male as well as her older brother, but he was still just a male. In their current dynamic, Nexrra's status was above his. Kuvrro touched his throat in apology.

Then he gave Ledrra a long, searching look. She returned it passively.

*****

After waiting long enough for the external shell to cool, Nexrra gave the order to leave the scout. One by one they stepped into the sanitizer—more out of habit and tradition than anything—and through the hatchway and onto the surface of Otsanda.

Cavrra gasped, and for a moment she was completely immobile. She had only visited the surface once before, and that was in a suit. It was a completely different matter to move and turn freely and feel the fresh air on her skin. She sniffed, her nostrils widening and changing just a trifle so she could experience the complete olfactory symphony.

You haven't experienced anything yet, Nexrra thought. Then she took one last look around to make sure they were completely alone.

"Everyone change," she said.

Jarren waited for the moon to rise. He didn't have to wait; he could change whenever it suited him. But he wanted to feel the moonlight on his skin, wanted to feel that delicious loss of control. He wanted to feel the wolf as it woke up and took over his mind and body. He shivered a little, and his penis stiffened.

He told himself that he was only going back to Otsanda to explore. He was curious about the presence of the leap gate, and he wanted to learn more about it. He did not ask himself why he was going back in his wolf skin, or why he was waiting until night. Why he was waiting until his reasoning mind was at its weakest to cross over to the new world.

He sat on the cold ground with a numb rump. The silver orb slowly peeped over the horizon. It wasn't full yet; there were still a few weeks yet before the wolf became imperative. But the moon still held power over him. Jarren shivered again. The need to change was a deep, sexual hunger. Tonight the two were interchangeable. He closed his eyes and summoned his wild nature.

It seemed strange that he had once been afraid of this. The wolf was power, the wolf was hunger, and the wolf feared nothing at all under the sun or moon.

His jaw lengthened, his pelt sprouted, and his limbs creaked and bent. Jarren reveled in the pain. He remembered the last time he'd taken this form, the last time he'd been with Nedrra. That pain was still fresh, and it fed the wolf's lust. He would hunt well tonight.

The wolf leaped to the front of Jarren's mind, pushing the empathetic thinker to the rear. Jarren became a passenger in his own head, watching and savoring the wolf's wild senses.

Then it stalked through the gate.

It was late afternoon on the other side. Jarren blinked in the unexpected sunlight. A bit of his reasoning mind came to the fore, but the wolf clamped down and kept control. There was no moon here, but it was still Jarren's time to change, and the wolf knew it. He lowered his muzzle to the strange soil and set off in search of prey.

There were birds here, and burrowers much like the ones back home. The wolf took note of these, but his jaws hungered for bigger game. Jarren's simmering rage at Nedrra's death translated into actual hunger in the mind of the wolf. He knew what he was hungry for, though he barely understood why.

Then he smelled the prey he sought. It was large and heavy and walked on two legs as though it were civilized.

He approached the mound where Nedrra had died. There were strips of shiny yellow material strung up on the trees around the place. The wolf ignored it.

He smelled fresh meat. The wolf growled and salivated. He saw the meat now, a young male in a light brown outer garment. There was a chain around its neck, and some sort of medallion dangled from the chain.

The male poked at the ground where the two aliens had died. The wolf crept forward a few steps and waited. Crept forward and waited. The stupid alien was deaf and blind, and it saw nothing until the wolf charged forward with its teeth bared.

The wolf went for its throat, smelling the salty sweat of fear as his jaws sought the tang of fresh blood. The alien reached under its garment and pulled out a black instrument. The wolf's front paw knocked it away, and there was a blast of sound and a burning smell.

Then his jaws closed together, fresh hot salty blood poured down his throat, and he buried his muzzle in the delicious glory.

When the alien was dead, the wolf tore at its garments and snapped its metal chain. When most of its soft, naked belly was exposed, the wolf began to feed.

Chapter Eleven

It had rained recently, and Kuvrro could smell wetness and life in the soil beneath their paws. But then he smelled something else, and his hackles rose. Someone growled. He thought it might be Drrak.

Fresh blood. He sat down and sniffed the air. Blood, sweat, and burning metal. All together it told a clear story. A sentient Otsandan had been attacked, possibly killed.

Nexrra looked at him. He smelled her confusion and fear.

Kuvrro took a few steps toward the smell and stopped. Nexrra was alpha here, but she was uncertain and afraid. Kuvrro hoped to encourage her without showing her up. He took another step and waited again.

Nexrra looked from him to the other three. They waited silently for instructions. She looked back at Kuvrro. He sniffed the air again. The blood smell was cooling, and valuable information was being lost while she dithered. But he kept his ears and tail still. He waited for instructions from his alpha.

Finally Nexrra took the lead and trotted past him. This new death might be related to their reason for being here. The fresh body could tell them much. They passed under the strips of yellow plastic. Kuvrro knew that these were put up to mark the places where a violent death had occurred, since the Otsandans lacked the nose to figure it out on their own. *Deaf and blind children,* Kuvrro thought randomly. He wasn't sure if they were more deserving of contempt or sympathy.

Nexrra stopped short and backed away, whining. When Kuvrro saw what was left of the Otsandan male, he was grateful for the strong stomach of the wolf. In his two-legged form, he might have vomited.

The man had been eviscerated and partially devoured. There were traces of saliva in the wounds, and the scent was unmistakably that of a hunter. One of their own had done this. Otsandans were not hunters, but they were so similar to his kind that he felt the natural revulsion that any thinking creature has toward cannibalism. He was revolted.

Drrak sniffed all around the corpse, keeping a healthy distance from the bloody horror. The ground was scuffed and torn from the struggle, and there were paw prints all around. Drrak spiraled outward, sorting out the scents. Then he looked up and growled. His ears angled back. He'd found a trail.

Ledrra followed Drrak away from the others. Kuvrro swallowed a worried whine. He was suddenly afraid for them and had no idea why. He didn't want the pack to split up. Nexrra looked up, catching a whiff of his anxiety. Then they heard the engine.

Kuvrro was disgusted with himself. The internal combustion engines the Otsandans used were loud and smelly, and any self-respecting wolf could hear and smell them from a mile away. They had been distracted by the horror on the ground, and now they were seconds away from being spotted.

Nexrra bolted, and Kuvrro and Cavrra followed close behind. They ran around the base of the mound, and behind him Kuvrro could hear the motor roar up to the death scene and stop. There were slams and shouts. Kuvrro knew only a few words in the local Otsandan language, most of them curses. He was hearing those now.

Nexrra stopped running. Cavrra and Kuvrro drew up, and Nexrra nudged Cavrra hard. She cocked her ears and sat very still, listening to the talk. She was the only one of the three who understood the language well enough to translate effectively.

Then she tensed. The Otsandans were running, running away from them. There was purpose in their gait, and their voices sounded strong and determined. They had seen something. Kuvrro whined. Had they seen Drrak and Ledrra?

Nexrra started running back the way they had come. The scout had landed near a copse of trees, and Nexrra went there now. The three wolves slipped into the thick brush and crept on their bellies until they found a thick fallen tree. They dug and scraped at the soft soil until they could nestle their bodies more or less underneath the tree. Then they waited.

Kuvrro breathed deeply and tried not to transmit his distress. He focused on the fresh rain in the soil, the mold and moss coming alive on the dead tree. Drrak and Ledrra would lose the Otsandans easily, and when it was safe they would find their way back to their pack. Kuvrro closed his eyes and waited. Nexrra was half-buried in the earth in front of him, and he felt her tremble very slightly.

They waited as the alien sun slid by overhead. The unnatural blue sky deepened to purple, then black. Kuvrro longed to leave their hiding place and run in the open so he could see the stars. He knew the very one he would sing to.

*****

Ledrra smelled the Garouean wolf, and in a sea of unfamiliar scents its familiarity struck her hard as a slap. Drrak was already running, nose to the ground. She had to rush to catch up and keep up.

The trail led up and over the mound. It was entirely open here, and Ledrra felt exposed. But she kept up with Drrak, trusting his nose and his judgment. They ran across the mound and down the other side, and then a gold glint in the wet grass caught her eye.

Drrak stopped dead. Ledrra stood very still behind him, breathing slowly and trying to control her racing heart. Half-hidden in the thick grass, against the base of the mound, was a leap gem. The black jewel glinted gold in the dying afternoon light.

The trail led directly into the spot, and a quick search confirmed that it did not lead away. Drrak sniffed at the gem, took a deep breath, and stepped forward. Even though she had expected it, Ledrra still felt a shock when the wolf disappeared into the thick grass as though through a doorway. She followed.

She opened her eyes on a maelstrom of light. Her eyes burned from the colors, every color in the universe flung into her sensitive wolf's eyes. She kept moving forward. She was in a rogue gate, and any hesitation could mean death or madness. It was probably madness to have come, but Drrak's solid form was a comforting reality.

Then she felt soil beneath her paws again, and electricity jolted through all her limbs. Drrak let out an involuntary howl, and Ledrra's voice joined his. Warm, familiar smells, solid ground so familiar it was shocking. She hadn't touched this soil in five years. They were on Garou.

And the moon was almost full here. She felt the wolf move forward and take control.

There was another male wolf in front of them who stood still for only a moment. Then it charged silently, taking Drrak by surprise. Drrak was knocked off his feet by the bigger wolf's charge. Ravenous teeth found his throat.

Drrak was taken aback and could scarcely find the wits to defend himself. Ledrra was as stunned as he was; who was this wolf and why was it attacking one of his own kind? Drrak snapped and scrabbled, drawing blood but accomplishing little. Ledrra slammed into the stranger and snapped at his neck. The other wolf was larger and heavier, but she managed to take his attention off Drrak long enough for him to stagger to his feet.

She backed away slowly. Social law forbade any hunter male to attack a female, but this wolf did not look normal. His green eyes were vacant and empty. There was no sign of the intelligence that lurked in the back of every wolf's mind no matter what the phase of the moon.

Ledrra lifted her lips in warning, but the stranger only lifted his own and stalked forward. His eyes. They were so strange. Like the eyes of an artificial wolf, a construct.

Drrak panted heavily, bleeding heavily from his neck and head. His eyes were glazed with pain, but he somehow managed to leap forward and place himself between his mate and the stranger.

The stranger moved so quickly that even Ledrra's keen wolf eyes could scarcely follow. Without a sound, Drrak crumpled to the ground. Ledrra leaped over his fallen body and attacked the stranger without a thought. She snarled and bit and dashed in and out like a stinging insect. The stranger could not score on her; all the fight had gone out of him. Finally he fled, tucking his tail between his hindquarters.

She went back to Drrak. He was already dead; his heart had stopped and his blood slowed. She licked his face. She hoped that he could somehow feel her love before consciousness faded completely.

Then she sat down, lifted her bloody muzzle to her own familiar moon, and howled. She sang for Drrak, for the mistakes he had made and for his atonement and forgiveness.

She hoped that somehow he could hear her.

*****

The Otsandans had gone; Kuvrro was sure of it. But still Nexrra waited, and her followers waited with her. Kuvrro knew why. She was afraid to move. Not out of fear for their safety, but fear of what they would discover. Drrak and Ledrra should have come back a long time ago. The trail to their hiding place was clear to any wolf. If all had gone well, they would have come back.

Finally Kuvrro slipped out from under the tree. Nexrra was alpha, and this ought to be her command to give. But Nexrra was still frozen. She really didn't have the initiative to lead. This wasn't a flaw, but it did mean that someone else had to do her job.

He shook himself, sending leaves and soil flying. He sniffed around and sneezed. Nexrra stayed put for a few extra seconds, then slowly followed him out. On the other side of the tree, Cavrra did the same.

Kuvrro looked around. He felt strange and cold. He had decided that it was time to move, but it was hard to take the necessary steps. He sniffed perfunctorily at the ground, stalling for time. He wished Mirra was here.

Cavrra growled at them both and started walking back the way they had come. Kuvrro and Nexrra followed silently with heads and tails lowered.

They had not taken more than twenty steps when they heard a familiar gait approaching. Kuvrro sat down, relieved. Drrak and Ledrra were finally coming back. The pack was together again.

But something was wrong. There was only one set of footsteps.

Ledrra limped into view. Her tongue hung out, and there were streaks of blood in her fur.

Drrak was nowhere to be seen.

Then she coughed and spat something dark onto the ground. It was solid black, shiny with saliva, and it glinted gold in the sliver of moonlight. The rogue leap gem.

Chapter Twelve

Jarren did not run far.

As soon as the strange female had gone back through the gate, Jarren limped back to the tree and collapsed. He sprawled out on the ground like a dead thing. His wounds hurt, but they hurt far less than the pain in his heart and mind. The wolf was frightened and confused. He had never struck a female before.

He closed his eyes, savoring the cool depths of unconsciousness.

When he awoke, the wolf was asleep again. Jarren touched his neck and chest. Scratches, mostly. The female had not scored well. But he still had a problem. He looked over at the corpse on the ground.

The stranger had shifted back to man form before dying. He looked familiar. Jarren supposed that it was because he'd seen images of the Star Pack's crew. Somehow they had found their way south to the wild gate. Jarren wondered why. In every report Mirra had indicated that they intended to keep to a small area in the far north. They wanted to avoid places heavily visited by the intelligent natives.

But now they knew about the gate. They knew that a hunter had killed on the surface of Otsanda. Jarren should have killed the female. He had been weak. She would tell the others, and they would hunt him and catch him.

But that would take time. He could make a plan for survival. If nothing else, he could flee into the woods and live wild. He was a good hunter. He would survive.

But he would not survive long if he left the body of his victim lying here, so close to the ancestors' home. The ancestors' assistants routinely searched these woods for the bodies of old ones who had wandered away. He had to hide it, hide it well enough that no wolf could track it.

The corpse reeked of fear and fresh blood. It was impossible.

No, not impossible. Impossible to hide here, on a world filled with sensitive and intelligent beings who hated murder. But there was a better place. A place filled with slow and stupid aliens who couldn't smell a rotting creepfur right under their noses.

It would be dangerous. The Star Pack crew would still be nearby. They would want to investigate the gem and the wild gate. But Jarren thought he'd rather take his chances with a dozen wolves than a million.

He climbed to his feet—ugh, his muscles ached. But he stretched and limbered up so he could hoist the dead stranger onto his shoulders. With a grunt and a curse, he stumbled into the tree and through the gate.

*****

Nexrra thought she might be sick. Ledrra had told them the horrible tale, and now they all waited in silence for instructions from their alpha. But Nexrra could not think of instructions. She could not think of anything but Ledrra, who had lost first her sister and now her mate. A wild leap gate and a rogue wolf—how was any of this possible? It wasn't. It just wasn't possible. But there it was. The gem was on the ground in front of her.

Ledrra looked calm and collected. Maybe she just couldn't be shocked anymore. The worst had already happened, and there just wasn't anything left.

They were in two-legged form to facilitate communication. Nexrra kept her ears pointed so that she could listen for approaching Otsandans. They would be coming; there was no doubt about that. They would be in a complete panic this time. The first set of murders had been upsetting, but this one would make them frightened and angry. The cold deliberation with which the Otsandan had been disemboweled was not that of an unthinking beast. Even they would know that.

Nexrra had seen the badge on the dead man's chest, and Ledrra had told her what it meant. "Chief" was their word for alpha. He had been an alpha police officer. Police officers were socially powerful; they were a sort of alpha in their own right. But this one had been an alpha among police officers.

They would scour the mound and all the woods for anything, two-legged or four, which they thought could have killed their chief. Nexrra and her people needed to move. The problem was that she wasn't sure where to go. The scout was equipped with an emergency leap gate, powered by a chip of gem that would only work once or twice. But Nexrra didn't know if they should go back to the Star Pack yet. They had found and retrieved the gem, but they hadn't identified the rogue wolf, who could kill again. Nor had they helped Ledrra find closure for her sister. If they took the emergency gate back to the Star Pack, there would be no coming back to this spot in a hurry. They had to finish their business here and now.

"Where should we go from here?" she asked. Maybe one of her pack had a good idea.

"Into the Otsandan world," Ledrra said. "We can pass for natives."

"Out of the question." That one was easy. "The police will be looking for strangers, outsiders. They always look for strangers when a crime has been committed; you told me that. We'll be caught, especially if we try to use our false identification."

"We could pass for Otsandan wolves." Cavrra spoke without looking up.

"Wolves may not be safe either. The murder of the alpha police could have been committed by a man or a beast, in their eyes. They will look for both."

"Maybe we should just go back to the ship." Kuvrro looked at Ledrra as he spoke, gauging her reaction. "We learned what we came to learn. There was a wild gate here and a rogue wolf gone mad. We should take this information back to Mirra."

They were all silent then. Ledrra was completely still. Her face was very pale and still, and her eyes shone with suppressed emotion. They flicked back and forth between brown and gold.

"I want my sister," she said softly.

"I understand," Nexrra said. She said to Cavrra and Kuvrro, "You two go back to the ship. Use the emergency gate on the scout. I will stay with Ledrra and help her recover her sister."

"This is very dangerous," Kuvrro said. "You risk being captured by their police."

"We are two attractive females traveling alone. We will be less suspicious than the entire pack together. As long as we appear frightened and helpless, they will not suspect us of the murder."

"All right. You are alpha." Kuvrro touched his throat.

"Go quickly. Tell Mirra everything. And tell her we will follow as soon as we can."

Kuvrro was scared for his sister and anxious about how Mirra was going to take this turn of events. But even so he would not soon forget his stupidity in leaving the rogue leap gem lying on the ground where Ledrra had dropped it.

*****

Jarren carried the body through the gate, and the vertigo hit him like a blow. He staggered, and his feet swam in nothingness. He felt as though he was drowning; he couldn't breathe, and he couldn't find the surface. He let go of the body and thrashed around, kicking wildly and trying not to scream. If he screamed, he would lose all the air in his lungs, and he would smother.

Bright stars swam in front of his eyes, and Jarren felt his consciousness slipping. He made one final lunge forward, and he felt cool grass under his hands and knees. He collapsed onto his belly.

Jarren lay like one dying and panted senselessly. His tongue lolled out onto the ground, and he could taste Otsanda.

At last Jarren raised his head and looked around. It was night, and he could see the bright foreign stars poking down between the trees.

The trees looked different. Where was he?

Jarren sat up, but he was dizzy and sick from the trip through the gate. He lay back down quickly before his vision went completely black. There was some rustling nearby, and it sounded like a hunter. But he was in no shape to move right now.

Jarren closed his eyes and hoped for the best.

At least he had lost the body. It hadn't happened in the manner intended, but the body of the dead hunter was gone for good. If he could get back through the gate, he would be safe.

Until those other wolves reported their discovery of the wild gate. Then there would be a full investigation.

Jarren wondered how many wolves he could kill before he was taken down. Enough to be remembered, he thought. Right now, that was all that mattered.

He dozed off under the alien sky. His sick, exhausted body collapsed under the stress and exertion of the night, and his mind fled into dark dreams.

Chapter Thirteen

Cavrra followed Kuvrro through the dark, unfamiliar night. She was winded and near exhaustion. She had changed too many times today; once or twice a week was normal for her. Her joints ached, and her body felt dehydrated. But she kept Kuvrro's bushy tail in sight. She would not fall behind. She would not fail her pack.

She could still smell the blood and death on Ledrra's breath. Before parting ways, she had wiped her muzzle on Ledrra's face. Once she made it back to the ship, the saliva and blood samples could be used to identify Drrak's killer.

Cavrra tasted foulness on her dry tongue. How she longed for a bath and a cold drink.

When Cavrra felt she was near collapse and was ready to beg Kuvrro to stop so she could rest, the little scout appeared in front of them. Kuvrro slowed to a walk, and when he turned around Cavrra saw that he too was almost exhausted. His entire body shook with the force of his panting. Cavrra could smell fear and anger on his hot breath.

The wolves limped to the scout, and Kuvrro put a paw on the panel that opened the hatchway. It slid open with a wheeze and a thump, and Cavrra smelled cool, fresh air.

There was a canine whine behind them.

They spun around, Kuvrro a little slower. A wolf stood there, an Otsandan wolf. It was a female and smelled like an alpha type under the dirt and fleas. She cocked her ears and studied them both. Cavrra sensed curiosity and fear. Not of Kuvrro and herself, Cavrra felt. Fear of what was happening to their home.

Cavrra sighed. It was too complicated to explain to this stranger what was happening in wolf language, which was largely nonverbal and contained almost no abstract concepts. Cavrra doubted she would understand anyway. She turned to go into the scout. Kuvrro had already gone.

Fear, confusion, curiosity, concern, you smell like the man-wolf killer?

Cavrra jumped and almost fell over. The feelings and thoughts were in her head, but she had not thought them herself. She felt like they had been pushed into her mind, pressed there like a fist into soft compound.

Come on, come on. Curiosity, impatience, fear—they're coming, tell me, must go, fear.

Cavrra had no idea how the wolf was doing this, but she tried to copy her. She formed a picture of the killer and consciously tried to remember the fight beyond the gate. Then she pushed the images forward, at the she-wolf.

The wolf blanched. Too loud – hurts — careful — curiosity — fear — the killer is here now — fear.

Are. You. Sure? Cavrra pushed back.

Impatience, anger — dumb and blind like men — must go, the killer is near—the killer sleeps—fear, men are coming, fear.

The wolf ran off into the night. Cavrra stared after her. For a moment she had forgotten her exhaustion.

Kuvrro yipped impatiently from inside the scout. Cavrra went in after him. She wanted to talk to him about what had happened, but she was too tired to change so that she could speak. The wolf was stronger and faster, but she wasn't a conversationalist.

The emergency leap gate was in the center of the pod, between the two control panels that faced the seats. The leap gem was small and weak, and it would only work a couple of times. Kuvrro nosed the switch that turned it on, and then he looked at Cavrra.

Cavrra knew what he was feeling. It was not right to leave their alpha in such danger. The wolf had told her that the killer was coming; the killer was nearby. Should they stay to face him? But Cavrra was completely exhausted, and Kuvrro was little better. She didn't know how they would fare against the rogue in a fight. This killer had attacked aliens and females. He was capable of anything.

They needed to tell Mirra what had happened. She would know what to do.

Cavrra walked through the gate. As the disorientation dizzied her senses, she felt Kuvrro at her tail. He was a solid, comforting presence.

They limped out of the gate onto the main deck of the Star Pack. There was nobody in sight, but their passage through the gate would alert Mirra. She would be here soon.

Cavrra lay down on the cool floor, and Kuvrro curled up beside her. She sighed as his body warmth surrounded and comforted her, and she fell asleep.

*****

Jarren tried to ignore the howling of the wolves as he rested. It was eerie how their voices resembled those of his people, but there was difference enough that he knew he was safe for now. The Otsandan wolves were only dumb animals, and they feared the two-legged Otsandans. They would fear him too, and they would avoid him.

Finally he awoke completely. His body ached, and his eyes burned with fever. He was sick with something; as soon as he was done killing everyone here he needed to get home so he could see a medical. He might have picked up some foreign germ here. His tongue felt swollen and dry.

He left the copse of trees and started walking. After a few minutes, he came to a deep gouge in the earth, a sort of channel that extended for several leaps. Then he saw the scout. Those interfering hunters had used a scout to track him down. The hatch was open, and Jarren crept close, wondering if anyone was inside.

He kept very still and listened, but there was no sound. The scout was empty. But that female would come back to it, he thought. This would be her den away from home until she found her way back to the ship. And when she returned, Jarren could kill her and finally be safe.

Jarren found a grassy spot next to the scout and curled up. He would sleep for a few minutes more, and he would gather his strength. Then he would settle the score with that female who had dared fight him.

His head ached so much.

*****

Nexrra and Ledrra walked side by side toward the alpha officers. They walked stiffly and with their heads up, moving almost in tandem. Ledrra had studied videos of the Otsandans and yet another thing they had in common was that a lowered head implied shame or submission. If they walked like alphas, they would be treated as alphas.

There were two males at the scene, and Ledrra could see the flashing lights of an emergency transport speeding away down the trail. Ledrra generally deplored the pollution and energy waste caused by their vehicles, but she thought that having such fast transport for medical emergencies was no bad thing when one was trying to save the life of a two-legged creature as delicate as an Otsandan.

Both males turned to stare as the attractive but sweaty and disheveled females approached. They put their hands on their hips simultaneously. Ledrra grabbed Nexrra, and they stopped. Touching one's hips was a threat among these people, like the baring of teeth. The men were warning them.

One of them relaxed and moved his hand away once he had a good look at the females. His eyes moved to her breasts and then back up to her face. "Can I help you?"

The other hung back and kept his hand on his hip.

Speaking very slowly, Ledrra said, "My—sister. Killed. Shot. Here." It was hard to speak in this particular Otsandan language. Her tongue kept wanting to curl under itself.

"Your sister?" The officer looked at his companion, whose hand dropped away from his hip. "Was that your sister that was killed near here two weeks ago?"

Ledrra nodded. She pointed to her face. "Born as one. My sister. She died. I—want her."

"Jane Doe has a twin," the second officer said. "She must not be from around here. She barely speaks English, and look at her clothes."

Nexrra stayed behind Ledrra and said nothing. Ledrra was grateful that Nexrra was not an alpha type like Mirra, who would have insisted on taking charge of the interaction. Nexrra was letting Ledrra do all the talking, which made this easier.

"I want my sister," Ledrra said again. "To howl—to honor her death."

Both males were silent. They looked at each other, then at Ledrra several times.

"I'll drive them over to the station," the second male said. "Then I'll call Spencer."

"Are you sure?"

There was more silence. Ledrra frowned. She was not fluent in their spoken language, and their unspoken language she understood even less. Something was being said, something was passing between them, and they did not want her to know.

Could they suspect that Ledrra and her sister were from further away than another land mass?

"My sister?" she said once again, when nobody had spoken for a while. They appeared to be arguing with their eyes.

"Come on, ladies," the second officer said at last. "I'll drive you down to our police station. The medical examiner will meet us there. He's the one who can talk to you about your sister."

He walked away, and Ledrra followed. Her stomach felt hard and knotted, and she knew she was making a mistake. But she needed to see Nedrra. And she needed to know what they knew.

They reached a black and white vehicle with a row of lights on top. They were turned off at the moment, but Ledrra had seen these cars before. It was another emergency transport, this one for catching and carrying rogues.

The officer opened a back door. "Hop in," he said.

Nexrra stepped forward, but Ledrra grabbed her arm again. Nexrra sensed her tension and squeezed the hand gripping the fabric of her shirt. "I can ride front?" Ledrra asked.

"Sorry," the officer said. "Nobody rides in front but me and my partners. Those are the rules."

"I am no rogue. I am good."

"I know you're good. You're not under arrest. This is just for your safety."

"Where will you take us?" It was getting easier to speak the language, but it was getting harder to speak. Ledrra was very afraid. There was something in the man's posture that she did not like or trust. He seemed too calm, too free and easy. He was working at putting them at ease, and somehow this made her nervous.

"To the police station. We'll meet the medical examiner and talk about your sister."

"She is there?"

"No, she's—" Then the male recognized his mistake. He lunged forward and grabbed Ledrra's arm, but she twisted away and started running. Nexrra was close behind.

"Why?" Nexrra panted.

"They were going to lock us up. The 'police station' is a place of cages. Can he see us?"

"No. He's too far behind, and their night vision is poor."

"Then change. We're going home."

*****

Officer Garnier chased after the women, but he knew he didn't have a hope of catching them. They looked tired as all get-out, but they ran like deer. After running pointlessly through the woods for almost an hour, Garnier found a scattering of clothing on the ground. But the women were gone.

He gathered the garments and tucked them under his arm. He decided that he didn't need to make an official report; they hadn't seemed dangerous, and they were not suspects in the strange murder.

The clothes felt strange under his hands, and they smelled odd. He smelled sweat and dirt of course, but something else as well. Something animal, but his brain could not pinpoint exactly what it smelled like. And the material—it felt slick as metal, but it moved like cotton. It had fit the strange women like a second skin, like spandex, but it was too thick and earthy to be the synthetic material.

Bob Garnier had been hunting aliens for most of his life. His very first memory was of standing in his back yard, looking up at the stars and waiting for the inevitable visitors. Since joining the force he'd let up on the search, but holding the strange women's clothing brought back that tickle of curiosity—and wonder.

Could they be aliens? The ME hadn't said anything about the Jane Doe's physiology that seemed out of the ordinary, but he probably hadn't looked very hard either. The cause of death had been simple enough.

Garnier decided that he'd like to go back and have another look at that body. It was technically part of an ongoing investigation, so he shouldn't have any trouble getting time alone with it. Maybe he'd figure out a way to run some of his own tests on it. His very own alien autopsy.

The hair on his neck and arms rose, and his heartbeat picked up to a gallop. This was going to be epic.

Chapter Fourteen

Ledrra and Nexrra ran themselves to exhaustion. This was bad, this was very bad, Nexrra thought. The Otsandans knew about them. They wanted to capture them. She had seen enough of their video stories to know that if she did survive such captivity, she would wish she hadn't.

Finally they stumbled to a halt within sight of the large mound. Ledrra collapsed onto the cool ground, and Nexrra joined her. They lay together, terrified and exhausted, trying to catch their wind and control their turbulent thoughts.

They must have dozed, because the next thing Nexrra remembered was the sun creeping pinkly over the horizon. She leaped to her feet—and immediately regretted it. Every muscle and joint ached. She felt like she had the one time she'd tried to resist the change. Her muscles felt like they'd each been torn lengthwise and then set on fire.

Ledrra got up much more slowly. She stared back the way they had come, and Nexrra knew her thoughts. Nedrra's body was gone beyond recovery. She was lying in one of those refrigerated coffins, being cut apart and examined by curious aliens. Nexrra licked Ledrra's face and tasted salty tears.

Together, they lifted their muzzles to the sky and howled. Ledrra howled for her sister's death, and for the deaths of the innocent Otsandans. Nexrra howled for Nedrra, the Otsandans, for Ledrra, and for all of them. Now that the Otsandans knew about them, now that there was physical evidence of their existence—well, there was just no telling what would happen.

*****

Jarren lifted his head. The wolves were howling again, but they were not Otsandan wolves. He recognized the Garouean voices. Two females, mourning the loss of a pack mate.

He rose and shook himself. The others were coming for him. But he would be ready. His head swam, and his stomach felt sick. He coughed and almost fell over.

He sat down and braced himself against the shifting ground. He was a little dizzy and tired, but no matter. He would still take care of anyone who tried to hurt him. He could do that. He could do anything.

*****

At last Ledrra's song for her sister ended. Nexrra lowered her muzzle and started back to the scout ship. Ledrra followed slowly. They both hurt all over, in body and mind.

As they traveled Nexrra was aware of eyes on them. They were not human eyes; if they were Nexrra would have heard and smelled them easily. Whatever it was meant them no harm, Nexrra felt. Her hackles were flat, and she did not feel tense or nervous. She just felt watched.

The scout ship was just ahead. Nexrra trotted a little faster. Soon they would be safely on the ship, and Mirra would know what to do about the rogue. Mirra always knew what to do.

Her relief was broken by a sudden shock of fear. She stopped in her tracks, and Ledrra stood like a statue behind her. Nexrra's hackles flexed, and Ledrra growled. They couldn't see it yet, but it was there.

Something sick and dying was waiting for them. It smelled like a wolf, but it also smelled like disease, like death and madness. It meant to kill them.

In the shadow of the scout, something moved and growled.

*****

"I don't know what to do," Mirra confessed.

"Nexrra and Ledrra are right behind us," Cavrra said. "They may have more information about the rogue."

"Or maybe it killed them both," Kuvrro growled. He paced Mirra's den tirelessly, like a trapped animal.

Since coming back to the Star Pack, he had been snappish and unpleasant. Mirra understood and did not discipline him. He was chief security officer and lone surviving male. He felt that he should have stayed on the surface to look after Ledrra, instead of letting his sister go into danger. Only Mirra's firm command had kept him from turning around and going straight back to the surface after giving her his report.

He was also furious with himself for losing the rogue leap gem. With it they could have captured the rogue hunter and protected Nexrra and Ledrra from one of many threats. Nexrra had been alpha; technically it was

162

her responsibility to take care of the gem. But Kuvrro was chief of security. Keeping everyone safe was his job.

"Ledrra and Nexrra are on their way," Mirra said. "And when they do, we can discuss together how we should handle this."

"How much does the Council know?" Kuvrro asked.

"Almost nothing. I haven't sent a report since our last exchange. Something about their response raised my hackles."

"What was wrong with their response?"

"Nothing at all. That's what troubles me. They have given me no reason at all to distrust them—and yet I do. Until I understand this, I won't send another message."

"It's been too long," Kuvrro said. His pace quickened. "I request to go back through the gate, to fulfill my duties as chief of security."

"Request denied." This was his fourth attempt, and Mirra was getting tired of it. "The emergency gate will be low on power, and it may not have enough to take you back and send three of you through again."

"I could take another leap gem as a replacement."

"That would mean building a live leap gate and leaving it perpetually unattended, right on the Otsandans' doorstep." Mirra stared at her mate. He had gone mad, surely.

"I can trigger the scout's self-destruct mechanism before we come back. There will be no evidence that we ever landed there, except for the hole in the ground."

"And destroy a fully functional gem in the process."

"She's my sister."

"If she's gone, she's gone. You must accept that."

"I won't."

Mirra sat back in her chair. Kuvrro's face was pale, and his eyes shone with emotion. It was plain on his face that if Mirra kept him prisoner here and Nexrra died, he would never forgive her.

One of her pack had already lost a family member. But what Kuvrro proposed carried tremendous risk. Which was the safer choice? Mirra was at a loss.

"What do you think, Cavrra?" she asked.

Cavrra's eyes widened, and she could not speak. Mirra had never asked her opinion of anything before. "Excuse me, captain?" she asked, in case she'd misheard.

"You smelled the rogue. You saw the condition Ledrra returned in. Could she face him again? Could she and Nexrra beat him?"

"In a fair fight, yes." Cavrra shivered. "But that smell was full of sickness. It might weaken him, or it might make him more dangerous."

"And what about the Otsandans?" Kuvrro asked. "Will they try to harm them? Will they be able to get to Nedrra's body?"

Cavrra shook her head. "Ledrra's the one to ask about that. I just don't know."

Mirra closed her eyes and put her head in her hands. Finally she took a deep breath and leaped into the abyss. "Permission granted, Kuvrro. Take one of the Class B leap gems from the midway gate. There are only two left. I hope you know what you're doing."

Kuvrro was out the door before she'd finished speaking. "I don't!" he called back over his shoulder.

Mirra bared her teeth.

*****

There was a special storage room near the exercise arena, and Kuvrro went there now. It was a narrow closet, dimly lit. The far wall was covered from floor to ceiling with small doors, each no more than two hands across.

Most were empty, but ten or so that were labeled, each with a series of numbers and symbols. Kuvrro went to the door labeled B—3^ and opened it. The compartment within was lined with tungsten to keep its contents secure. He reached in slowly, as though it were an animal that might bite, and he took out a tungsten-lined carrying case. Inside was a single leap gem.

He held the case in both hands and ran his fingers over its smooth, unremarkable surface. The gem within had been trained and attuned to the main gate on the Star Pack, and Kuvrro was going to destroy it to save his sister.

He kept the gem in its case while he crossed the ship and found the central gate that would take him back to the scout. With Nexrra's face in his mind, he stepped through. The dizziness was less this time.

When the world returned, he was back on the scout. And it sounded like he was just in time. Outside, the world was coming to an end.

*****

Jarren's head ached, and his tongue felt dry. Something about this world disagreed with him. As soon as he was done here, he would go back to that gate and never set foot on Otsanda again.

Two females trotted into view. One was familiar, but the other was not. Jarren should have known that there would be more than just the two down here. Killing them might be harder than he'd thought.

The wolf in front lowered her head and growled. Jarren did not engage in any preliminary fighting etiquette. He charged silently, going straight for the female's throat.

She leaped back just in time, and Jarren's jaws closed on air. The other she-wolf waded in, knocking Jarren off his feet. As he rolled he saw more wolves behind them. How many were there?

Then he saw that they were natives, Otsandan wolves. Their muzzles were thinner, their heads not so large. But the resemblance was still striking, enough to distract Jarren for the moment it took for one of the females to pin him down, putting a heavy paw on his neck.

Jarren struggled and snapped at the offending limb. Distantly he heard a shout. "Fear danger his bite is death disease fear!" Odd, it felt as though Jarren was hearing the voice from within his own head. It must be the fever.

The female pinning him jumped back. The two females looked at each other, and Jarren took advantage of their distraction. He rolled to his feet and lunged at the nearest female, the one who had dared put her paw on him.

A wave of dizziness washed over his eyes, and he fell. He snapped at his target, but he had fallen short and his jaws closed on nothing but a tuft of fur.

The females backed away from him, and Jarren got up and staggered after them. Hot foam dripped from his jaws, and his head pounded as though he'd been struck. He was very ill, he realized. As soon as he was done killing these two, he would go home and visit the medical center.

His eyes burned, and his jaws ached. He had to finish this quickly.

He roared and charged.

*****

Kuvrro hit the power switch on the gate and removed the tiny leap chip that powered it. Then he pulled out the other gem—the larger gem, the most valuable thing he'd ever held in his hands—and slid it into the other gem's niche. The niche was too small, but that didn't matter. The gate itself, a powerful alloy of tungsten and titanium, held the gem in place and kept it from pulling back through space and time to find its mate. Instead, space would bend to meet it.

Then Kuvrro ran outside.

*****

Ledrra and Nexrra were at a loss. They could not kill the rogue; they could not even touch him. The native wolves' agitation infected them both and kept them backing away as the rogue advanced.

He was very ill; anyone could see that. He must have picked up some Otsandan infection. The Star Pack inhabitants had been immunized against most Otsandan illnesses, so perhaps his infection would not touch them.

But his burning red eyes and slavering jaws awakened a primal fear in them both, and they kept backing away.

As though the moon had come to earth, Kuvrro appeared in the doorway of the scout. "Jarren?" he shouted.

Ledrra tried to change, to warn Kuvrro about the sickness. But she was still very sore, and her body was worn out from too many changes in one day. Her face burned and ached as she tried to force her will onto her body. Just the mouth, she thought. That would be enough.

Something shifted and popped in her jaws. But slowly. Too slowly.

*****

Kuvrro backed away from the haggard, sickly wolf that had turned to stalk toward him. He recognized Jarren from the Academy; he'd been a lackluster student who graduated a year or two behind Nexrra. He'd heard that Jarren was on the Council for Alien Affairs. How had he ended up here, and in such a state?

Jarren was the rogue? It seemed impossible. But all of this was impossible.

Kuvrro looked into the bloodshot, sickly eyes and believed in the impossible.

And now he was in trouble, because he had forgotten to turn wolf before running out here, and it was too late to do it now.

Jarren gathered the last of his strength and leaped for Kuvrro's throat.

*****

Nexrra charged, but too late. She slammed into the rogue from behind just as his teeth closed on Kuvrro's bare throat. All three of them fell to the ground, and Kuvrro screamed.

The rogue let go of Kuvrro and staggered around to face Nexrra. She growled. Let him bite her; she didn't care. He would not hurt her brother.

The rogue growled back. Bloody foam dripped from his jaws. Then his eyes rolled backward, and he collapsed. Nexrra kept her guard up and her teeth bared, fearing a trap.

The rogue's breathing slowed, then stopped. He seemed to be dead.

Nexrra ran to Kuvrro and licked his face. He was already getting up, and he brushed her off. "Just a scratch. He barely touched me. Come on, we've got to go."

He looked around and saw the Otsandan wolves standing like grey statues a short distance away. "Can you tell them to get away? Mirra's authorized me to self-destruct the scout."

Nexrra threw her head back and shrieked. Instead of the deep, mournful song she had sung for Nedrra, this was a wild cry, full of fear and warning. The wolves scattered instantly, and within seconds it was as though they had never been.

"How did you do that?" Kuvrro asked. He had never heard his sister howl like that before. Nexrra did not reply. It was too complicated to explain in wolf form.

Ledrra stood a little ways off, staring at Jarren's body. She remembered him vaguely; they had graduated from the Academy at the same time. He'd worshipped Mirra, but she (rightly, in the opinion of most) considered him beneath her notice.

Jarren was the rogue who had killed those Otsandans, and somehow he had gotten her sister killed. She bared her teeth and growled at his corpse. If she could have, she would have killed him twice.

Jarren leaped to his feet and snapped at her, tearing her across the face. Ledrra fought back, biting and snapping until he fell down again. Then she sank her teeth into his throat and tore the life out of him for good.

Nexrra whined, looking from Kuvrro to Ledrra. Now two of them had been exposed to whatever disease had infected and killed Jarren.

"Come on," Kuvrro said. "We'll worry about it when we're safe on the ship."

The cut on his neck was bleeding profusely.

Chapter Fourteen

The wolves were a good distance away when the scout self-destructed, but they still heard and felt it. The power cell in the heart of the scout exploded, sending violent kinetic energy hurtling outward and deep into the ground. As the force hit the leap gem, it too self-destructed, pulling the scout and a good chunk of the surrounding earth into the space between worlds.

The gem lying on the ground in the copse of trees remained unscathed—and undetected.

When the Otsandan detectives found their way to the site, they found a burning crater, and in the center of it was the mutilated body of a man. An autopsy suggested that it had been killed by the same creature that had killed and mutilated the two poachers and Detective Kinsley.

*****

Kuvrro, Ledrra, and Nexrra were hustled into the Star Pack's medical bay, where they were hooked up to diagnostic machines. Cavrra soon joined them. Though she had not been injured by the rogue, she had still made fluid contact with him and was considered exposed. Results were inconclusive, so Tigrra played it safe and pumped them full of every antibiotic and antiviral treatment that was safe to give. After eight days of profuse vomiting and diahrrea, which Tigrra kept calling "the best thing for you," they were pronounced dehydrated but healthy.

Mirra finally sent her report to the Council, and she received a reply almost immediately. Some sort of plague had struck the Northeastern territory of Garou, and there was a strict quarantine in effect. The disease was unknown to the medical specialists, but Terra found several references to a similar plague in the Academy library. "It's an Otsandan infection," Mirra said. "It causes madness and death if left untreated. I'll have Tigrra send you the details."

Then she cut off communication. She had a lot of thinking to do, and she did not want the Council's interference while she did it.

*****

Mirra and Ledrra had lunch together in Mirra's office. They shared protein bars, dried yellowfruit, and a native fruit that Ledrra called an apple. Mirra found them tasty, though a bit tart.

Finally Mirra got to business. Ledrra stopped eating and gave the captain her full attention as soon as the captain opened her mouth. Mirra's attitude toward her pack had changed, and Ledrra respected her for that.

"The Otsandans are highly dangerous," Mirra said. "They allow religion to dictate their morality, they have weapons that kill at a distance, and they commit 'rape.' Their behavior is horrifying."

"True."

"They are also almost identical to us."

"Also true."

"My protective instincts tell me to leave this place and never return."

"Understandable."

"But they have leap gates here. Someone planted that gem on the burial mound and activated it, and there are probably others. Rogue gems with no tungsten gates around them. It's a frightening thought."

"This is almost definitely the case. The werewolf legends span the entire planet."

"I don't know what to do."

Ledrra looked down at her hands. "I think we should stay."

"I'm told their alpha-police may have seen you change, when you ran from them. They know we exist."

"It was dark… but I don't know what he saw. Perhaps."

"It will be dangerous for anyone to visit the surface now."

"It was always dangerous. But these people are our brothers and sisters. We are their pack."

"They killed your sister."

"And Jarren killed three of their people. The score is settled. I think we should stay. We still have much to learn from them."

Mirra sighed and leaned back in her chair. She picked up an apple and considered it. "All right. I respect your opinion."

Ledrra looked into Mirra's eyes and touched her throat.

Slowly, Mirra touched her own throat in reply. "We are pack."

"We are pack."

Part Three:
The People of the Gem

Chapter One

Mirra peered at the image on the wall eye. "What in the universe is it?"

"It's a dog," Kuvrro said proudly. "I found it on the surface, wandering around the woods. Ledrra and Cadrra can study it."

"It's marking on the exercise equipment."

"Isn't it fascinating? Just like us—only different."

Mirra had to nod. The odd little creature resembled a wolf superficially; clearly it was a carnivore of canine lineage. But its flat, shiny coat was completely inappropriate for survival out of doors, and its striking grey and white markings were useless as camouflage.

Its body language, too, was unlike that of any wolf older than a cub. A grown wolf taken by force and dropped into a strange place like this would be huddled in a corner, thinking only of escape or defense. This creature trotted all over the exercise room, happily sniffing at everything and pissing on everything else. It seemed oblivious to the danger of the watching hunters.

And yet... Mirra could not look away, for there was still some trace of the wolf in this beast. Just here and there, minor tics and twitches that made Mirra's hackles prickle with recognition. A turn of the head. The snuffling sound its nose made as it investigated a pile of balls. The way it stopped panting and pricked up its ears every minute or so, its eyes bright and focused. The wolf still lived in this animal, deep down.

"Is it safe to interact with it?" Mirra asked.

"Oh yes." Kuvrro tapped his throat. "It ran from my wolf, but when I went to two legs it came right to me. It showed throat and called me master, and when I told it to follow it obeyed. There is no aggression in this animal, not toward anyone who walks on two legs."

"That's not natural. It ran from the wolf, one of its closest relatives, but it submitted to the man? Is it ill?"

"Shall I fetch Ledrra? She can answer your questions better than I."

173

"Please do." But Mirra had already made up her mind that she would find her own answers. As Kuvrro left her side, she opened the door to the exercise room.

The dog bolted at the door as soon as it opened, and Mirra hastily closed it behind her. As the door closed the dog turned and went back to its constant pacing and sniffing. Then Mirra sat down on the floor.

The exercise room was most hunters' favorite place on the ship. It was the only room big enough to run and jump in, and there were plenty of platforms and toys to keep the wolf entertained and calm. So there were at least a dozen wolf scents scattered about the room, and the dog seemed determined to discover and classify every trace.

But its focus was broken when Mirra sat down. It ran to her with tongue lolling and proceeded to lick her hands and face and throat in submission. Its hindquarters moved almost constantly, and its tail whipped against her face.

Mirra tolerated this for a minute or two, then she held up both hands, palms out, and said, "Stop!" The dog could not possibly understand her language, but it recognized her tone and backed away with its ears down and tail tucked. It danced in place just out of reach, hindquarters wriggling frantically.

Something else to add to the piling mountain of evidence that Garou and Otsanda had some sort of common lineage. Hunters and Otsandan humans were light-years apart, yet they resembled each other closely enough to pass for one another—not only in appearance but in body language and tone of voice, too. A commanding tone in Otsandan was exactly like that of a hunter. This shouldn't be possible, she thought as she stared at the dancing, submissive dog.

But the leap gems were here. There was a rogue leap gate connecting this world with Garou. And that changed everything.

As Mirra stared at the submissive little creature, she felt a spasm of maternal warmth. "Come," she told it, holding out her right hand.

The dog didn't need further coaxing. It barreled into her, licking and rubbing frantically in an effort to bathe her in its scent. It's like a cub, Mirra thought, imprinting on its mother.

So that was the secret. Now Mirra knew what had been done to the poor beasts.

Ledrra slipped through the door behind her a minute later, and Mirra told her, "Their maturity has been stunted."

"Stunted how? Drugs?"

"Through selection and inbreeding. The Otsandans bred dogs to remain perpetual puppies, dependent on humans their entire lives. That's how they're able to train them with such unquestioning obedience."

"The poor things." Ledrra sat down next to Mirra, and the dog danced over to her to lick her face before returning to Mirra.

"But the breeding program gave the dogs power over humans as well. Look into its eyes."

Ledrra tapped the floor, and the dog danced back over to her. It never seemed to tire of wriggling. She ran her hands over its smooth pelt and scratched its ears. Then her eyes widened. "How is it doing that?"

"It's protective mimicry. They behave like cubs to please their masters, and the masters feel like parents and want to protect and feed them. A symbiotic relationship."

"Amazing." Ledrra scratched the dog's furry chest, and it finally stood still, closing its eyes with pleasure. "It's probably hungry, isn't it?"

*****

Meanwhile, Kuvrro and Nexrra explored what they'd managed to learn about the relationship among dogs, wolves, and the two-legged humans. Kuvrro felt that this was an important aspect of Otsandan life and might hold the key to the link between Otsanda and Garou. Nexrra was less sure.

"Dogs are a biological anomaly," she argued. She tapped at her wrist eye and scrolled through a dozen pictures of dogs that she'd gathered from the Otsandan "web." She highlighted the tall, shaggy breed, then the squat, big-shouldered one. "They're freaks. They don't even look like us. Just because the Otsandans decided to manipulate the natural order— again—"

"Dogs share genetic material with our Otsandan doppelgangers," Kuvrro said. "They're close enough that I believe they can still interbreed. But they've evolved to depend on the two-legged ones for survival. I think this is fascinating, don't you?"

"It's interesting, but I don't see the link to the rogue leap gate." Nexrra shut off her screen and shook her head. She smelled of exhaustion and frustration.

Kuvrro didn't understand the link either, but his inner wolf was growling. There was something here that they needed to investigate and understand; that much he knew. And he wanted his sister's help; she was better at "thinking" tasks than he was.

Nexrra looked at her brother. Her eyes were wide and golden, and her pupils were enormous. *Black and gold,* Kuvrro thought.

"That rogue leap gem is still out there," she said.

"I know." It was Kuvrro's own foolishness that had gotten it lost, and the memory made him want to bite himself.

"There's no safe way to retrieve it," he said. "Our encampment on Otsanda is many days' run from the spot, and our second drop pod was destroyed. I don't know what to do."

"Is Mirra still avoiding contact with the Council for Alien Affairs?"

"She responds to their queries with polite ignorance. As far as I know, she hasn't told them about Drrak's death or Jarren's madness."

"Do they know that the aliens have evidence of us?" Idly, Nexrra turned her wrist eye back on and flipped through a few random pictures of Otsandan humans. Kuvrro stared at them, and he felt his incisors lengthen. There was a news story featuring the use of weapons in places of learning. There was another story about a dead infant and its rogue mother. He knew that it was wrong to impose hunter morality on an alien race, but their physical resemblance to his own kind made it hard to maintain objectivity. *You walk on two legs!* he wanted to shout at them. *You should be better than this!*

"I don't think so," Nexrra said. She paused on a video of two aliens in the throes of mating. It was an odd coupling; the male's penis was fully engaged and the female's vagina was receptive, but the participants barely looked at each other. The male's grunts were half-hearted, and he stared at his own member rather than his partner. Ledrra's notes indicated that this was called pornography, and Otsandans used it for sexual stimulation. She hadn't been able to explain why they needed it.

"I don't know how much the aliens actually know about us. If they know what we are and where we're from, there should be stories about us on their news. But there's nothing." Nexrra flipped away from the pornography and brought up a web page dedicated to mostly-true stories about the goings-on of Otsandan natives. She tapped a small green button in the corner, and the Otsandan text flipped to hunter tongue, relieving Kuvrro. He knew just enough of the local tongue to make his head hurt.

"Perhaps the aliens who found Nedrra's body are keeping it a secret," Kuvrro said. "That would be ideal. Then we could just kill a few of them, and our presence would be a secret again."

Nexrra glanced at him. "Kill them? But they've done nothing to harm us."

Kuvrro looked down. Killing the aliens didn't feel like murder to him; it felt like eliminating a dangerous rogue. But he knew that was wrong. He was still imposing mature hunter morality on a new, young species.

"We'll never find them again anyway," Nexrra said. "The only way back to that location is through the rogue leap gate, and its twin is back on Garou."

"So it is." A glimmer of an idea formed in his mind, but he pushed it away for now. Nexrra was too good at sniffing out his thoughts, and he wanted to keep this one private.

"It's time for me to change," he said, changing the subject. "Will you come to the surface with me? I'd like the company."

"Mirra won't go with you?"

"She hasn't been to the surface since the first landing. She says that a captain's place is always with the ship, but I think she's afraid."

"Then I'll go with you." Nexrra's time was still a week away, but there was no harm in exercising the wolf early. "I miss running under the moon."

Chapter Two

Council Alpha Terra opened up her desk screen and scrolled through the files the Star Pack had sent regarding Otsanda. Early reports from the crew had been quietly optimistic, then disconcerted as quasi-intelligent life was discovered. Then she'd gotten several reports of an odd nature, discussing the Otsandans' resemblance to the hunters themselves, and whether or not that could be a coincidence. Of course it had to be, Terra had thought initially. But recent developments here on Garou had struck her as both odd and alien, and now she didn't know what to think.

Then—nothing. Mirra had given one very brief report, mentioning that a landing pod had been destroyed and two hunters had died, and nothing else. A brief mention of a rogue wolf from Garou, which shouldn't be possible. But Mirra was a brilliant, levelheaded captain, and she would not make such an extraordinary claim without extraordinary evidence.

But nothing was so unsettling as the mysterious plague that had struck the Northeast territory. And together with the timing of Mirra's peculiar account, Terra felt downright nervous.

Hrraz insisted that they had the plague under control, and they were well on their way to developing a vaccine. So at least the population was safe. But still. The virus had broken out in the lone hunter neighborhood, where solitary males lived when they had no cubs to care for. Generally, when there was an outbreak of illness, it started in the family sector or the ancestors' sanctuary. This virus had struck the strongest and healthiest hunters first. It was unnatural and terrifying.

What if the virus came back?

What if it came back and began to work its way down the population? Terra shook that train of thought away. She could go mad herself, thinking about what might happen, rather than what was.

She went back to the early reports from the Star Pack's first days on Otsanda. Mirra had quickly determined that Otsanda would not make a suitable home for hunters. The inhabitants were still in the messy stage, still biting and clawing at each other like cubs at the teat. They had nuclear weapons capable of poisoning their entire planet, and they still had religion. Not a healthy combination for themselves or the visiting hunters.

Terra shut down her computer and left the little cottage she shared with her mate. She was antsy and uncomfortable, and she wanted to bite something. Fresh air and exercise would calm the wolf, so she went for a run.

The wolf was eager for release as soon as the bright sunshine hit her face. Terra stretched and yawned, and her yawn became a wide-mouthed howl as her fur thickened and the wolf surged forward. A few cubs were scuffling in the dust next to the road, and they howled back at her as she ran past.

The air was fresh and warm with only a hint of coolness in the breeze to indicate the impending cold season. The equinox was only a few weeks away, but the weather had stayed hot despite the shortening days and changing leaves. Terra lolled her tongue out in a wolfish grin, and she dashed away down the road and into the nearby woods.

It was cooler among the trees, and the wolf's brain was alive with the smells and sounds of a healthy forest. Reptilian flyers dashed from branch to branch, startled by the passage of the predator, and something small and furry dashed away near her feet. The hunter's thinking mind remained, but it was quietly content in the hindquarters of the wolf's wild mind. Terra's only concern was for the run, the hunt, the feel of fresh air in her face, and the scent of life in her nose. It felt wonderful to lose her complex, civilized worries for a moment and just run.

The trees closed in tightly around her, and dead leaves crunched under her paws. Terra left the narrowing path and dove into the thick brush. There were ripe yellowfruits here, round and plump and delicious. The wolf gobbled a few, savoring their sweetness. But she was too hungry to settle for fruit. She licked her chops.

A faint rustle alerted the wolf to the presence of living meat. Not a scuttle or a hop; her keen ears detected a grinding slide. A ground worm. Not the most filling meal, but soft and tasty.

Terra hunkered down and waited. The sliding sound came again. Moist body over damp leaves. Ground worms came to the surface when the ground was warm and damp in order to mate. If Terra was lucky, she might get two at once.

The worm was close, just on the other side of a thick fallen branch. Terra had to be quick. The ground worm was slow-moving on the surface, but if it managed to get underground Terra would have no chance of catching it. Ground worms had hundreds of tiny sharp teeth that could tunnel like lightning through anything but solid rock. Terra would have to move fast.

Another slow, sliding slither. This was it. She needed to strike while the thing was in motion, before it had a chance to change course. Terra tensed and sprang.

It was perfect. She cleared the branch and landed almost directly on top of it, which was gratifyingly large. It was at least as long as Terra's own body and as big around as her left paw. Its body was mottled green and grey, and it oozed black where Terra's jaws cut through its flesh. As the worm fell in two, its blind head swung around and snapped at the wolf's muzzle. She flinched back from the needle-sharp teeth, which were not large enough to cause serious harm but would break off in her flesh and itch for days. The wolf put one paw on top of the head and bit off the rest of its body. She ate the ground worm's flesh with gusto, leaving the snapping, hissing head to die slowly among the leaves.

Her belly was somewhat full. Terra wandered aimlessly through the trees, sniffing this and pissing on that. It felt good to have nothing to do. Somewhere in the back of her mind she was aware of the obligations awaiting her, but that part of her was mercifully far away. The wolf was in charge now.

Voices. The wolf tensed. Hunters on two legs, walking so stealthily that she might not have heard them had not one hunter spoken suddenly in a hushed whisper. The wolf had nothing to fear from hunters, but something about the creature's tone rose her hackles. She found a thick bush nearby and crawled underneath. There she waited. She didn't wonder why she was hiding from her own kind, or whether her fear was valid. When the wolf spoke, the wise hunter obeyed.

The ground was slightly concave below her feet, so Terra was able to conceal most of her body under the bush. She shut her eyes to conceal their reflective glow. Her ears and nose were her keenest senses in this form, and these she focused as the hunters drew near.

"We've lost the trail," one said. His voice was soft, barely a breath in the wind, but Terra's ears still caught the words faintly.

"We'll circle around and make another pass," the other said. Terra tensed. That was Hrraz's voice. She dared open one eye, but she could not yet see either of the speakers.

What was he doing out here? He'd told her that he was going to the medical center to discuss a pain in his shoulder. Had the medicals fixed his trouble already, and he'd decided to celebrate by hunting?

But then why did Terra still not want to come out of hiding?

"It might have gone back through the rogue gate," the strange hunter said.

"Unlikely," Hrraz said. "It would not have the intelligence to know what to look for. More likely it caught some local infection and is dead in a hole somewhere."

"And you're certain that this creature is a—"

"Cat. The Otsandans call it a puma, which is a type of 'cat.'"

"So you're certain that it came from there. It's not a rogue ungula or clawed creepfur?"

"Hoof strikes look nothing like claw marks. And a clawed creepfur would not drop down out of a tree at its enemy."

Now Terra knew what they were up to. They were looking for the strange animal that had attacked Jarren and his cousin. She'd thought, as she'd likely been expected to, that the rogue animal had been identified as a clawed creepfur. They were big and tough, and in self-defense they could do enormous damage to an unprepared hunter.

That did not mesh exactly with what Jarren had said about the animal, but Terra had dismissed most of his words as the ramblings of an inexperienced hunter. It was well known that Jarren usually preferred to stay indoors during the change. He'd only gone out the one time to impress a female or something.

But she should have realized that a clawed creepfur was still no match for two wolves on the hunt. She'd been led to believe something, and she'd blithely believed it. That did not make her feel good about herself.

The hunters drew closer, then stopped. "Someone's close by," the stranger said. "I smell wolf."

Terra opened the other eye and peeked through the bushes. Hrraz and his companion were on two legs, but their pelts were thick and shaggy for such a warm day. Wolf noses protruded from otherwise hairless faces. It looked odd and painful to Terra, but she supposed they wanted to use their wolf senses but still communicate. Wolves were capable of rudimentary language, but for subjects like leap gates and rogue animals, the two-legged form was ideal.

"Probably some cubs hunting," Hrraz said. His eyes passed over her—and moved on. "Let's turn back now."

"Alright." As they turned around, Terra recognized the black and grey patterns in the stranger's fur. That was Cyrr, head of the Council for Medical Studies, Southwest territory—not from around here. He was a nice enough hunter though overprotective of his mate, Terra remembered, not one she would have suspected of keeping secrets.

What would they do if Terra came out of her hiding place now? Would they flee, or would they explain themselves? Terra decided to stay put. She would ask Hrraz about it later, when they were both home and alone.

"What should we do if the animal attacks again?" Cyrr asked as they moved farther away.

"A nest of clawed creepfurs, deathly ill with the same plague that struck…" And then they were out of earshot.

Terra lay still for a long time, waiting to make sure the others were completely gone. She'd sensed apprehension but no real fear in their body language, which was a good sign. There was probably a perfectly good explanation for Hrraz's behavior.

This wasn't the first time her wolf had reacted badly to her mate. Ever since Mirra and the Star Pack had landed on Otsanda, he'd behaved oddly off and on. Nothing she could pinpoint, but whenever she'd discussed the matter of the two-legged natives, he'd gotten very distant and thoughtful. As though he knew something she didn't, and he wasn't sure if he wanted her to know.

Terra left the bush and started back the way she'd come, but then she reconsidered. She didn't want to be home when Hrraz returned. The wolf couldn't explain why, but it felt—confrontational. Like a situation that could turn into a fight. Instead she circled around to the road that led to the ancestor's retreat. It was quiet there, and the ancestors were good company.

Chapter Three

Terra panted as she ran. She liked the ancestors. They were usually calm and pleasant, accepting of their stage of life. Once in a while one would go rogue, biting and snapping as though she didn't remember her own pack. But such were rare and easy to put down. Mostly they just seemed tired and willing to rest.

As she approached the retreat she slowed to a halt and shifted back to two-legged form. Terra shook the excess hair out of her pelt and yawned. Her age was showing; she was already tired after her brief stint as the wolf. Maybe that was why she felt drawn to the ancestors' retreat. Her youth was further away than the day she would ride the train.

But that day was not yet. Terra had work to do. She couldn't possibly think of retirement with so much going on, both here and on other worlds.

She walked into the cluster of huts and burrows and looked around. She'd heard the ancestor train, so she'd expected to see at least a few newcomers out wandering around, exploring their new homes and finding a comfortable shelter. One or two would self-euthanize immediately, either via the vials of painkiller that could be found in all of the huts or just by walking into the woods and never returning. But the average length of residency was at least two moons. Some even lived for a year or more.

There was nobody in sight. Terra breathed the mint-green summer air and stood very still. She wasn't sure what to make of this.

It might mean nothing. They might all be out hunting together. It was hard to picture a collection of dying hunters working together, but it could happen.

Or possibly the plague had struck here.

Terra swallowed. The plague was blood-borne, so it wasn't possible to transmit through the air. She didn't even have any breaks in her skin at the moment, so she was perfectly safe. But the wolf reacted with animal panic at the thought of being so close to a disease that brought madness and death.

Males had even attacked females, while the virus was in full force. If the plague struck here, it would be like a rain of blood. Terra shuddered.

She forced herself to approach a nearby wolf burrow. It was dark inside of course, but Terra's nose easily determined that it was empty. No smell of blood or disease either.

She moved on to the next. This one was also empty, but her nose told her that it had been recently occupied. There was still a trace of body warmth in the sandy soil of the burrow. A male, she thought, old but healthy. No injuries or serious diseases. No reason for him to creep off by himself to die. He was just gone.

Terra turned away from the burrows. She wouldn't get much useful information here. She had to enter one of the huts. Her heart picked up speed at the thought. She wasn't sure why, but that seemed like a more dangerous proposition to wolf. But she had no choice if she wanted answers.

The closest hut was made of strong lunawood, but it was faded and weatherbeaten with age. Even lunawood did not last forever, and these huts had been here for generations. Terra stood outside the door for several minutes and patted the wooden door with both palms in case the occupant inside could not smell her. She did not want to take anyone by surprise, but she was hesitant to shout aloud here. Finally she entered.

There was no occupant here, either. This should not have surprised Terra, but still she felt shaken. The one-room hut had an empty feel, as though nobody had ever lived here. She smelled traces of elder wolf, but they were faint and far away. The nest in the middle of the room was clean and empty. A pile of blankets was stacked neatly next to it as though awaiting the next occupant. The wall eye was off, and the lights were cold and dark. This was an empty hut.

Not every hut was occupied all the time, though. Often there were multiple vacancies, during lulls in the population. Terra needed to keep looking if she wanted real answers.

But this was the third empty home she'd inspected, and something told Terra that this wasn't right. Her wolf was growling faintly.

She checked two more huts just to be sure. The first felt as empty as the other, but the second had a faint scent of occupancy. So there were elders about. They just weren't here.

Well, why shouldn't they go out together as a pack? It seemed like a difficult accomplishment, since many of them could barely run and others were trapped in their forms. But the ancestors were free people, just like anyone else. They could do what they wanted.

Terra hunkered down and sniffed at the grass. The hut occupant's trail led past the other homes and towards the thickest part of the woods. Terra hesitated. There was no real reason to follow them. There was no sign of violence or plague here. She was head of the Council for Alien Affairs, not Ancestor Affairs. She could go home right now, and maybe she should.

Was she afraid? Terra marveled at herself. Afraid to go into a dark wood after a pack of aging wolves? But yes, her wolf confirmed. She was a little afraid. Things were strange here. Not strange enough to trigger flight, but her hackles were up nonetheless.

So should she go home or follow the trail? Terra pondered. If she went home, there was the matter of Hrraz's lie to contend with. She wasn't ready to deal with that yet; thinking about it gave her a sick feeling that she pushed away as quickly as she could. She would explore the woods, and she would discover what had happened to the ancestors.

She might even find a clue to what Hrraz and Cyrr had been talking about, and why they had kept their excursion a secret. Maybe she'd even find the creature they'd been hunting. If she could find it, she thought she might understand everything.

Terra loped into the woods after the elder's trail, the hunter's curiosity overriding the wolf's caution.

It was dark and cool under the trees. The leaves were changing but had not yet fallen, giving the light a sunset glow. Creepers scurried away underfoot, and there was a warm smell of soil and life. Terra lowered her face to the ground and sniffed. There were many ancestors here, possibly the entire community had passed this way. They'd moved in a rough line, marching like creepers. So they weren't hunting. What, then?

Terra picked up the pace. There was no reason to shift back to the wolf; the scent of ancestors was thick and strong even to her inferior nose.

She could run at near her top speed and still keep to the trail. At any rate, the trail was mostly a straight line. It only wavered in areas with rises and falls in the ground that an elderly body might be unable to manage.

The scent of ancestors grew stronger, and Terra ran faster. When she caught up to the group, she literally fell into them. She tripped over a grey-white wolf lying on the ground and tumbled headlong into three more. There were a few yips and groans, and someone bit her calf.

Terra rolled onto her back and tapped her throat in apology. The wolf she'd fallen over twitched an ear, but otherwise he did not move. Was he ill? No, Terra's nose answered. Just exhausted. Worn out from the long walk here. She looked around at the rest of the pack. They were all tucked together nose to tail, all sitting or lying down. Some on two legs, some on four, all still and silent.

"What are you doing?" she asked. Her incisors tried to sharpen, but she pushed them back firmly. She must not give in to the wolf's fear until she understood what frightened her.

"Watching," a white-haired female croaked. Terra remembered her; Grrifa had worked at the medical center for a number of years, helping the sick and dying find peace. She had ridden the ancestor train a year or two ago. It was amazing that she was still alive.

She gestured at a large lunawood tree on the far end of the crowd. Terra saw that they were all facing or angled toward it in some way, even the ones who looked ready to die of exhaustion. The trek here must have almost killed a few of them. Why had they come all this way, to look at a tree?

Terra suddenly felt angry and fierce. Her hackles sprang up along her neck and back, and she growled.

The white-haired one nodded. "You feel it too. It's that." She pointed at the tree again. Terra bared her teeth. Why did they care so much about a stupid tree?

Then a stray sunbeam pierced the leaves overhead, and a gold glint flashed in Terra's eyes.

A golden glint from a black gem.

The strange creature. Hrraz's secrecy, and his connection to the Council for Medical Studies, Jarren's madness, and the plague that had struck this territory. It was all coming together.

Mirra had suggested in one of her last reports that there might be a rogue leap gem on Otsanda. One of her own pack had touched it, carried it—but had not been able to show it to the Council. Somehow it had been lost, and the Council had dismissed Mirra's concerns as bizarre and unsubstantiated. Terra had decided that Jarren had somehow used the trail of leap gems the hunter ships had laid across the galaxy to reach Otsanda. He'd been mad with plague, and he'd once been obsessed with possessing Mirra. Hunters who went rogue were capable of bizarre and seemingly impossible behavior.

Hrraz had dismissed her concerns. He had been the one to suggest that Jarren had murdered Nedrra, perhaps under some sort of fever-induced delusion. He might have dumped her body on the surface, or he might have buried her somewhere on Garou and forgotten. Mirra said that Nedrra's body had been discovered by the Otsandan aliens, but Hrraz had pointed out that the aliens' news was composed of equal parts truth and falsehood, cobbled together to tell an exciting story rather than transmit truth. Nothing on their "Internet" could be trusted as fact.

Terra stepped carefully around the prone elders and approached that fierce golden glint. Hrraz knew that this thing existed. Why hide it from her, though? They had mated for life. She'd thought she could trust him. The wolf never acted without thinking first of the pack. Did this mean that he did not consider her pack?

Terra's heart hurt.

The tree was enormous, and it smelled of clean soil and age. It must have been here for a thousand years. The leap gem embedded in the bark flickered at her like a wolf's eye. Black and gold, the colors of the hunter.

Terra came no closer. She knew where that leap gate led, and she had no desire to visit that mad, foreign planet. She sniffed in the direction of the gem, and she fancied that she could smell the madness that waited on the other side. Pure imagination, of course. Only matter could traverse a leap gate, not mental illness.

"Why are you here?" she asked the nearest wolf, a black and grey female who regarded her with weary curiosity.

The wolf cocked her head and whined. "We don't know," said Grrifa. "The wolf spoke, and we answered. It called us here."

Terra looked back at the gem. Very slowly she ventured closer and reached out with a single finger. A gold spark flashed, and Terra jerked her hand away. The gate was live. Anything could just walk through. From either side.

The leap gems had a psychological effect on hunters; it brought out the wild instinct to roam, to explore and hunt. A hunter who encountered a leap gem could hardly resist the urge to step through and explore the other side. That was why the ancestors had come here. But being old and frail, perhaps they lacked the physical strength to cross over. The shift in reality would probably kill them.

It had killed Jarren. Terra took a step back away from the tree. It danced in her eyes with golden glints that floated like dust in sunlight.

"Terra, what are you doing here?"

Terra turned around to face her mate. "I am the Council Alpha, Hrraz. I should ask the questions."

Hrraz stepped over and around the silent ancestors. He touched the gem, and the gold light flashed. The ancestors began to shift and yawn as though waking up from a dream.

"It affects the old ones' minds when it goes rogue," Hrraz said. "I've been trying to get it under control, but the things that have been happening lately—ever since the cat came through—"

"Cat?" Terra tasted the unfamiliar word.

"The creature that attacked Jarren and his cousin. It fits the description of an Otsandan creature called a cat."

"So this gem does connect with Otsanda directly," Terra said. "Jarren went there, and the air made him ill. He had no immunity. Then he brought the plague here…"

"I know."

"You knew about this. Jarren went rogue and killed at least two hunters, and his madness jeopardized the Star Pack's mission. They are in danger still, from the natives who might know about them. And you knew all this."

"Yes." Hrraz stared at her. Terra met his gaze and could not believe what she was seeing. He was confessing to a terrible deception with no sign of shame or remorse. He hadn't even touched his throat. And now he stared at her, as though he was challenging her.

Hrraz was not rogue or ill. This could only mean that he believed that he was doing the right thing. So Terra bit back her anger and said, "Explain yourself."

He turned and walked away. The ancestors were slowly climbing to their feet and shuffling back the way they'd come. Terra had to hop and dodge around them to catch up with the stranger she'd thought of as her mate. Her incisors lengthened as her anger returned. How dare he?

She cuffed him across the back of his neck. "I said, explain yourself!"

Hrraz spun around. His incisors were at full length, and his cheeks were dusted with grey fur. Terra blanched, but his response was calm and measured.

"I am returning to the lone cabins," he said.

"Why?"

"In the Southeastern territory."

Terra's face felt cold and pale. Her incisors receded. "Why?" she repeated.

"It is time. We have spent too many years together. It's unnatural."

She couldn't believe what she was hearing, but Hrraz's eyes did not waver. He did not smell like anger or fear; he was perfectly calm and smelled only of strength. It was an attractive scent, but it made Terra feel ugly and small.

And when Hrraz turned and once again walked away, Terra had to let him go.

Chapter Four

Mirra was not pleased when Kuvrro told her that he and his sister wanted to run under the moon. But she only told him to be careful. "Stay in wolf form," she said. "And if you see those mad aliens, run back here. Immediately."

Kuvrro nodded and touched his throat. Mirra was less edgy and controlling than she had been when they'd first come to Otsanda, but she still put the safety of her crew ahead of everything. She would let him do what he wanted, but she would hold him responsible for anything that went wrong.

He turned to go, and Mirra said, "Wait." He turned back, and she stepped close until they stood nose to nose. He blinked.

"I want to try something," she said. "It's an Otsandan custom." Then she kissed him.

Kuvrro froze, and his mind went temporarily blank. He knew what a kiss was; he'd seen them in the aliens' entertainment stories. But he'd never thought about it, never wondered what it might feel like.

It felt amazing. Mirra's lips were full and soft, and her tongue flicked softly inside his mouth. Kuvrro thought that he was probably expected to reciprocate, and he kissed her back, moving his lips in sync with hers. Mirra wrapped her arms around his waist, and he felt his sex stiffen. He closed his eyes and wished that this moment would never end.

All too soon it did. Mirra withdrew, looking as stunned as he felt. "That was—interesting," she breathed.

"Now I understand why they're all so mad," Kuvrro said. "Do all their mating rituals feel like this?"

"I don't know. Maybe we should run some experiments when you come back."

Suddenly running on the surface held less appeal for him than before. Kuvrro licked his incisors, and Mirra ran her hands over his buttocks. Kuvrro decided that his sister could wait a bit longer for him.

*****

Nexrra sat on the floor next to the leap gate, down the hall from Mirra's office. She was already in four-legged form, and she sneezed when he approached.

"I apologize for my tardiness," Kuvrro said. Nexrra's tongue lolled out in a canine grin, and she pawed at him playfully.

"Stop that," he said. Then with a self-satisfied yawn and stretch, he joined her in wolf form. The change was fast and easy this time; it was his time of the month, and the wolf was eager to run.

Then with a hungry growl, he followed his sister through the leap gate.

The original landing pod where they'd first touched Otsandan soil was functional but dormant. They padded through the circular seating in the center and past the medical bay and disinfecting shower. Nothing was turned on, and the wolves padded quietly through the darkened cave and out the main hatch.

The moon overhead was like a ripe, orange fruit. Kuvrro threw his head back and howled, and Nexrra's voice joined his. They sang together to the constant moon and to the strength of the wolf. This was not their moon, and Kuvrro sensed a slight discord in their harmony. But he sang on in the hopes that it would become their moon, that Otsanda would someday be a real home to him and his pack. As long as they could avoid the two-legged rogues, Otsanda was a marvelous place.

As their song ended, Kuvrro heard howls and yips in the distance. Native Otsandan wolves, responding to their voices.

Nexrra loped away from the voices, and Kuvrro followed her. He wasn't sure what sort of reception they'd get from the natives, and he wasn't in the mood for a fight. His throat still ached where the rogue Jarren had bitten him.

The terrain here was steep and rocky. There was a chill in the air; autumn was well under way, and winter was only a month or two off. Kuvrro would probably spend next month's change on the Star Pack. This part of the planet was known for bitterly cold winters.

There was a scum of ice on a nearby pond, and Nexrra pawed it away so that they could drink. The water tasted of animal life and insect casings. It was rich in protein and oxygen, and Kuvrro licked his chops. Nexrra dipped her muzzle deep in the water, washing her face in the scent.

His stomach growled, and he glanced at his sister. She wolf-grinned and took off at a run, and Kuvrro followed. She seemed to have a plan.

With the cold season coming, the smaller burrowing prey was dug in deep and would be hard to find. But Nexrra seemed to know where she was going. The air was fresh and brisk in his nose, and he savored the multitude of scents that carried on the chill night breeze. Dead leaves, flying birds, water and bacteria and excrement and life. It was so new that it made Kuvrro's nose tingle, yet it was also deeply familiar. This world was only unlike Garou on the surface. Beneath its fur, they were pack.

But the two legged ones, he lamented. They were so mad and frightening. Look at what they'd done to wolves. They'd turned them into dogs!

Over a rocky hill they ran, and Kuvrro's claws scrabbled in the damp moss. There was a deep, wide stream on the other side, thick and smooth. Nexrra trotted down to its edge and looked back at him. She wanted to go fishing.

Why not? They weren't likely to find many rodents in this sort of weather, and bigger game would be harder to kill with a pack of two. Kuvrro followed his sister along the edge of the stream to an area where it narrowed and deepened to a sort of throat. Then he braced himself and stepped into the stream.

Nexrra loped away upstream until her tail was a grey flash in the darkness. Then she waded in herself, and Kuvrro heard her splashing and snapping at the water. He raised his paws one by one to keep his circulation healthy, but otherwise he kept as still as possible.

Nexrra splashed closer, and Kuvrro saw a flicker in the surface of the water. Dinner was on its way.

Kuvrro lowered his nose to the water, and muscles in his legs and shoulders tensed.

The flicker came closer, and Kuvrro struck. His jaws closed around the body of a fat fish, and he flung it onto the pebbly bank. Another flicker, and Kuvrro struck again. Now two fish flopped and gasped on the bank, and Kuvrro decided that he'd had enough of the cold water. His paws were numb, and his bones were beginning to ache.

Nexrra was already out of the water and pouncing on their catch. Kuvrro joined her, and together they crunched up the sweet, tasty fish. The flesh was cold and almost devoid of fat, not nearly as satisfying as a red-blooded kill. But it was enough that they had killed on the surface of Otsanda. It made Kuvrro's wolf feel strong.

Then they went for a run. The cold air was brisk and pleasant, ruffling through Kuvrro's fur. Nexrra ran ahead, and he chased her playfully. She spun around, nipped his ear, and took off again. Kuvrro growled and ran faster, but she managed to stay just ahead.

Someday, he hoped, he and Mirra would run together like this. It would be so pleasant to chase his mate over this beautiful land, to hunt and kill with her. But Mirra was not the sort to take risks just for the sake of wind in her fur. She was too much a pack leader.

They scrambled over another low rise and found themselves in an open space. Now they could really stretch their legs. Nexrra howled breathlessly as they ran, and Kuvrro yipped in response.

Then she stopped dead in her tracks. Kuvrro had to turn to the side to avoid slamming into her. Her body was stiff, her ears and tail alert and still. Kuvrro pricked up his own ears, but he heard nothing out of the ordinary.

Then he heard it: a stealthy footstep from somewhere on the far edge of the open space. It was ahead—no, behind. The footsteps were all around them. Predatory steps, something was stalking them. A whiff of wild scent touched Kuvrro's nose.

Native wolves. All around, watching them.

Nexrra whined. She wasn't afraid, at least not of the wolves themselves. But there was apprehension in the way she sniffed the air, the way she held her tail perfectly still, straight as a tree.

The wolves were just out of sight at the edge of the clearing, and now that Kuvrro was paying attention he could hear and smell them plainly. Some security chief he was. He'd been so wrapped up in his freedom, so excited to stretch his legs under the moon, that he'd been completely oblivious to the potential for danger. The four-legged natives had never shown signs of aggression towards them, but that did not mean they never would.

Nexrra lowered her head and approached the edge of the clearing, where two luminous, golden eyes watched them. Kuvrro followed her lead, keeping a few paces back. If these wolves wanted a fight, Kuvrro would be ready to oblige.

He had never seen a wild wolf so close before. When last he'd been on the surface, he'd been fighting for his life and for the life of his sister. The wolves had been there, but he'd barely noticed them. Now they stood in front of him, calm and regal and alert. They were the true rulers of Otsanda.

The wolf who approached them was smaller than the Garoueans, and his markings were lighter and more varied. His skull was smaller and flatter, indicating lower thinking intelligence. But a thinner body and longer legs, making him a better runner and possibly a better fighter in terms of speed and agility. Kuvrro thought he could take the wolf, if he had to. But he would have to work for it.

Then two more wolves stepped forward: females. Kuvrro could not fight them. His instincts and the law of the pack forbade it.

The lead male sat down, and the two females sat as well. So they did not intend to attack. Kuvrro sighed with relief and sat down.

Nexrra still stood, frozen in place like a stone. Her head was low to the ground, and her legs were stiff as branches. Kuvrro cocked his head at her. She wasn't frightened or angry, but he sensed confusion and shock. He wished that he could shift back to two legs so that they could talk about this, but it would probably not be safe.

As the thought crossed his mind, Kuvrro heard voices. But the sounds weren't coming through his ears. They were inside his head, voices like thoughts, speaking in the back of his head.

One voice sounded like Nexrra. The other was male, and foreign. How was he hearing a strange voice in his own head?

Kuvrro concentrated, and he tried to pick up what they were saying. Nexrra's tone was apologetic; the stranger's voice was angry and apprehensive. They weren't arguing, but it had the feel of an argument, one that his sister was losing. Finally Nexrra lowered her head and sniffed the grass, and then she backed away. Kuvrro followed, confused and a little worried. There had been no exchange between the two, no visible communication, but Nexrra acted as though she'd been soundly chastened. What had just happened?

Nexrra kept her head down and her pace at a steady lope the rest of the way back to the gate. Kuvrro paused and look around before following his sister back into the pod. It was early yet, and the moon shone down at them like a silver eye. But he saw other eyes watching: golden eyes that flickered among the trees. The natives had followed them, and they meant to see them off.

Kuvrro wasn't clear on why, but it was plain as daylight that the Garouean wolves were no longer welcome here.

He followed Nexrra through the gate and back to the Star Pack. He would finish the night in the exercise cave, alone. Nexrra watched him plod away, and behind him he heard her whine an apology.

Chapter Five

Nexrra felt terrible about cutting their trip to the surface short, but the natives had been adamant. If she and her brother hadn't left the area, they would have been attacked. She and Kuvrro might have been able to fight them off, but they would have been forced to kill a higher alien intelligence for essentially no reason.

She distracted herself by visiting the dog. Mirra had not yet decided what to do with the beast. They couldn't turn it loose in the wild and expect it to survive, nor did they know how to locate its human pack. So for now it was being kept in the cave that had once belonged to their entertainment officer, Drrak. As always it leaped into the air and licked frantically at her face, as though it had been kept in isolation all its life. Nexrra pitied the poor thing. How terrible to be so stunted that one's only hope for happiness lay in the approval of another creature.

She led the beast down to the medical office to perform a scan. She thought about the extensive equipment back home on Garou and wished that she could take the dog there. DNA scans, bone samples, parasite analysis… there was so much more she could do with a full laboratory to work with. But she ought to be grateful for what she had, she knew. The Star Pack was the biggest and best-equipped ship ever built. It needed to be, since it was the most widely traveled ship and would always go further than the hunters had ever gone before.

One advantage she did have here was access to local information. She turned on her eye screen and tapped into the Otsandan's information network. The "web" as it was called. Like a spider's web? Was it designed to catch the unaware, or was that just more of the natives' imprecise language?

Different dogs were used for different functions, and there was a wide variety in size and temperament. Using visual clues Nexrra was able to eventually identify the dog as something called a "pit type." But that did not narrow it down as far as Nexrra would have liked. There was a variety of pit-type dogs, and all of them were capable of interbreeding. This dog could be any number of breeds or types.

197

Nexrra gave up on that line of inquiry. It didn't matter very much. What she was more interested in was information that could teach her more about its human masters.

She fed the dog a sedative wrapped in dried ungula meat. It gobbled the meat down and licked anxiously at her fingers, then it cocked its head at her. Its ears made furry little triangles that Nexrra found endearing. She flipped her eye screen over to her science notes and started typing. Mirra had explained the symbiotic relationship between humans and dogs, how dogs had found an evolutionary loophole that had protected them from extermination in the manner of larger, more aggressive predators. Nexrra felt the effect of that relationship, the chemical rush that indicated the onset of parental instinct. She wanted to record every moment of this.

She noted the dog's behavior and her own biochemical response, and then she made a list of the areas she wanted to study further. The dog's biochemistry, for example. Were the feelings of familiar affection reciprocated, or was this a sort of protective coloring, like the eyespots on insects? If the dog felt the same way she felt looking back at it, that would be a remarkable discovery. Everyone back on Garou would be shocked and amazed, and nobody would call her a fluff-headed cub ever again.

The dog lay down on the metal floor and closed its eyes. Nexrra stroked its soft fur, and it stretched out its limbs in what looked like contentment. She noted the stimulus and response in detail, but she made sure to make no judgments about its psychological state. Visual data only. Later, when she had more information, she could interpret that data without prejudice.

Once the dog was unconscious, she ran the body scanner over it. The dog was male, and unsurprisingly it had been castrated, probably while still a pup. This was a common practice; according to Ledrra the humans considered it cruel not to geld their pets before sexual maturity, to curb aggressive behavior as well as reduce the population of unwanted animals. Nexrra understood the logic, but the practice still made her queasy. The dog looked and acted too much like a wolf cub. It was affecting her scientific detachment.

At least Mirra had met the beast first, and she had been charmed by it as well. Nexrra did not have to worry about the captain mocking her for her sentimentality. Not that there had been much mockery lately. Ever since the disaster on Otsanda that had killed Drrak, Mirra had been quieter, calmer, more respectful of her crew. She'd always acted like she thought she was older than the rest of the hunters; now she acted as though she really was older. Almost maternal, like a true pack leader.

A proper pack leader knows how to treat her followers like family, Nexrra thought as she stroked the sleeping dog's furry side. That's not something you can learn from books at the Academy.

She drew three vials of blood from the animal and placed them in a storage receptacle in the wall. Then she went back to studying the body scan. There was something funny about the dog's neck. She zoomed the scanner in on the mass at the dog's neck and took another picture. It was a device, she realized. A computer chip of some kind. Some sort of identification, she wondered, or a locator?

They had devices that could pinpoint a carrier's location by using satellites. They were called GPS. Was this a GPS? The Star Pack orbited Otsanda behind the moon, out of range of their satellites. She hoped. But Mirra would not want to take the chance. As attached as she was, she would want the dog destroyed.

Nexrra had to get the dog out of here. She wasn't finished studying it, but at least she had blood samples that she could study at her leisure once the dog was gone.

But what could she do? She couldn't just drop it back on Otsanda where they'd found it. If cold and hunger didn't kill it, those territorial wolves probably would. She could probably surgically remove the chip and destroy it, but that wouldn't solve the ultimate problem of what to do with the dog. They surely couldn't take it back to Garou with them. What would Mirra do?

Mirra would make the hardest decision, because that was what she always did. Mirra did not believe in taking foolish chances.

But she did believe in making sacrifices for the good of the pack, and Nexrra thought she knew what she had to do.

Chapter Six

Terra walked back to her empty home alone. She saw a few other hunters, but they sensed her sorrowful body language and kept their distance. A pair of scuffling cubs stopped their fighting and lowered their heads as she passed by, her distress like a beacon.

The little cottage seemed cavernous now, huge and hollow without Hrraz. Now she saw all the little signs she should have caught before. All of his personal belongings were gone, even his favorite foods were gone from the cold box. He'd cleaned out his half of the home while Terra had been distracted by Mirra's troubles.

Would he resign from the Council for Alien Affairs? Terra hoped he would; she did not want to see him every day at work. But maybe—she frowned. Maybe he'd left her like this in an attempt to shame her into quitting. Quitting and leaving the alpha post to him.

That was not going to happen. Terra wanted to get to the bottom of this.

That leap gem. That was the key to everything. Who had put a wild gem in that tree and just left it unattended? And why? Hrraz seemed to know something about it, enough to keep its existence a secret.

The rogue gem was dangerous; it had let animals through on both sides of the gate. But the hunters who knew about it had left it in place. Mystery added to mystery.

Terra curled up in the central nest and turned on a soothing music-and-scent program on the eye. She fell asleep listening to the rhythmic sound of wolves running through grass and the scent of sunshine on soil. Her brain was exhausted and cluttered with questions, and it needed to shut off for a while.

She slept deeply and remembered none of her dreams. But somehow the puzzle pieces had fallen in a pattern, somewhere in her resting mind. When she awoke, she knew where she needed to go next.

To the Southeast territory, and the leap gem mine.

*****

It would be a fairly long journey, at least two days on four feet and five days on two. Terra decided to take the longer, two-legged journey. Traveling as the wolf was faster, but she would be limited to nonverbal communication. She would also need more sleep, and when the trip was over she would be all but useless for a week. So Terra filled her travel pack with fruits, a water pouch, and several other portable foods. Then she strapped a hunting knife to each thigh and set out. She used her wrist eye to send messages to everyone on the Council except Hrraz, that she was taking half a month's leave of absence. She had a research project to work on, and she would be away from home the entire time. None of this was technically untrue.

Terra stood outside her little home and stared at it for several minutes. She and Hrraz had lived here for years and raised a cub together. She wanted to leave it behind, as Hrraz had left her behind. But was that a practical idea? Anywhere she went would be empty of Hrraz.

She wished for a moment that she could go to Otsanda. A new world, new people, new problems. It was a scary place, from what Mirra had told her, but maybe that was good. The fear would distract her and ease her pain. Maybe.

She tapped out the code on her wrist eye that would lock and seal the house. All electronics inside would go dormant, conserving energy until her return. The windows darkened, protecting her privacy from curious cubs and troublemakers. Then she turned her back on her home and set out.

It was a warm, clear morning, and Terra felt good as she stretched her legs and breathed the sun-warmed air. The cold season was coming, but its beginning was still a good two months away. The nights would be chilly, but for the most part Terra would travel in comfort.

Near midday Terra saw a sign for a paradise. She decided to stop here for a meal. Fresh meat would be harder to come by as she moved away from the forests and into the arid, scrubby lands to the south.

She found the attendant station and dropped off her travel pack for safekeeping. The attendant took it and grimaced at the weight. "Traveling far?" he asked.

"I don't know," she said. "That's why I packed so much."

"Fair enough." He gestured at the wall behind him. "Need a blade, or are you going wolf?"

"Got my own." Terra patted her thighs.

"You're well prepared." The younger man tapped his throat and gave her an unmistakable look. "I like that in a female."

"I'm past season." Terra ran her fingers through her hair, ruffling the feathers of white that adorned her pelt.

"Nobody's past friendship." The young male cocked his head and leaned forward a trifle.

Terra's whiskers tingled, and her incisors sharpened. The young male was attractive, and Terra was all alone. Hrraz had left her. She'd thought they'd mated for life, but he'd left her anyway. She would not make that mistake again, but that didn't mean she couldn't have companionship.

"Do you need to stay at your post all day?" she asked.

"Only until midday. And I'm hungry; I haven't eaten all day. I want to go hunting." He licked his lips.

"Then I'll see you in half a turn—if you can catch me." Terra leaned forward and licked his nose, then she took off running into the brush, shocked by her own boldness.

*****

Hours later, Terra moved on south. She was very late; she'd wanted to be on the territory border by now. But she was too full and satisfied to be upset with herself.

The male's name was Grrun, and he had just graduated from the Flight Academy and was awaiting job placement. He had not yet mated, nor did he plan to in the near future. He'd said that he wanted to save his wealth and explore the galaxy first. He'd been an eager and willing partner and a good hunter too. When he decided he was ready, Terra thought he would make an excellent mate and father.

He'd also grown up in the southeast, so he was able to give her additional information about the leap mine. It was heavily secured, of course; the mine was dangerous in at least four different ways. Grrun had told Terra which office to visit first in order to get a pass to enter the mine. As head of the Council for Alien Affairs (a title that had impressed him deeply; he'd almost skipped the sex in favor of asking her questions about the different worlds Garou had pissed on), she would have no trouble getting in, but she would have to talk to the right people and explain why she was there.

"The mine isn't very big," Grrun said between mouthfuls of Terra's neck, "and most of the gems they find are too weak to use for leaping. But if they find a strong vein they'll lock the mine down until it's been excavated."

"Where can I go to learn more about the gems themselves?" Terra asked. She squirmed beneath him and presented her silky rump.

"Probably the Tech Academy." Grrun's voice hoarsened as he pressed forward to engage. "There are libraries... professors..."

And that was the end of the conversation.

Now Terra jogged briskly south, savoring the late afternoon's sweet air. It was astounding how much better one felt after a good meal and a bout of athletic sex. She needed to do that more often.

Hrraz's memory twitched in the back of Terra's mind, but it was far away, like the memory of long-ago pain. Terra pushed him away, and he vanished without a ripple.

She would not make the border until nightfall. Should she sleep outdoors or look for lodging? There was no shelter nearby but bushes and weeds, but if she turned wolf she could probably dig herself a comfortable ditch in the dry soil. The alternative was to look for a village where she could find someone to house a lone hunter for the night in exchange for food or currency.

Terra wanted company—particularly if she could find another tasty young male—but her wolf spoke up and advised caution. Hrraz was behind her, but the mystery was not. There was a secret here, and Terra's purpose was to find out its meaning. The more she stayed out of others' eyes, the easier this would be.

She found a slight rise in the land, not quite a hill, and settled down in a small divot at its base. It smelled faintly of wolf; others had used this spot as shelter before, but not recently. Terra lay her travel pack down to use as a pillow, curled up into a tight ball, and fell asleep. Her muscles ached faintly, but the pain was comforting rather than uncomfortable. It was nice to be on the move, to have an active purpose. Sitting on the Council was rewarding in its way, but sometimes that was too much sitting.

She dreamed of the leap gems, of blackness in space that glinted gold. Small black holes that could be held in the hand. They were as big as the universe, but somehow Terra was bigger. And when she looked deep inside one, it looked back at her.

She awoke puzzled and hungry.

For two more days she walked and slept rough, eating fruit and cheese from her pack and meat whenever she could catch it. Finally she awoke to a dull, overcast morning that smelled of rain. It would be a cold rain; the morning had a chill that Terra thought was not likely to dissipate. Tonight she would want to seek shelter rather than sleep wild.

By midday she'd come to a large village that she thought must house the Tech Academy. There were roads and houses everywhere, and the air was filled with wolf scent. All ages Terra detected: adults, children, and elders. Did they have an ancestors' retreat close by? Or did this territory have a different method for ancestors who had come to the end of their useful lives? Terra hoped that she could find out while she was here. This place was very like her home, but the sights and sounds were different enough to excite her curiosity. She wanted to learn all about this place before she had to leave.

"Excuse me," she said of a passing male with pale yellow hair. His eyes were the lightest blue she'd ever seen, and his body pelt was almost white. He must spend most of his days outdoors, she thought. "Where's the Tech Academy?"

The male sized her up and dismissed her. Disappointing but not surprising; he was probably looking for a female who could still bear young. "You're going the right way." He pointed behind him, down the road. "It's just down that way and to the left. You can see part of it behind that hill."

Terra saw, and she thanked the male. He tapped his throat and moved on.

The Tech Academy was wide and squat, nothing at all like the high-ceilinged Flight Academy. But of course this building did not have to house rockets, space simulators, or any of the other bulky equipment necessary for teaching young hunters how to fly.

Terra walked up to the building with her head high and her neck stiff. Her wolf was twitchy, and she felt anxious walking into this strange

204

place. But she saw nothing that indicated that strangers were unwelcome. Just inside the front door of the building was a lounge area equipped with chairs and couches as well as wolf nests. The air vents wafted in the scholarly scents of grass and paper. This lobby was equipped to make everyone feel comfortable. So why did Terra feel so nervous and alone?

An elder female, grey-haired and shaggy of pelt, approached her. "Hello, I'm Prrua. Are you a new student?" She looked Terra up and down, nostrils flaring. It was not unheard of for a hunter Terra's age to start a new education program, but it was peculiar enough to pique curiosity.

"No. I'm from the northeast territory. Terra, from the Council for Alien Affairs." She tapped her throat and leaned forward, inviting Prrua to investigate.

Prrua's examination was perfunctory. It would have been rude to make a great show of sniffing over someone of Terra's importance. "How may the Academy be of assistance?"

Terra decided on discretion. Until she understood why Hrraz and that other fellow from Med Academy wanted the matter of the leap gem kept a secret, she would follow their lead and be quiet about it as well. "I've been head of the Council for Alien Affairs for a dozen years," she said. "In all that time, I've never bothered to learn about the leap gems. I don't even know how they work. Can you help me? Is there someone available who can educate me or show me where I can go to educate myself?"

Prrua nodded, and her expression brightened. "I can take you to the library," she said. "All of our professors are in classes right now, but there should be someone in the library who can answer any questions the books don't."

"I thank you." Terra touched her throat, and Prrua politely reciprocated.

Chapter Seven

Prrua led her down an adjacent hallway. The carpet beneath their feet was thick and rough, reminiscent of scrubby grass. Terra inhaled and smelled fresh grass and soil. Their ventilation system was of high quality, giving students the feeling that they were working outside. Terra liked that. The Flight Academy students spent a lot of their time in simulators, so even when they were indoors all day they didn't feel confined. But Tech Academy would be different. Areas of study here included chemistry, and math, hours spent in close quarters staring into tiny instruments. The wolf would get bored and restless without some sort of release.

The library, too, was designed to simulate the outdoors so perfectly that Terra felt exposed. Then she looked up at the sky and realized that the ceiling here was an enormous window. It was angled slightly to allow precipitation to run off, but the lines in the glass were so thin that Terra had to look hard to find them. A cool breeze ruffled her hair, and she had to look around until she found the cleverly placed vents that kept fresh air blowing between the stacks of books. In addition to chairs and couches, in the main common area there were huge wooden blocks just the right size for climbing and jumping on. Terra felt light and comfortable just standing here; were she a student, she would never want to leave.

Prrua watched her reaction and nodded. "Our library is the envy of other academies," she said. "There is almost no scuffling in our halls, and the students have excellent study habits."

"I can see why." Terra looked for the wall eyes, which would connect to the library's database. "Where would you recommend I start looking for information on leap gems?"

"What do you want to know?"

"How they work."

Prrua snorted and shook her head. "You're going to start your climb at the top of the mountain. All right. The books about leap gems are this shelf over here." Prrua led he toward the back of the library and showed her a long, low shelf against one wall. "And the database is right over there." Prrua pointed to the adjacent wall, which held an eye about half a length across. There were two females standing in front of it, tapping around what looked like a series of books about mating rituals on other planets.

"Thank you so much for your help," Terra said. She tapped her throat, and again Prrua returned the gesture.

"It's part of my job. I always like seeing visitors from other territories take an interest in our work."

"What other territories?" Terra asked after her.

"From yours." Prrua paused and looked over her shoulder. "That other hunter from your Council was here last month. Didn't you know?"

"Of course," Terra said. "I remember now. Thanks again for your help."

"I'm happy to do it." Then Prrua was out of the library and gone.

Terra wandered over to the shelf she'd indicated and examined the books. They were the newest model, the electronic books that engaged the reader's senses as well as her mind. The books lit up as she tapped them, illuminating their titles and releasing a whiff of soothing, stimulating scent. Fresh and green, like leaves and sunshine. She breathed the scent and read the titles. *Leap Gem History*, *Quantum Gems*, *The Discovery of the Leap Gem*... Terra carefully studied the entire shelf as the sun inched across the sky. She had already resigned herself to spending her entire day here, so she felt no need to hurry.

She picked up *The Discovery of the Leap Gem* and took it to a nearby nest. The cushions were soft as a cub's fur and smelled of grass trimmings. She curled up among the cushions and opened the book.

Terra opened the twin plates and tapped the left hand screen. The first pages appeared, and Terra tapped each screen twice to enlarge the text. It was getting harder to read; she thought briefly that she ought to see a medical about her weakening vision.

She might never get a chance though.

Now why would that thought appear in her head?

She pushed that thought away. But it did occur to her that she'd never been to the Medical Academy. It was fun to travel like this and see new places, experience new technology. And make new friends, she thought wistfully as she thought of Grrun's hard, hairy body. Maybe she wouldn't hurry back to her own territory. It all depended on what she learned here.

Discovery was a fascinating read. Garouean society had gone through its messy stage centuries before, the wolves fighting among themselves and the scientific community struggling to find a cure for the "curse." During that time, technology had fought against nature instead of alongside it, and huge swaths of the southern territories had been destroyed. It had been an ugly time.

During that period, though, while the hunters' heedless mining of precious metals was at its peak, a peculiar mineral had been discovered: jet-black and hard as iron. Terra tapped the page and watched a small video that showed the mineral being chipped out of the rock with special tungsten tools. Unseen hands used a chipper to knock a chunk of black stone out of the wall and toss it into a metal box. Terra had learned at Flight Academy that tungsten was one of the few elements that could shield the leap gem and contain its space-bending properties. Tungsten, lead, and something else, some compound she couldn't quite recall. No doubt this book would tell her eventually.

The book described, in detail, the terrifying and exciting first days after the discovery. The miner who'd first found it, a female named Agrra, had almost lost her fingertips when she'd played around with a few broken pieces. The stuff was inert when buried in the rock, but exposure to warmth and oxygen activated it. Then when the pieces were separated, they created a loophole in space between them. And from there…

Fortunately that first vein had been weak and thin, the gems no more than chips. But the gem's potential had been identified, and life on Garou would never be the same again.

Terra read on about the world-wide social explosion the gems had brought to her world. Wars and bickering ground to a halt; suddenly nothing seemed as important as the ability to leave the solar system and travel among the stars. There might be other people out there. Other hunters. Other prey. They could piss on new trees, run under a different moon.

Best of all, or so it seemed at the time, space travelers would be free of the moon's compulsion. Turning wolf would no longer be inevitable, no longer forced on every member of the population older than eight. Further experimentation eventually indicated that they still needed to change, but it could be at a convenient time of the hunter's choosing. And those travelers would come back with new data about how to tame and control the wolf. Now it was no longer a curse but a gift.

Discovering the leap gems had meant an end to Garou's messy stage. What if it could mean the same for Otsanda? Terra filed the thought away for future reference and kept reading.

The book wrapped up with a few video simulations depicting how the leap gems were currently being used. They were mined by hunters, wearing specially shielded suits, and the gems were kept in tungsten transport boxes until they could be taken to the lab at the Tech Academy. There they were subjected to an array of exposures to gases and radiation until their quantomagnetic properties had been damped enough to make them safe to handle. Finally they were carved and shaped to fit the leap gates that would be installed on the new planets that Garou discovered. On the voyage they were kept in lock boxes in pairs so that the two gems would naturally attune to each other and no other. Terra pictured a star ship trying to reach a distant star and instead found itself landing on Morteloup and wrinkled her nose with amusement.

There were a few videos simulating a ship's structure and technology as well as its travels through the leap gates and to the farthest reaches of explored space. Terra tapped the gate as the ship passed through, and she could see the golden glimmer around its invisible edges. The leap gems in space were fixed to large asteroids that the Council for Alien Affairs could track in their orbits, and instead of a metal frame the gate was a field in space that followed the asteroid like a tail. Terra knew all of this already, but she enjoyed the rhythm and style of the book, and the videos had been well-designed with interesting scents.

A warm, furry body slid into the nest beside her. "Do you mind some company?" asked a female voice.

Terra shook her head no. She smelled that the female was in estrus, but that did not concern her. Terra was past breeding age, and she was no threat to this healthy young thing. She glanced over and saw with no surprise that the girl's pelt was thick and shaggy, and her eyes were golden. Females in that time of the moon were frequently haunted by the wolf, even during the day.

Terra wondered why she was not taking suppression drugs. Why would she want to breed now? She would have to quit the Academy, at least temporarily. Perhaps she wanted to quit, or she was close to graduating and wanted to start a family right away. It was not of Terra's business.

"I'm Terra," she said.

The younger female tapped her throat. "Mistrra. I'll be no bother. I just want to sleep for a bit before my next class."

Terra gave her a friendly pat on the shoulder and went back to her book. Hormone swings could make a female moody and sick; it was no wonder she needed a rest. And she'd chosen a female companion who would not be moved by her scent to try to engage her. She'd actually be able to sleep, here. Clever Mistrra.

The book was connected to the Tech Academy's library database, and Terra "asked" it by tapping the final page what book would be best to read next. The screens blinked a few times, then *Quantum Gems* appeared. That was one of the books Terra had just looked over, so that was convenient. She got up and put *Discovery* back on the shelf. When she got back to the next with *Quantum Gems*, Mistrra was curled up into a tight, furry ball and fast asleep.

Terra settled in as quietly as she could. *Quantum Gems* was a more difficult read that assumed a deep understanding of quantum particles and potential energy. Terra frequently had to tap the sidebars that showed video clips illustrating what the text was talking about. Normally she enjoyed puzzling out the meaning of written words, but this was too much puzzle for her.

One section she had to tap and re-watch several times. In addition to descriptions of gravity and sinks reminiscent of black holes only smaller and containable, the book kept describing the gemstones in terms of evolution. How was that possible? Rocks didn't evolve. The book itself seemed confused, contradicting itself in several different sections, and Terra gave up on it. She closed the book and put it away; she needed a break.

She'd go for a walk and maybe find the local paradise. Then she'd look for lodging. Tomorrow she wanted to be well on her way to the mine. Maybe someone there could explain what the gems really were.

Mistrra was staring at her.

Terra blinked. "Are you all right?" she asked.

The other female did not reply. Her eyes were unblinking gold moons, and the pupils were fully dilated. Terra met her gaze and tensed for either a fight or a run. Mistrra was in prey mode, and a single wrong move could bring the wolf down on Terra's throat. There was the faintest of rumbles coming from nearby, but Terra wasn't sure if it was Mistrra or herself who was growling.

What was wrong? Estrus sometimes made a female cranky, and the wolf would be wild and unpredictable. But no wolf went rogue in minutes. Terra had smelled nothing but sleepy discomfort on the female until this moment. Now she smelled like anger. And madness.

Terra hooked one foot over the edge of the nest. She didn't want to fight. She wasn't sure she could win.

In the back of her awareness she heard others in the library, muttering and whispering. Slowly the nearby students were becoming aware of Mistrra's condition, and they were as shocked and disturbed as Terra herself.

"Not like her at all," she heard distinctly. This did not make Terra feel any better. Mistrra could be ill, and it could be contagious.

It could be the plague.

If it were the plague, the entire Tech Academy was in danger. At the very least everyone here would have to go into quarantine, and Terra would never make it to the mine.

She propped herself slowly up onto her hands. If she fell backwards and rolled out of the nest, she might make it to all fours before Mistrra struck.

"Mistrra, what's wrong?" A sharp, startled cry from the entrance.

Mistrra spun around with a snarl, and Terra caught a glimpse of a thick, bushy tail before the rogue hunter was out of the nest and away. The young male who'd cried out tried to shift, but he was too slow. He went down like a stone into a pond under two hundred pounds of mad wolf.

Terra took off after her. She was no longer afraid, just angry. All she'd wanted to do was relax and read and learn about leap gems. Now she was caught up in this fight that might kill her, at least it would send her to the medicals. She would never make it to the mines at all if the female killed her.

She caught the rogue around her throat and pulled upward, against her jaw. Mistrra dropped the hapless male and tried to spin around. Terra felt hard muscles under her arms and thighs as she gripped Mistrra tightly and held on for her life.

Mistrra flung herself onto her back, and Terra's head thunked against the grassy floor. The surface was soft, but the floor underneath was hard as stone, and Terra's brain felt rattled.

Her grip loosened, but thankfully there were others around them now, all working together to grab and restrain Mistrra. They held her front and back paws, her head and jaws. Mistrra growled furiously but could not move. Terra lay on her back on the library floor, panting. Her incisors had grown past her bottom lip, and she licked them self-consciously.

Mistrra quieted and lay still. There was a moment of stunned silence, then the rogue lunged again, leaping and snapping at anything within reach. But the others still held her firmly, and she could not score.

"What happened?" a nearby female asked. She was a slender little thing with reddish-golden hair.

"I don't know," Terra answered. "She was sleeping. Is she ill?"

"She smells ill," said one of the young males holding her. "But she wasn't sick this morning. I saw her in the eating hall. She smelled perfectly healthy then."

"Could her estrus have made her ill? Why was she not suppressing her cycle?"

The reddish-gold female lifted her lip and showed a single tooth. "She likes the attention."

Terra looked at the faces of the other females and guessed from their expressions of smug superiority that Mistrra was not well-liked. But that was irrelevant. How had she become so ill so quickly? The plague had been a fast-acting virus, but even then it had taken several days of lethargy and fever for the madness to set in.

Maybe Mistrra's estrus had concealed her symptoms. Or—Terra's stomach tightened with fear—maybe the virus had mutated. Maybe this was how the plague would strike next.

"The medicals are here," a female from the back of the crowd announced.

The group parted and shifted to allow three dark-haired females through. Past them Terra saw two more administering aid to the young male Mistrra had attacked. Terra thought he would be all right. The rogue had scored on his throat, but she had not had time to bite deeply enough to kill. She hoped.

That could have been me. Terra shuddered. And there was nobody who had been close enough to intervene, if anyone would even try. She had almost died today.

She wanted to go home now. Go home and curl up in her comfortable nest and shut out everything. She wanted to sleep for a month.

But she could not. Even if the medicals let her leave, which was unlikely, Terra had a strong feeling that there was a deeper mystery here than a simple sickness. The wolf told her that Mistrra's illness was related to Terra's presence here, and she wanted to know how that could be possible.

More than ever Terra felt that she needed to see the leap gem mine. Her wolf insisted that she would find the answers there.

Chapter Eight

Ledrra ran through the obstacle course again, and the dog chased her eagerly. Nexrra stood next to the door and watched them. They acted like sibling cubs, chasing and tussling over and around the climbing equipment. She felt a glow of maternal warmth, though neither of them was her blood kin.

She thought that this meant it was time to settle down and breed. Nexrra had never been serious about a male; the only one she'd ever felt close to was her brother. But Kuvrro was bonded to Mirra, at least for now, and it was time for her to find someone too. This strange, dangerous mission was sure to bring respect from the groundlings, and once she was back home she'd be able to take her pick of the local males.

Ledrra trotted back to her, panting. The dog panted at her heels, grinning happily in the manner of humans. Another fascinating aspect of their evolution: mimicking their facial expressions. Dogs could bare their teeth in the wolf manner to indicate anger or distress, but when they were relaxed and happy their jaws hung open and their teeth showed in a very different manner.

"I wish he didn't have to go," Ledrra said.

"I know, but it's for the best," Nexrra said. "He belongs with his own kind, and with the species he knows best."

Ledrra nodded and then leaned in closely. "Are you sure you want to do this?" she asked quietly. "Those folk are mad, and you're going to walk right up to them."

Nexrra's reply was barely audible. "This is the only way I'll get close to them. I need to do this. I need to know."

Ledrra glanced around, though they were still alone in the exercise room. "Try to find out what happened to my sister," she said.

Nexrra nodded once, quickly. Then she knelt down and scratched the dog under his chin. "Are you ready to go home to your pack?" she asked. The dog wagged his tail.

*****

Nexrra had planned her visit carefully. The scout pod was stationed in the wilderness of a territory called Canada, and the area was mostly empty of humans except for a few who retained enough of their instincts to enjoy hunting and running under the moon. Nexrra didn't think she'd have any trouble with this sort; all she had to do was emulate an Otsandan hunter. She used vegetable extract to dye her coverall with splotches of green and brown, and she borrowed one of Ledrra's coveralls to create a bright pink cap to cover her grey hair. Internet images suggested that orange would be the ideal color for her cap, but pink was an acceptable color for Otsandan females. She thought she would pass.

Her plan was to travel to the nearest Otsandan settlement—probably something called a campground, a sort of tame paradise—and try to give the dog back to his pack. Hopefully she would not find them right away. She wanted to make contact with as many humans as she could, so she would have more data to take back to Ledrra.

Nexrra filled her travel pack with dried fruit, meat, and a bladder of water. She tightened the straps across her back and just as she was preparing to leave Mirra appeared in her doorway.

"Are you sure about this?" the captain asked. Once again Nexrra was struck by the change in her. At the beginning of this mission Mirra had only issued demands, never questions.

"The only alternative is to destroy the dog," Nexrra said. "And the ethics guide says never to kill a native species if there is another way to solve the problem."

"Mm." Mirra put her hand out, and the dog licked it eagerly. Its hindquarters danced back and forth with excitement, and Nexrra felt a twinge of jealousy. Even the animal recognized Mirra's social superiority.

Then Mirra stood up and looked Nexrra in the eye. "So you think your wisest course of action is to go down to Otsanda and confront the mad aliens directly," she said.

"Yes, of course." Nexrra relaxed a trifle. Mirra was criticizing her choice, but she was not forbidding it. Everything would work out.

"Of course, if you are discovered, you will have jeopardized the lives of every hunter on this ship." Mirra's eyes flashed gold, and her pupils were enormous.

"So Nexrra, I hope you'll be careful. I don't want to lose any more of my pack."

Nexrra rubbed her throat desperately; a single tap seemed insufficient. Mirra turned on her heel and walked out of the room, satisfied that her message had been received.

If you fail, if you are discovered, you're as good as dead. Don't even try to come back.

*****

Nexrra decided for the sake of convenience to name the dog Happy Face. Creatures who ran on four legs and lived by their noses scarcely needed names, but since Nexrra would be living on two legs for the time being, she needed to communicate with the dog using two-legged language. And even when Nexrra tied a length of wire cord to his collar and dragged him away from Ledrra to the leap gate, he kept his tongue-lolling human grin. Happy Face seemed to fit.

What does my name mean? Nexrra wondered as she tapped the leap gem and waited for it to recognize her. Odd that she'd never thought about it before. A name was just a sound that meant a person, a scent, a feeling. Kuvrro meant family, love, and protection. That was all she knew. Maybe that was all there was to it, for her people.

The Otsandans gave their offspring names that meant other things. They seemed to want to inflict certain traits onto their children that they deemed desirable for themselves. *More Otsandan madness,* Nexrra thought. *What if the child didn't want to be strong, regal, or beautiful?* Not every hunter could grow up to be the best. It seemed cruel to force that kind of expectation onto a helpless cub.

The gem flashed gold, and Nexrra gave Happy Face a tug with the makeshift leash. Instantly the dog sat down and looked at her, awaiting her command. "You're going home," she told him. Happy Face panted stupidly.

She kept the dog close to her side as they stepped through. The disorientation of passing through the gate was brief, but she had no idea how the dog would react. She wanted to be ready for anything, so she held the dog within touching range of her leg as they stepped forward, into the dark.

This was a mistake.

When they passed through the gate and into the darkness of the empty pod, at first Nexrra had no idea what was happening. There was a brutal pain in her right leg, and a horrible growl, like a wolf gone rogue. Nexrra tried to kick her leg, to shake off the pain, but it wouldn't move. Something was biting her, and she was pinned to the spot by the weight.

"Happy Face, stop!" she commanded, trying not to cry from the pain. The dog's growl intensified, and it gave a little shake of its head.

"Happy Face, stop!" she screamed, and she felt the wolf swarm out of her mind and take over. Her ears and teeth sharpened, and her heavy paws swiped the ignorant pup across its stupid face. The wolf howled, and the dog scrambled frantically away.

Nexrra tried to push the wolf down and regain control, but she was bleeding badly from her leg, and the wolf smelled the perpetrator, scrambling and cringing in the dark. Ears back, teeth bared, she stalked the whimpering, pissing dog that scampered around the little pod, desperate for egress.

Then Happy Face happened to jump and fall against the switch that released the pod's hatchway. It was deliberately simple so that even a four-legged hunter could operate it, and something four-legged had. Happy Face fell backwards through the sliding hatchway and into the cool daylight of early Otsandan morning. The wolf snarled and charged after it.

Once outside, the cool air and open space calmed the wolf, and Nexrra was able to regain control. Once she was back in two-legged form, she wanted to chew off her own leg in chagrin. Happy Face was gone. She'd tried to save him by returning him to his pack, and she'd failed. Now he was lost in the wilderness, and she was still bleeding and in no condition to chase him.

She had nobody to blame but herself. Data concerning the leap gates and less intelligent creatures was uncertain, since it was rare for one to need transport. Once or twice hunters had moved ungula to a new planet for colonization, and for the most part they handled it the way they handled everything: placidly. But once or twice an ungula had gotten so agitated it tried to kick or bite its handler. Nexrra should have foreseen this possibility and clamped the dog's muzzle.

Should she try to track it down and win it back? The hot trickle down her leg suggested that this was not a safe idea. Her wound wasn't life threatening, but an infection could make her very ill. Also, she admitted to herself, she sort of didn't want to find it again. Her leg hurt badly, and she'd been frightened and horrified by its sudden attack. She knew in her head that it was just a dumb animal from an alien world, but in her heart the dog had felt like pack. Now she felt betrayed, though she knew that was foolish.

She stood uncertainly, favoring her injured leg. She looked back at the pod, then out at the Otsandan wilderness. She ought to go back to Mirra and report her failure. The captain would tell her what to do next, if anything.

But that idea didn't taste good. She didn't want to go back, and she certainly didn't want to listen to Mirra's sympathetic, superior voice saying but not saying I told you so.

The cord on its leash, she thought. The dog's pack might get curious about what it's made of, and I don't think bluetree fibers grow on Otsanda.

She felt relieved. She ought to spend at least a day or two looking for the dog before she headed back. She was obligated to keep all forms of Garouean technology out of Otsandan hands, no matter how simple.

But first she ought to see about this leg. She took off her travel pack and fished around for her med kit. She smeared sweet-smelling poisontree sap over the bite wound, then she covered it with a thick grey bandage that blended in with the grey hair on her leg. When she got to fresh water she would wash the wound more thoroughly, but this would do for now.

Her very next order of business was to find a cozy hole where she could sleep off her nerves. She ached all over from the adrenaline rush and from the pain of changing so quickly without preparation, and her cheeks felt flushed and feverish.

Nexrra went back into the pod and curled up on one of the thinly cushioned seats. It was less comfortable than the ground outside, but she was too tired to look for shelter outside. Her head pounded like a hammer on stone.

Chapter Nine

Three days passed, three of the longest days of Terra's life.

The academy was quarantined, as she had expected. Everyone had been tested—blood, saliva and stool—for traces of the plague virus that had struck the northeast territory. She herself was placed in isolation, for which she did not blame them. A rare virus had affected her home territory, and now seemed to have followed her here. Terra would have insisted on this precaution herself.

But knowing this didn't make her captivity any easier to bear. They'd let her stay in one of the empty office caves on the lowest level of the academy building. The furniture was comfortable, and there were plenty of books. There was even a wall eye, so Terra could watch all the picture stories she wanted. She still had her wrist eye, so she could call the Council at home and tell them what was going on here and to tighten precautions since it seemed the plague wasn't gone yet.

But she was completely alone. The sight and scent of other hunters through screens was not the same as their physical presence. She'd told the medicals repeatedly that the plague was transmitted through blood contact, but they'd pointed out that Mistrra had seemed to contract it with no contact at all. So here she was.

Terra paced back and forth tirelessly, aware but uncaring that she was being watched and evaluated by the medicals. Let them think she was going mad. Two more days of this treatment and she would do just that, virus or no virus.

Finally, on the fourth day, there was a click at the door and a young female with pale brown hair and a medical badge entered. She touched her throat, which heartened Terra. Perhaps the quarantine was over, and they were about to apologize for the inconvenience and let her go.

"I am Leykrra," she said. Her tone was quiet and apologetic. "I need to ask you a few questions about your purpose here."

Terra's nose wrinkled. "My purpose? What does that have to do with the rogue female?"

"Mistrra has been studying the leap gems as part of her final training. She spent half a day walking in and out of gates last moon. She could probably tell you anything you want to know about leap gems. Except that she's still in the med unit and probably won't be released for at least another ten days. Her blood is clean of the plague, but her hormone levels are elevated, so the medicals have determined that her estrus triggered a behavior shift. They're putting her on stabilizers, and she'll have to stay until the scent of estrus is gone."

Leykrra sat down in the floor nest and curled her legs beneath her. Terra sat in the nearby chair, establishing her rank as the higher female. "What is this about?" she asked.

"The other medicals think I'm mad," Leykrra confessed. "But please verify: you were reading about leap gates when Mistrra went rogue, right?"

"Correct." Mistrra had been studying leap gems as part of her education, and Terra had been studying leap gems when the female had joined her. It was an odd coincidence, but Terra still didn't understand Leykrra's point.

She sat silently for a long time. Terra observed that the hairs on the younger female's arms were raising and lowering. She was confused, afraid, or both.

"I've been studying the gems as well," Leykrra said at last. "I wanted to go to Flight Academy when I was younger, but I failed the aptitude test. I don't have the nerve for space."

Terra could see that. Light fur was sprouting along Leykrra's jawline, and her nostrils were beginning to flare. The youngster was stressed enough just discussing this matter—whatever it was—with Terra. There was no way she could handle the life threatening conditions the space travelers experienced every day.

Finally Leykrra leaned far over and murmured something so quietly that Terra's ears had to expand to catch it.

"I believe the gems are alive."

Terra stiffened. Had Leykrra gone rogue as well? Was she trapped in here with a rogue wolf? She wasn't sure she was up for another fight.

"I assure you, I am not ill," Leykrra added. As most rogues did. "I've studied the gems. I've dissected them. They share multiple properties with living things."

"Oh, really?" Terra leaned forward. "How do they eat?"

"They absorb molecules from their surroundings. It's a form of very small osmosis. Only a few molecules a century will feed a gem the size of your claw."

"How do they excrete?"

"The energy they excrete is what powers the leap gems. It passes through the gates between the linked gems."

"How do they move and grow?"

"Like a virus. Completely inert until they get close to an organism they can use. Then they fasten onto it and absorb its energy. Just a few molecules a century, like I said."

"Like a virus..." Now Terra thought she knew where Leykrra was going with her thoughts.

"Mistrra has been exposed to the leap gems. You are studying the leap gems. And now she's gone rogue in the manner of the plague that struck your territory, though she is not infected."

"Has she been to the north east territory? It's more likely the blood test was faulty."

"She did, as part of a study group that visited your Flight Academy. But she was the only one of that group who went rogue. And she had no symptoms at all until she came into contact with you."

"Are you saying that the gems made her ill somehow? That just passing through the gate exposed her to this virus, and then my presence triggered it?"

Terra stared at her, and Leykrra looked down at her hands. They were thick and furry. She was truly upset, and Terra didn't blame her. Such a tale must have gotten her mocked out of the medical center with her tail between her legs.

"I'd like to guide you to the mines," Leykrra said.

"So I'm being released from quarantine now?"

Leykrra nodded, and her pelt receded. "All of your blood tests came back negative for the plague, and you have shown no signs of illness since the start of your confinement. The med techs have instructed me to escort you back to your home territory, where you are to remain. Permanently."

"But you said—" Then Terra stopped. Leykrra had said that she'd been instructed to make Terra go home. She hadn't said that she would. "I see."

"We should go quickly. It's nearly nightfall, and we'll make better time when it's dark."

*****

It felt good to have a packmate again, even one as strange as Leykrra. She seemed friendly and agreeable despite her strange ideas. Terra supposed that too much time spent studying living organisms had made her see organic characteristics in everything. Leykrra had wanted to go to space, but her natural limitations had balked her. So she'd turned instead to medicine, and boredom combined with frustration had fostered delusions in her young, pliable mind.

Terra thought maybe she could help her. After they returned to Terra's home territory, she would talk to the rest of the council about finding her a job at the academy. Just because she wasn't suited for space exploration didn't mean she couldn't be useful to the space explorers. She could study the alien diseases they found on other living planets and develop vaccines for them to be kept on Garou. Such a system might protect them from a future plague.

They ran all night on two legs. Leykrra wanted to run as a wolf, but Terra thought they should keep to two legs for now in order to optimize communication. Also, she didn't want to admit it, but changing back and forth was exhausting. She wasn't getting any younger.

Terra smelled the mine before she saw it. It reeked of metal, dirty water, and something else. Something cold and sterile that reminded Terra of deep space.

"That's the smell of the gems," Leykrra said when Terra curled her lip. "You don't notice their scent when they're part of a gate. But here, they're raw, and there are a lot of them."

There was a repellant fence around the facility, which surprised Terra. Very few places on Garou were completely off limits to visitors, so repellant was a rare technology. The fence itself was a solid sheet of metal: iron, aluminum, and Terra thought tungsten. It was an expensive alloy. The ground in front of the fence was seeded with a foul scent that made Terra think of vomit and disease. Her stomach clenched a little as a light morning breeze wafted the stench her way. It was synthetic and completely harmless, but any hunter who lingered here would soon be very uncomfortable.

It was possible, with a good running jump, to scale the wall and leave the bad smell behind, but running along the top was an electrified rail. Bright sparks flew off of it at regular intervals, both to warn off curious hunters and to discourage flying animals from landing on it.

Leykrra coughed into her arm. "This way," she said, and Terra followed her along the fence to the main gate. There was a small square eye set into the wall here, and Leykrra put her right hand on it. The screen beeped, and she held up her red medical badge. Another beep, and the gate slid silently open.

"Won't you get into trouble for this?" Terra asked as she followed her in.

"It doesn't matter." The gate clicked shut behind them, and Terra flinched. After so recently being held in captivity, Terra had no love for enclosed spaces. "I've been 'encouraged' to seek employment elsewhere. Preferably in a different territory."

Terra was sorry for Leykrra, but she thought it was probably for the best. At the Flight Academy, wild ideas were encouraged. Free thinking led to new discoveries.

But then why was the rogue leap gate kept a secret? Terra intended to find out, and she felt that this was the place to learn. Her hackles rose as they crossed the tiny, grassy courtyard and approached the mining center.

The center building was a squat metal square built into the side of a rocky hill. This was where the workers stored their equipment, and educational lectures were given to the advanced Academy students. Leykrra led Terra through the blank metal doors and into the dimly lit caves beyond. "Is nobody here?" Terra asked. She would have expected to see at least one hunter stationed here, even if the mine wasn't currently in operation.

Leykrra shook her head. "One of the miners was injured yesterday, so the shaft is closed." She led Terra down a smooth, empty hallway, past several classrooms and a large office. "The best way to get down is through here."

"How was he injured?" Terra's throat tightened. She was used to the idea of being caught or arrested by the authorities. She didn't want to walk into any actual danger.

"Something happened in the lab. A piece of gem he was working on burned him." Leykrra glanced at Terra, and her eyes flashed gold in the dim light.

"Do you know how?" As far as Terra knew, heat exposure wasn't part of the process of conditioning leap gems.

"Nobody knows. They said it was an unauthorized experiment. I saw him, after. It will take months to grow his skin back."

"An unauthorized experiment." Terra's voice was flat. "You don't believe that, do you?"

"This way." Leykrra led her through another set of doors, and they were in the dark. Again Terra was hit by the scents of metal and deep space.

Directly in front of them was a dark tunnel. Terra looked up, and she saw a thin sliver of moon directly overhead. She paused a moment to drink it in. She could feel the late summer air, even down here, and it felt cool and soothing. The stars stared down, unblinking, as they had for millions of years. Terra felt the cool stone beneath her feet as she stared up the channel and into the vastness of space. It was all up there, all real, alive and brilliant before her eyes. Though she was deep under the ground and could barely see the moon, Terra let out a low howl. A moment later, Leykrra's voice joined hers. They sang quietly together of life and death, of soil and stars. Terra didn't understand what was happening or why she was here in this strange place, following a mad hunter's rogue notions. But there was life all around, and Terra sang to it. She could do nothing else.

Finally the wolf song came to an end, and without a word Leykrra turned and trotted down the tunnel in front of them. Terra followed silently.

Moments later Leykrra stopped. "We're here. Try not to touch the walls. It's a small vein, but even small gems can hurt you when they're wild."

The stone floor was wet and cold under Terra's feet. It was completely dark down here, and all she could smell was metal and bad soil.

Mining the leap gems was a destructive task, which was why there was only one mine on the entire world. The gems were infinitely valuable, and it was easy to understand why.

At least Terra could still smell Leykrra. The other female was nervous but composed, which reassured Terra. "Why are we here?" she asked.

"You wanted to learn about the gems." There was a swish in the darkness, as though Leykrra had turned briefly to look at her.

Terra looked behind them, but she couldn't see anything. Her heart picked up a little, and her eyes felt raw from trying to see. "Yes, I do," she said, "but I thought we were coming here to talk to someone. A scientist, or a miner, or—"

"What better way to learn about the gems than from the gems themselves?" Leykrra asked. Her voice was pleasant, but Terra heard the baring of teeth behind her words. Terra's heart beat faster, and she took a step back. Her back struck the wall of the tunnel, and she shivered.

"Touch it. Right here." Leykrra seized Terra's hand unerringly—how had she done that in such darkness?—and pulled her around.

Terra tried to shake her loose. "You said don't touch the walls!"

"I'll show you where it's safe to touch. Now." Leykrra pulled Terra's hand again, and this time Terra complied. She was frightened, her wolf was growling, but she was also curious. She wanted to see what this mad female was talking about.

Her hand touched the cold, damp stone. Jagged like crystal, with smooth facets here and there. The raw, wild leap gem in its natural state. Harmless one moment, deadly the next—

Leykrra screamed.

Terra looked in the direction of the scream. The mad one was behind her, not even touching the gems as far as she could tell. What was happening?

Leykrra screamed again, and her scream became a deep-throated howl as the wolf surged forward. Terra felt her own hackles raising, and her incisors cut into her lower lip. She forced her wolf back. She needed to understand, and for that she needed her two-legged brain.

Terra's hand stroked the edge of the gem-studded wall, and she gasped as a sharp point cut her finger. She tried to pull her hand away—

225

and couldn't. Her hand was cold and numb, and the numbness crept up her wrist and her arm. Terra grabbed with her other hand, and it was like grabbing nothing. Like grabbing a cold piece of meat.

Then her left hand went cold and numb as well.

Terra screamed Leykrra's name, but the other female had troubles of her own. She'd gone full wolf, and the wolf sounded maddened and sick. She snarled and thrashed like a dying burrower, and Terra was pinned against the wall, helpless to come to her assistance. Her skin crawled like a thousand insects as she tried to brace herself for the crush of mad wolf biting into her neck.

And still the cold numbness crept up her arms and toward her face.

"Help!" Terra screamed. Surely they couldn't be completely alone here; there had to be a guardian stationed, or a wolf running outside. Maybe someone was close by, maybe he could come help them.

The coldness was still coming, and Terra felt like she was slowly sinking in thick, cold blood.

Then it spread all the way across her face, and Terra let out a despairing, dying howl.

And as the coldness shivered through her brain, Terra finally saw. She finally understood.

She knew.

Howling and tumbling, she hurtled through the wild gate.

Chapter Ten

Nexrra awoke completely disoriented. Her head and neck ached as though she'd been beaten, her throat was raw, and her tongue felt dry and fat. She jerked awake and tried to leap to her feet, but she only succeeded in tumbling flat onto her face. Her forehead slammed against the floor with a sickening jolt, and she tasted blood.

She pulled herself into a sitting position and hugged her knees. She still felt dizzy and sick. Was the dog infected with some virus? But she'd tested its blood herself, and it had been healthy. Nexrra touched her cheeks, and they felt furry and hot. She had a fever.

It was the plague. The sickness that had maddened Jarren, driven him to kill his own kind and even attack females. He'd given it to Nexrra after all.

But Jerr had pumped her and her brother full of antivirals on the ship. She'd pronounced them both healthy. And that had been weeks ago. Surely she should have shown symptoms before now.

The plague might be the sort that lay dormant, though. Resting below the surface, waiting for the right stressor—an animal attack, for instance—to strike.

Nexrra had to get back to the Star Pack. Her life was in immediate danger. It might be too late now.

But what if it was already too late? What if she went mad and attacked her packmates when she went back?

What if she attacked Kuvrro?

It was a horrifying thought, and Nexrra trembled.

But she had no choice. She couldn't stay here, and let the humans find her body. She would send a message to Mirra before going back through the gate. Then the captain could prepare for her. And euthanize her, if necessary.

Nexrra groaned as a white blast of pain ripped through her head. She would almost welcome death if it would bring relief from this pain. No wonder Jarren had gone mad.

She turned on her wrist eye and tapped out a message to Mirra. She kept it vague; her message would reach the Star Pack by piggy backing the Otsandan Internet, and such messages were easily intercepted. Nobody would understand the language, of course, but Otsandan humans were perpetually curious. Even about things that could not possibly concern them, like the mating rituals of inedible insects. Nexrra thought that their constant curiosity explained a lot about their behavior. Curiosity was like having a strange little animal that bit and gnawed at the mind.

So the message was brief but to the point. NOT FEELING WELL. DOG RAN AWAY. COMING HOME. BE READY FOR ME. PACK LEADER.

The last two words were most important, and Nexrra studied them for a long time before tapping the green button that would send those words to Mirra. Pack leader. Not captain. Nexrra was invoking Mirra's instincts with those words, the instincts that that led one to guard and protect rather than lead. To kill, if necessary.

Mirra would understand what Nexrra meant, and she would not hesitate to kill Nexrra if she threatened the rest of her pack. Even if Kuvrro left her for euthanizing his sister, she would put her pack before an individual. It was the duty of all leaders.

Nexrra went to all fours and crawled out of the pod. She felt weak and nauseated; she lacked the strength to even change to wolf to make crawling easier. The leap gate was only a few lengths away, and hand over hand she crept over to it.

Now Nexrra had to get to her feet to activate the gate, and she shivered with the effort. She was really going downhill fast. Jarren had worsened over the course of days before going completely rogue. Why was it striking her so fast and so suddenly?

It didn't matter. Nexrra put her hand on the activation eye and leaned her face against the frame of the gate. She was going back home to the Star Pack. So much for finding the dog's human companions; she couldn't even sniff the ground in this condition. So much for finding out what had happened to Nedrra's body.

The leap gem brightened, and Nexrra smelled fresh air. The gate was open, and she stumbled through.

Then she thought, This isn't right, this isn't the ship. The air smells too green--

Then consciousness ceased.

*****

When she awoke, her head felt clearer. Her face still felt warm, but she no longer burned with fever. Nexrra opened her eyes and looked around.

She wasn't on the ship. She was in a thick wood that resembled the one she'd just left, but the air smelled different; there were motor vehicles close by, a lot of them. The soil smelled different too. She was still on Otsanda, but she was in a very different part of the world.

Wait. She knew where she was. Nexrra staggered to her feet and rubbed her face with both hands. She knew where she was. She'd been here once before, with Kuvrro.

This was the place where Jarren had attacked them. But how? The leap gate she'd passed through had been keyed to the one on board the Star Pack.

Nexrra wondered if she'd blacked out and somehow re-keyed the leap gate. But that was almost impossible without careful planning. As sick as she was, she doubted that she could have done it.

"Nexrra, is that you?" A female voice, sounding as weary and confused as she felt.

Nexrra knew that voice and when she turned to face the older female standing behind her, she thought that she ought to be shocked. But so many impossible things had happened since they'd come to this impossible planet, nothing seemed surprising anymore.

It was Terra, the head of the Council for Alien Affairs. Nexrra had never met her face to face, but she'd seen her often enough in the communication eye.

"How did you get here?" Nexrra asked.

"The leap gem brought me here." Terra looked around fearfully. "I came here straight from Garou. Will the air kill me?"

Nexrra shrugged. "I'm sick," she confessed. "And I've been fully vaccinated. I don't know."

But she didn't feel sick anymore. Ever since falling through the gate, her malaise seemed to have faded. Maybe it had been psychosomatic.

Terra shook her head. "It doesn't matter. I'm old, and if I die I die. The gem must have brought me here for a reason. It must have brought you, too."

"What gem?"

"That one." Terra pointed at the ground, and Nexrra saw that it was the wild gem Kuvrro had lost. Somehow she'd passed through a harnessed gate and come out through the rogue. That should not be possible.

Terra knelt and picked it up. In the bright morning sunshine, it flashed like a golden star. Nexrra growled.

"Why are we here?" Terra asked. "Why did you send us here?"

"Who are you talking to?" Nexrra knew Terra couldn't be talking to her. She didn't know any more than the council female did.

"The gems are alive," Terra said. She stared at the gem in her hand as though she'd never seen one before. "They spoke to me. They sent me here."

Terra was sick, Nexrra thought. She didn't look or smell ill, but obviously the plague had struck her mind. She inched away, hoping to get a running start before Terra tried to attack.

Then Nexrra's limbs went numb, and she couldn't move. A dark, cold voice filled her mind.

Nobody believes the solitary human, who sees aliens around every corner. Dispose of the remaining gems, and your lives will be safe.

"What was that?" Nexrra asked.

"The leap gems are alive." Terra's words were mad, but Nexrra saw no trace of madness in her eyes. Exhaustion, fear, and elation. But no madness. No sign of the rogue wolf. "They spoke to me in the mine. They sent me here. They sent you, too."

"They're stones," Nexrra said. "They exist under the ground, with no light and no food. How are they alive?"

"Under the ground they're dormant. Like a virus. They existed for millennia, asleep. But when we created the gates, they started to wake up. And they saw."

"What did they see?"

"Our world and this one are linked. But it's not safe for us here yet. We have to leave, and we have to take the gems with us."

Why not? Nexrra mused. She'd been forced to believe all sorts of impossible things here on Otsanda. And every wolf bone in her body was insisting that she trust and believe in her elder. "How?" she asked.

"We need the Star Pack," Terra said.

Nexrra tapped at her wrist eye. She still wasn't sure that she could get a message to the Star Pack from here; she'd never gotten a response to her last message. But Mirra would want to hear this.

Nexrra tapped again, but the little screen remained dark. "We're too far from Otsandan civilization to hijack their Internet, and the Star Pack is out of direct range," she said.

"We'll wait," Terra said.

"For what?" Neither issue related to their communication problem was likely to resolve itself with nothing but time.

"I don't know. But the gem wants us to wait."

Nexrra's stomach flopped uneasily. Terra had never been likable; much like Mirra she'd been a cold and controlling alpha. But this new Terra frightened her. There was still no scent of sickness or anger, and Nexrra did not sense that Terra meant her harm. But she was spouting impossibilities. None of what she was saying could possibly be true. Could it? But if it weren't, how had Terra gotten here alone? It was barely possible that she could have followed the Star Pack's leap trail across the galaxy, but she could not have gotten to Otsanda without passing through the Star Pack itself, and alerting Mirra.

Nexrra tapped again at her wrist eye, even though she knew it would do nothing. She needed Mirra, and she wanted her brother. She couldn't make these kinds of decisions by herself.

"He's coming," Terra said. She raised her face to the air and sniffed. "He's still looking for us."

"Who is?" Nexrra smelled nobody. She still felt a little weak, and her head ached.

"I can't smell him yet either. The gem told me to watch for him. He's been tramping all over this mound for days, and the gems have been watching him."

So now the gems could talk. Nexrra felt irritated, but only for a moment. Because then she heard the Otsandan crashing through the brush in typical human fashion. Leaves crunched under his feet, and a fresh breeze carried his scent straight into their noses. She could tell by the way he stepped slowly and carefully that he thought he was being stealthy. Nexrra almost wanted to pity him.

"What did the gem say about him?" she asked Terra. She was tired and sore, and she couldn't handle the strain on her nerves anymore. She officially made up her mind right then to give up control and follow Terra as alpha. She could always run away if Terra went completely rogue.

"The Otsandan who wants to capture us is a lone rogue," Terra said. "His pack mates think he's mad."

That did not sound good to Nexrra. "Can we run?" she asked.

Then he crashed into view. His face was naked and shining with sweat, and his Otsandan garment—patches of different shades of green, and black footwear—reeked of sweat and liquid poison. He'd been drinking what the Otsandans called "cocktails," and he smelled like he'd been doing so for days without a break.

"No." Terra bared her teeth.

Nexrra's heart raced. "We mustn't kill him."

"Why not?" Terra asked. "He's the only one who knows about us. If he dies—" she stopped.

Nexrra didn't answer. As she stared at the burly, unarmed male, panting and glaring at them with weak vindication, all she knew was that he could not be killed. Something bad would happen, though Nexrra had no idea what.

The male spoke. Nexrra could not understand the words; her grasp of the local Otsandan language was shaky, and the male's voice was slurred with exhaustion. He spoke again, and she tapped her throat apologetically. Then she held up both hands in the Otsandan gesture of submission.

"He's the only one who suspects us," Terra insisted. "If he dies, we'll be safe."

Terra had not studied Otsandan culture as Nexrra had. "If he dies, all of the Internet will suspect us," Nexrra said calmly. Keeping her hands up, she stepped close to the male. His ruddy face paled, but he did not retreat.

"Otsandans love fantasy," she went on. Her voice was calm and soothing, and though the words were not directed at the alien, he seemed to relax a bit. "They want to believe in magic and monsters. If we kill this man, others will believe that he spoke the truth about alien visitors. They will come looking for us. And they will find the gems."

Terra held up the lone gem in her hand. It flashed like brilliant eye, and the male's eyes widened.

"This isn't the only gem," Nexrra said softly. "You know. You can sense them too."

"All over the world," Terra whispered. "Our two worlds are linked. But now the gems are awake, and they know that our worlds aren't safe. They want the link closed. For now."

"He can help us." And Nexrra moved closer to the male, who stared at the gem like a starving dog looking at food.

She licked her lips, bared her teeth, and spoke in Otsandan English. "We are friends. Are you friends?"

The male straightened, and some color returned to his cheeks. These creatures love magic and mystery, Nexrra thought, but not too much. Like cubs, they are reassured by the familiar.

"Yes, I am friends," he said. His voice was deep and raspy, and he spoke each word carefully.

"You look for—aliens?" Nexrra's tongue stumbled over the strange word, but the male brightened.

"Yes!" He stepped forward, and Nexrra jumped back. She didn't think he was dangerous, but she didn't want to make direct contact unless she had to. He could be crawling with disease.

The male stopped and put his hands up, mimicking Nexrra's pose.

"I will show you our alien boat," she said.

"Nexrra what are you doing!" Terra snarled, her teeth extending. The male whimpered and stumbled away, and Nexrra stepped between them.

"Do not frighten him!" she growled. "He can help us, but not if he runs away!"

"Nexrra, you're going mad," Terra said, but she backed away and raised her hands as well. Nexrra relaxed.

"Put the gem in the fork of that tree."

The tree she indicated was a slender sapling with smooth bark. Terra obeyed, and Nexrra lowered her hands and approached the male.

"Alien boat," she repeated. Then she bared her teeth in what she hoped was a friendly Otsandan smile.

"You'll take me to your ship?" The male smiled back. "Are the other aliens as pretty as you?"

"Am not human. Hands off," Nexrra said.

"Yes, ma'am." The male glanced at Terra, no doubt remembering those incisors, and deflated.

Nexrra reached out slowly and took his meaty hand. It was sweaty and reeked of fear. They'd have to fix him before he would be any use to them, which meant flushing out all the poisons and toxins he'd put into himself recently. He needed to lose weight, too. She could hear his heart struggling to keep pace with his body.

She could fix him. It was what she did.

Nexrra tugged on the male's hand and led him to the sapling. She put her other hand out, a finger away from the gem, and she said, "Take us to the Star Pack."

Then they stepped forward, into the tree.

Chapter Eleven

The stranger's arrival caused a commotion, to say the least. Kuvrro turned wolf and would have attacked him on the spot had Nexrra not thrown herself in his path. Mirra kept her two-legged form but wanted to know in loud, firm tones why Nexrra had brought a dangerous human into their home. Jenrra took one look at the commotion and set to work scrubbing away the filth and dirt the human was dropping all over the floor. That was how Jenrra operated; when stress levels got too high, she looked for something to clean. Ledrra wanted to know what had happened to the dog.

Once Kuvrro was somewhat under control and the floor was immaculate, Mirra instructed Kuvrro to escort the stranger to the exercise gym and keep him there. "What should I do if he turns rogue or tries to escape?" he asked. His golden eyes almost glowed.

"He won't try to escape," Nexrra said. "He wants to be here; he wants to help us. Don't you dare kill him. We need him."

"We need to go home," Kuvrro grumbled, but he led the human—who smelled like urine now—away down the hall.

Ledrra followed Nexrra and Mirra to the captain's office. Without asking permission, Nexrra tapped open the control eye to the gym and turned up the soothing scents. Kuvrro was still on edge, and they needed the human alive. Even though none of the others seemed to know this yet.

Mirra sat down in the nearest chair and curled her legs under her. "Explain yourself," she told Nexrra. "Succinctly. All of our pelts are on the line because of what you've done today."

Nexrra told Mirra and Ledrra everything she knew, and everything Terra had told her. Mirra's brow furrowed. "That Council female is here?"

"She came through a rogue gate, just like Jarren did. But the gems are not rogues anymore. They're waking up."

Mirra straightened in her chair.

This was where Nexrra got confused, because she didn't fully understand it herself. When the gems had spoken to her, she'd had the impression of something very big trying to say something very small. The gems had imparted their wisdom to Terra and partially to Nexrra, but they did not have a spoken language. It had been like—listening to the stars. Nexrra felt like her brain was not big enough to understand everything the gems were trying to say. "The gems were scattered across the universe, and they went to sleep. Now they're waking up, and they're trying to fix some of the holes they've made."

"What scattered them?" Ledrra interrupted. "The gems were here before us. Who planted them here? It wasn't us, and it couldn't have been the Otsandans."

Nexrra shook her head. "Something old, older than Garou. They're extinct now. All that's left of them is bits of satellite and radio signals. The gems don't have eyes, so I don't even know what they looked like."

"We should form a mission to seek those signals," Ledrra mused. "We could learn so much—"

"That is a matter for the Councils at home," Mirra said. "Our current mission is to survive the madness that Nexrra has brought to my ship."

"This human—" Ledrra leaned forward. "Does he know what's become of my sister?"

Nexrra touched her throat and looked down. "I saw her in his mind as we were crossing the gate. He stole her body from the cold place where they were keeping her, and after taking her body apart he burned her along with the clothes he found. The alphas caught him and cast him out of their pack, but they didn't learn anything about us. Bob is still the only one who knows."

Ledrra nodded slowly. "At least I know what became of her. Now—"

Mirra snapped her teeth impatiently. "I'm sorry about your sister Ledrra, but we need to get back to the leap gems. Your brother wants to kill this Bob rogue, terminate the mission, and go home. I don't think he's wrong."

"Because we need to collect the gems," Nexrra said. "They told us that they were scattered all over Otsanda, but most of them have been buried and gone dormant. There are three still active, and we need to find

236

them and get them off this world. They're all around the planet, so we need someone who can pass for human and travel across territories."

"Why do we need to get the gems?"

Nexrra curled up in the floor nest and hugged her furry knees. "Because it's not time yet," she said. "Otsanda has enormous potential, and its people are capable of wonders that could change the entire galaxy. Their stubbornness, their imagination—they could revolutionize the stars. But I saw a bit of what their world is like, through the eyes of the wolves. They think they live outside of nature, and they're still trying to master it instead of get along with it. They're like us, when we were still looking for a cure. If they gain access to the stars now, before they've matured, they could turn the entire solar systems into wastelands and dead worlds, like Morteloup."

"But what about this human? He's as volatile as the rest."

Nexrra shook her head. She hoped that she could explain what the gems had imparted to her as they'd passed through the gate. "He only wants to see aliens. He wants to prove aliens exist, and he'll do anything we ask as long as he's allowed to explore the Star Pack and take pictures with his hand eye."

"Let him take pictures? So all of Otsanda can see that we are here?"

"You ought to spend more time exploring their Internet," Ledrra said. "There are pictures and video stories of aliens everywhere. All of them false, tricks created with fancy effects and colors. Nobody will believe him. And what if they do? We're terminating the mission. We'll be light years away. We'll never see these creatures again."

Nexrra felt saddened by that, but she knew that it was for the best. She thought of the clever wolves with their speech of the mind. But then she thought of pollution, war, and rape, and she knew that this species needed to be left alone for now—to succeed or fail on their own feet.

"So tell us about the gems," Mirra said. "How do we go about collecting them?"

Nexrra sat up and willed herself to be calm, professional, and commanding. The pack leader was asking for her help. "Terra and I can both find the gems, since they've spoken to us several times. Bob Garnier can make all the travel plans, since he knows how their currency works, and one of us can go with him."

Mirra leaned forward. "What do you need from me?"

*****

To Nexrra's disappointment, Terra was chosen to be the human's companion. But she had to admit that it made sense. As an elder female, she would be accorded more respect than a young, attractive one, and nobody would look too closely at her trumped-up identification. The human, Bob, introduced her as his mother who spoke no English, and she was left completely alone. It helped that the Council female had already mastered the haughty expression of a matriarch forced to consort with inferiors. It came, she said, from too many Council meetings and it was an expression that spanned the two cultures.

Nexrra was concerned that Bob would be missed if he just left his home pack without a word, but her worries were unfounded. What helped more than anything was that each location of a leap gem was a hot bed of myths and legends about werewolves. Bov was well known by his family and friends as a story-chasing rogue, so when he told them he was going on vacation for a month to hunt werewolves, nobody thought it odd at all.

Nor did anyone seem to notice when a certain tree in the forests of Romania was suddenly gouged and left bleeding sap in the middle of the night. The few who noticed assumed that it had been some sort of burrowing animal or woodpecker. It was more concerning when an ancient California redwood was similarly damaged, but the forest ranger assured tourists that a poultice of hot tar would patch it right up.

"Maybe a werewolf did it," suggested a young man in the audience, and his mother cuffed him across the back of his head. The group laughed.

The third gem, in the wilds of Germany, was the trickiest to get at only because the arrival of Bill and Terra coincided with some sort of festival that celebrated the discovery of alcohol, or its fermentation process, or something like that. Terra reported to Mirra that Bob seemed determined to drink his weight in the concoction known as beer, which slowed their progress exponentially. They wound up extending their trip by another month, until the festival concluded.

What Terra didn't tell the others was that she was slowing down the journey as much as Bob. They would soon leave this planet forever, and all of its mysteries and beauty would be lost to Garou. On this last leg of the journey, she made up her mind to partake in cultural festivities and make an actual attempt to learn. She never developed a taste for beer, but there were other activities that engaged her attention. The Otsandans were fascinating to watch, and Terra took to studying their behavior and interactions with their young. The young males were marvelous to flirt with; none of them took her seriously as a mate, but they were handsome and charming. When they'd been imbibing in the beer tents all afternoon, they got less charming but far more amusing.

Her favorite, though, was the forest of huge whirling machines called carnival rides. She rode them over and over again, shrieking with glee, while the humans around her laughed merrily. At night the rides lit up the sky like colored lightning, and Terra tried to keep her night vision minimized so she could get the full effect. One ride tossed her straight up into the air while strapped snugly into a metal compartment, and she howled as the rainbow of lights blurred her vision.

A collection of adolescents started following her around, sharing her riding compartments and calling her "Grandma." She assumed that it was a sort of ancestor honorific. They introduced her to sausages, expensive cheese, and a baked concoction known as the soft pretzel. She tucked a piece of the pretzel into her travel bag; she would take it back to the Star Pack to be analyzed and reverse-engineered. It would revolutionize the Garouean diet.

Every morning of the festival started the same way though: with Bob Garnier groaning and vomiting and swearing that he would never touch beer again. By nightfall he was intoxicated again. She was sympathetic the first several days, but her sympathy was drowned in the smell of sour sick by the end of the first week. She was having far too much fun to feel sorry for his self-indulgence.

"He's like a puppy gorging himself on the teat," she complained to Mirra via her wrist eye.

"It's almost over," Mirra said. "Get those gems back to us, so we can return them to Garou, and you can go home too."

"Can I kill him, then?"

"No!" Nexrra said before Mirra could respond. The captain glanced at her, then she bared her teeth in a fierce expression of amusement. No. Nexrra straightened. Mirra was smiling.

Nexrra touched her throat uncertainly, then she smiled back. She had never felt more at home.

Epilogue

Hrraz and Cyrr shared a wild ungula in the paradise close to Hrraz's new lone quarters. Cyrr brought it down with his teeth, and Hrraz butchered it cleanly with a heavy, serrated blade. Over strips of raw flesh, they discussed the new development.

"Mirra's last report stated that they're coming home," Cyrr said. He tore off shreds of red flesh and tossed them into his mouth thoughtfully.

"No mention of rogue leap gems, gates, or plague-ridden wolves," Hrraz said. "It was a very short, simple message."

"It will fit neatly into our official report, then."

Hrraz leaned over and buried his teeth into the meatiest part of the animal. He tore off a chunk with relish and chewed vigorously for several minutes. Finally he swallowed and said, "And as for our unofficial report?"

"The one we keep buried in the leap mine, that only we and our ancestors have seen?"

Hrraz nodded at his brother. "That's the one. Is the story of our two worlds ended then? Now that the gems have been retrieved?"

Cyrr growled. "Hardly. The stories remain. And—we'll go back there again. When a century or two has passed, and the Otsandans have bred out some of their aggression."

Hrraz lay on his back and stared up at the stars. "I wish I could go up there," he said softly.

"There's still one wild gem left," Cyrr pointed out. "Near the ancestors' retreat."

"No. I removed it. Right after Terra disappeared."

"Why?"

"Because... she wanted it so. Her eyes—the way she looked at me—the will of our ancestors was not worth losing her that way."

Cyrr got up and moved closer to his elder brother. "But we have the recordings. The words of the old ones. You've seen them. They wanted our peoples to grow side by side."

241

"The old ones aren't here. If they were so all-knowing, they would have survived and stayed to guide us. We're on our own, and we have to do what's best for our people now."

Cyrr sighed and picked off another shred of meat. "You're right. I would have liked to have seen Otsanda, though. Just once."

"Me too."

And they stared together upwards, at the bright, eternal stars.